"You'll never guess what I'm thinking."

"Will I like it?"

"You should. It should make your ego swell up like a balloon."

"Then tell me, by all means."

"I was thinking that of all the honeymoon couples I've seen here in Hawaii, none of the guys measures up to you. You're every woman's ideal of the perfect bridegroom. I was also thinking—"

"Yes, yes," Jack put in with humorous anxiety. "You were thinking. So far I'm crazy about your thoughts."

"I was thinking that this trip isn't the trip I'd planned to have. I feel a little guilty admitting this, but I never expected to have this much fun. Do you think it's awful of me to feel that way? Can you imagine a woman enjoying her honeymoon more because her bridegroom didn't come along?"

Dear Reader,

Spellbinder! That's what we're striving for. The editors at Silhouette are determined to capture your imagination and win your heart with every single book we publish. Each month, six Special Editions are chosen with *you* in mind.

Our authors are our inspiration. Writers such as Nora Roberts, Tracy Sinclair, Kathleen Eagle, Carole Halston and Linda Howard—to name but a few—are masters at creating endearing characters and heartrending love stories. Their characters are everyday people—just like you and me—whose lives have been touched by love, whose dreams and desires suddenly come true!

So find a cozy, quiet place to read, and create your own special moment with a Silhouette Special Edition.

Sincerely,

The Editors
SILHOUETTE BOOKS

SE-RL-3R

CAROLE HALSTON
Honeymoon for One

Silhouette Special Edition

Published by Silhouette Books New York

America's Publisher of Contemporary Romance

Thanks to faithful fans in my family for reading and
enjoying my books: Michelle, my sister, and Deana
and Jean, wives of two lucky brothers.

Special thanks and love to Ida Hall for being the
mother of Monty, my husband, and for being so
proud and supportive of my writing career.

SILHOUETTE BOOKS
300 East 42nd St., New York, N.Y. 10017

ISBN: 0-373-09356-X

First Silhouette Books printing January 1987

America's Publisher of Contemporary Romance

Printed in the U.S.A.

Books by Carole Halston

Silhouette Romance

Stand-in Bride #62
Love Legacy #83
Undercover Girl #152
Sunset in Paradise #208

Silhouette Special Edition

Keys to Daniel's House #8
Collision Course #41
The Marriage Bonus #86
Summer Course in Love #115
A Hard Bargain #139
Something Lost, Something Gained #163
A Common Heritage #211
The Black Knight #223
Almost Heaven #253
Surprise Offense #291
Matched Pair #328
Honeymoon For One #356

CAROLE HALSTON

is the wife of a sea captain, and she writes while her husband is at sea. Her characters often share her own love of nature and enjoyment of active outdoor sports. Ms. Halston is an avid tennis player and a dedicated sailor.

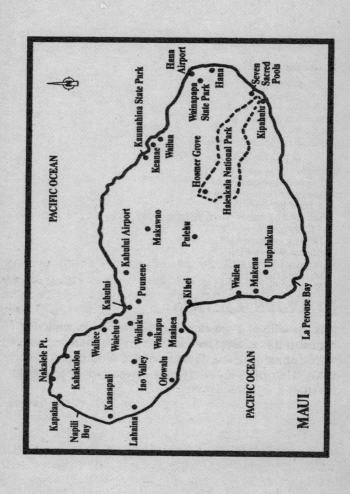

Chapter One

Rita had no sense of foreboding as she waited for Mark with his mother, shortly to be her mother-in-law, in the living room of Rita's Atlanta apartment, a source of pride for her. She had no inkling that the tastefully decorated room would become the setting for a nightmare, its neutral walls a backdrop of bitter humiliation for her. She was utterly unprepared for the death stroke about to be dealt to the life she had built so painstakingly for herself, at such great cost, upon secretive foundations.

As far as she knew, all was well. In fact, things couldn't have been better. It was just days now before the wedding, which was going to be a big, traditional affair. Mark's mother was overseeing the arrangements since the wedding would take place not in Atlanta, where Rita and Mark both lived and worked, but in neighboring Athens, where the University of Georgia campus was located and Mark's parents were entrenched, highly respected members of the community. Mark's father was a tenured professor at the university, his mother active in church and charitable organizations. Rita having long since established in everyone's minds the coolness of the relations between herself and her family, living in some distant unstipulated location, it made perfect sense to have the wedding in Athens. Katherine Pendleton was in her element planning it and happy to relieve Rita of all the headaches.

On several occasions prior to this one, Rita's future mother-in-law had found it convenient to stay overnight at Rita's apartment when she drove to Atlanta to do shopping related to the wedding and to consult with Rita. Rita was always the slightest bit nervous but welcomed the opportunity to play hostess to Mark's mother. To entertain a woman of Katherine Pendleton's breeding and social know-how was a test for Rita, coming as she did from her kind of background. She was becoming gradually more confident, able to relax a little around her future mother-in-law and even look forward to that time when she could take Katherine Pendleton's approval for granted. When that moment arrived, Rita would truly have succeeded in making herself over into the kind of person she longed to be, someone like Katherine Pendleton herself, the perfect wife and mother, a woman of impeccable taste and breeding and high moral character.

Naturally Mark was pleased that Rita and his mother got along so well. He had done the expected when he heard that his mother would be in Atlanta overnight, offering to squire his "two favorite women" out to dinner. The three of them, Mark, Rita and his mother, looked forward with some complacency to a pleasant evening free of those crosscurrents of friction that can be present when a man is marrying a woman his family doesn't heartily condone. Not one of the three had any reason to suspect that there would be an unexpected fourth joining them, disrupting the smooth course of the evening and redirecting Rita's entire life. If Rita had received some advance notice, she would have tried desperately to avoid what she looked upon as a visitation of cruelest fate.

Instead she was filled with a sense of self-congratulation that she would look back upon bitterly when the evening was over. It seemed to Rita that she was within reach of all her goals. Katherine Pendleton's bodily presence in her living room and the seeming certainty of Rita's upcoming wedding were proof that Rita had succeeded in teaching herself what her background hadn't been able to supply. If only her mother had been a woman like Katherine and home had been a place of pride, not of shame, life would have been so much easier and happier, not the long uphill struggle that it had been. But Rita was almost there, at the top of the mountain.

Being self-taught, she'd had to be cautious, as was evident in the decoration of the apartment and her own appearance. All the furniture and accessories in the living room were of good quality but very conservative in design. She'd taken no risks, played it "safe," using muted colors. The overall effect was restful and gracious, with no focal points of drama, true, but also with no jarring, telltale flaws as was evidenced by Katherine Pendeleton's total approval.

Katherine also thoroughly approved of Rita's appearance. After knowing Rita for two years, the older woman had no suspicion that her future daughter-in-law was deliberately hiding a flamboyant beauty. Rita used a shampoo rinse on her auburn hair to tone down the flame highlights, and she never wore it down. Fighting its natural tendency to curl and wave, she pulled it back from her face in a classically simple and severe French twist. Her discreet use of makeup steered clear of any efforts to maximize the exotic effect of huge dark eyes the shade of bitter chocolate, excellent bone structure, and a mouth that managed to be both sensitive and luscious.

The three-piece outfit she wore tonight was typical of her style of dress. She favored suits or dresses with jackets for both work and evening wear. The lines of her champagne beige skirt and matching jacket, teamed with a cream silk blouse the color of her single strand of pearls and pearl stud earrings, hinted at a slender figure underneath without making any issue of its shapeliness, as was Rita's wish. She never dressed to display her stunning figure, as her mother had always done. She had no wish to attract that kind of attention from a man. What had it ever gotten her mother besides promises from handsome losers and one failed marriage after another?

"That beige and cream combination is so becoming on you, Rita, dear," Katherine Pendleton complimented before she got down to discussing several minor problems that had cropped up with the wedding arrangements. "I think I like you best in the quiet beige tones."

Rita's smile was pleased. "Like mother, like son. So does Mark."

"My son is definitely a young man with good taste, especially in his choice of a bride-to-be."

Katherine Pendleton's complacent tone gave everyone concerned an approving pat on the back, herself for producing such a discriminating son, Mark for making a judicious choice of marriage partner in selecting Rita, and Rita for being so perfectly suitable. It wasn't the first time Katherine had openly spoken her approval of the match, of course, but Rita was warmed and gratified. The tiny core of insecurity lying at the center of her well-being was wrapped in still another thin layer of reassurance. Eventually there would be an impenetrable pearl.

"Speaking of Mark, he said he'd be here between a quarter after and six-thirty, depending upon the traffic," Rita said, consulting her slim gold watch.

"Good. That should give us a few minutes to talk about the wedding before he arrives." Katherine Pendleton clasped her hands in her lap and smiled her benign chairwoman's smile that she used with committee members. "As I mentioned on the phone, Cora Baskins, our church soloist, has been called out of town with a serious illness in her family. She won't be back in time for the wedding. I'm afraid we're going to have to pick out another song or else omit the solo. Betty Evans just doesn't have Cora's voice quality or range. Of course, it's your decision, dear, but my thoughts were..."

Rita appeared to be fully attentive and interested, but the discussion didn't really engage her thoughts. The decision on the choice of wedding music wasn't really hers to make. She would go along with whatever Katherine Pendleton deemed best. Any slight stir of irritation that Rita felt at her own lack of control over her wedding was fleeting, drowned in the placid sea of her sense of good fortune. She was lucky to be marrying a man like Mark, from his kind of background. It didn't concern her in the least that her affection for him was warm and comfortable, not passionate. In her mind, strong physical attraction between a man and a woman was associated with the lower classes. Educated, respectable people didn't act like animals.

It didn't matter to her that nothing about Mark awoke in her a sense of awe or intense admiration. She knew that he was basically a pleasant, average man, attractive but not strikingly handsome, not especially clever or witty. His interests were average male interests. Like most men, he scanned the front page of the newspaper and then turned back to the sports pages. He had no fascinating hobbies and was moderate in all his habits. He hadn't distinguished himself in law school and probably wouldn't have a brilliant or lucrative career. Currently he was on the legal staff of a large insurance company and didn't earn as large a salary as Rita herself. Rita expected to continue working as long as necessary and didn't mind, just as she hadn't minded contributing to joint savings for a future down payment on a house and furniture. She'd thought nothing of paying her half of honeymoon expenses.

Rita wasn't marrying Mark Pendleton for wealth or material comfort, though she intended always to have the latter. She knew she could earn it for herself. What Mark offered her was entry into a life of sterling respectability that she coveted for herself and for the children that she intended to bear, who would never know the tortures of being low class. They'd never be embarrassed by what their parents did for a living. They'd never feel inferior. They'd be among the charmed circle of children from wonderful homes with upstanding parents, not ostracized from it as Rita had been, for circumstances completely beyond her control. Mark had been one of those lucky children, and he bore the stamp. It had been immediately perceptible to Rita in his manner, dress, and conversation, with the easy, telltale references to his parents and background. That background, more than anything else, qualified him in Rita's eyes and made him desirable as a husband.

As she opened the door to him on this evening that promised to be pleasant, the sight of him didn't quicken her pulse, but it confirmed her belief in her good fortune. He was one of those men who felt comfortable in a suit and tie and was more inclined to wear slacks than jeans on a casual occasion. Rita liked the tendency toward formality. She took pleasure in his well-groomed appearance and his slightly courtly manners, especially when they were out in public view. She was always proud to be seen with him.

"Right on time, as usual," she greeted him with self-conscious warmth. The entryway was separated from the living room by a partial brick wall and thus visible to Mark's mother, who would be looking on.

"Wouldn't do to be late tonight, not when I have two good-looking gals as dates," Mark declared. Closing the door behind him, he took Rita's hands and squeezed them while he kissed her lightly on the lips and then gave her an admiring once-over. "Nice outfit," he complimented and then directed his attention beyond her into the living room. The welcome in his face and voice was genuine. "Hi, Mother. How are you? How's everything at home? Is Dad over his bout with the flu?"

Rita observed the tableau of mother and son greeting each other with both pleasure and envy. Mark so obviously loved and respected both his parents, but he was especially close to his mother. Katherine Pendleton's face was kindled with a possessive pride as she rose to her feet and offered her cheek for Mark's dutiful son's kiss.

"Shall we have a cocktail or glass of wine here before we go out to dinner?" Rita inquired when the greeting had been accomplished and she was included once again.

Mark glanced at his watch, his expression an advance denial in itself. "No, I think not. I made early dinner reservations." He smiled indulgently at his mother. "I know you and Father are used to eating ear—" He broke off in surprise at the sound of the door chimes, and both he and his mother automatically looked over at Rita, whose expression answered their unspoken question. She wasn't expecting a caller.

"Excuse me while I answer that," Rita said and went to the door, a little pleased smile curving her lips in response to the exchange taking place behind her back.

"You're a very lucky man, Mark. I'm sure you know that," Katherine Pendleton told her son in a fond tone that suggested he was deserving of his good fortune.

"You bet your life I know it," Mark replied complacently.

The smile froze on Rita's lips as she opened the door and, with no preparation for the sight that awaited her, saw her caller. Unable to speak, she stared in numb horror at a youthful apparition of her mother in cheap, trendy clothes, the flame hair a shoulder-length tangle of waves and curls, the pretty face heavily made up for sensual emphasis on the eyes and mouth. For Rita it was like looking into a cruel mirror and seeing herself nine years ago at the age of eighteen the way she could have been, if she hadn't been so determined to escape her origins.

"Hi, Rita, it's me, Edna. Your little sister. Remember me? Guess I've changed a lot. I was only nine when you took off from home."

Rita visibly cringed with the first words spoken in a brash, uneducated young voice into which uncertainty crept as Edna quickly read her lack of welcome and talked louder and faster as though to bolster her own ebbing confidence.

"Guess I'm the last person you expected to find on your doorstep, huh? Guess you're wondering how in the world I tracked you down. It wasn't as hard as I thought. Everybody knows you down at that big fancy store where you work. Sorry to bust in on you like this, but I don't know another soul in Atlanta but you and Vince, the guy I thought I was eloping with, and I'd rather sleep on the street than spend another night with that lying bastard. Mamma'd kill me if she knew I was here, asking favors of you. She never would even let us kids write you. She was mad at you for taking off the way you did, without so much as a goodbye, and then you wrote her that letter about how you didn't want to have anything to do with any of us anymore—"

"I never *said*—" Rita's voice seemed to come to her ears from a great distance. She felt strangely unreal. This was all some terrible nightmare.

"Maybe that's not what you said in so many words," Edna amended cheerfully, "but that's what you must have meant since you never wrote or came to visit. Course we moved again right after you left and you didn't have no way of knowin' the address. No hard feelings, honest. And it looks like you've done real good for yourself. When somebody showed Mamma that article in the society section of the Atlanta newspaper about you being engaged to some super respectable lawyer fellow with an uppity family and you with a good job with that big store, I could tell she was real proud deep down. Mamma always wanted to 'get' somewhere and 'be' somebody herself."

Edna nervously shifted the gold chain strap of her small handbag on her shoulder. She had been prepared for a possible cool reception, even hostility, but not for this numb despair. Rita's frozen pale features and dead eyes belonged to the next of kin at a funeral and made Edna deeply uneasy.

"I'm real sorry I barged in on you like this," she apologized, making a tentative gesture toward Rita. "I got myself in this pickle, and I shouldn't have bothered you. I promise I won't ever again. All I'm asking is a place to spend the night and enough money to take a bus back home to Florida. That's where we're living now. I'll pay the money back." Her voice grew philosophically bitter. "Lord knows I hate to go back and listen to all the 'I told you so' crap. Mamma told me Vince was just giving me a line so that I'd travel around with him on his salesman's job. She said he didn't really intend to marry me."

Edna blew out her breath in a loud sigh that deprecated and yet accepted her untenable position of having been proven wrong. Rita could feel the sound waves traveling past her into the living room, where Mark and his mother were entombed in silence, listening to Edna's every word spoken in the uncultivated tones that matched her appearance and condemned her to the ranks of the low class.

"You might as well come in," Rita said tonelessly, opening the door wider and standing to one side for Edna to enter.

The damage had already been done, and in her heart she knew it was irremediable. In those few minutes standing outside Rita's door, Edna had destroyed Rita's nine-year effort to establish credibility as a suitable mate for a man like Mark Pendleton. Numb with the conviction that all was lost, Rita couldn't muster the will to try to curb Edna or assert control. The strange sensation that it was all a terrible nightmare persisted. Her best protective mechanism was to remain numb with shock.

Inside the apartment Edna took in quick, nervous impressions of her surroundings and Rita's guests and felt more ill at ease than ever with no support forthcoming from her sister, who was continuing to act like a zombie. Taking matters into her own hands, Edna introduced herself and determined the identity of Mark and his mother. In the face of their shocked politeness, she felt called upon to apologize at length for her intrusion and to elaborate upon the explanation for her presence that she had already given Rita at the door. Unknowingly she managed to paint a graphic picture of her—and Rita's—background, the kind in which yelling matches with parents, even the exchange of blows, and dropping out of school are commonplace and home is a place to escape.

Edna would actually have welcomed stopping at any point, but since no one except her seemed inclined to say anything, she didn't know what to do but keep on talking, and the only subject she had in common with Rita's visitors was Rita herself. She supplied details of Rita's personal history that made Rita's soul curl up inside her, explaining that Rita was to be commended for leaving home when she was eighteen, Edna's present age, and breaking off contact with her family, having up until that time been a household drudge and unpaid baby-sitter. Edna and Rita's mother had always worked at night and needed to get her sleep during the day.

In the interest of fairness, Edna had to say that their mother had done the best she could to provide the necessities for her children, earning more than most mothers without the benefit of a high school education by waiting tables in cocktail lounges and nightclubs, where being pretty and having a fabulous figure got her big tips. Edna herself looked just like her mother and was the same personality type, liking the nightlife, glamorous clothes, and good times. She had hoped to have better luck with men than her mother, who always seemed to marry men with big ideas who let her down.

At this point Edna turned to Rita and filled her in on her mother's matrimonial history since Rita's departure from home, revealing that the current marriage was their mother's fifth and might be the one to last. She and her husband were faring quite well as proprietors of a honky-tonk that was doing great weekend business with live country-western entertainers.

Mark and his mother wouldn't have been human not to react to the unexpected appearance of a sister of Rita's with curiosity and interest, whatever she had turned out to be. Rita never talked about her family. Her past was a gray void to them. Edna was so different from anything they might have expected that they were understandably incredulous.

The physical resemblance between the sisters was apparent on first sight and all the more disquieting because of the marked contrasts. Seeing Rita and Edna side by side raised the distinct possibility that the older sister had tamed and subdued a natural beauty of the flamboyant variety, for Edna, dressed and made up to look like the understudy for a hooker, was nonetheless strikingly pretty with an earthy sex appeal that came from being thoroughly at ease with a body shaped to please men. She had an abrasive outgoing charm that her poised and perfectly groomed older sister lacked. Mark Pendleton was intrigued and intimidated by what had been lost in the transformation of an Edna into a Rita. He was eerily reminded of famous multiple personality cases and wondered what other secrets were hidden behind Rita's composed, deathly pale face.

Throughout Edna's rambling discourse, Rita watched Mark and his mother, noted the fascination with which they listened to the exposure of Rita's past and their discreet exchange of glances with occasional looks in her direction. Whatever contempt or pity or indignation they were masking behind their carefully polite expressions she was convinced that they were communicating those feelings to each other. It was this perception that Mark and his mother were solidly in league—standing on one side of an invisible line of class distinction, with Rita and Edna on the other side— that helped to pull Rita out of her lethargy. Mentally, she aligned herself with her sister. Through no fault of theirs, she and Edna shared the same background, whose liabilities Rita had so foolishly thought she could overcome.

Plunging the room into a dreadful quiet, Edna suddenly stopped midsentence, as though overwhelmed with the hopelessness of her efforts to talk them all into a restoration of the normal. Looking from one of them to the other, she let her gaze rest on Rita.

"I really made a mess of things showing up like this, didn't I?" she said miserably. "I'm terribly sorry. If you could just lend me the money for bus fare and a taxi, I'll get out of here and never bother you again." Her eyes touched on Rita's apparel and then made a glancing inspection of Mark and his mother. "Judging from the way you all are dressed up, you were planning to go out when I busted in. I just hope I haven't held you up from something special."

"We were about to go out to dinner," Mark spoke up, finally discovering his voice. Uncertainly he looked over to Rita for some indication that she wished him to include her sister in their dinner plans.

Rita did a mental recoil at the notion of transferring the incompatible foursome to the dignified restaurant where Mark had made reservations and continuing there what was an awkward and pointless situation. Apparently Katherine Pendleton's thoughts were running along the same lines.

"Perhaps Rita would like to spend some time in private with her sister," the older woman put in quickly. "I'll just pack my things and go to a hotel so that Edna can have the guest bedroom."

Rita's quick surge of resentment brought a flush of color to her pale features and fire to her dark eyes. As much as she would look forward to being rid of both Mark and his mother while she tried to come to terms with what had happened, it wasn't the place of Mark's mother to start organizing and bossing them all around. This was Rita's apartment, and she was the hostess, the one in charge. The cool courtesy of her tone as she addressed the older woman made that view pointedly clear.

"That's very kind of you to make that offer. I'm sure you'll be much more comfortable in a hotel. It's also thoughtful of you to suggest that my sister and I not join you and Mark for dinner. We do have family matters to discuss and so, I'm sure, do the two of you.''

Katherine Pendleton's sharp little intake of breath in response to Rita's unmistakable sarcasm was audible in the dead silence. Mark looked uneasily from Rita to his mother and back to Rita.

"Why don't you and your sis—" he began in an obvious peacemaker's attempt that was peremptorily cut off by his mother.

"Mark, perhaps Rita will be so kind as to permit you to use her telephone and make me a hotel reservation while I go and pack."

"Of course, Rita won't mind, Mother," Mark replied in a conciliatory tone, but he was speaking to his mother's erect back as she made her exit from the living room. The pained mixture of apology and reproach on his face was joined by uncertainty as he looked at Rita and read in her dark gaze a disdain he had never seen there before. "Or maybe you will mind," he said, shaking his head. "I'm not certain of much of anything right this minute."

Rita's bitter smile was no reassurance. "Don't worry, Mark. Your mother will sort it all out for you and tell you what to do."

Her words brought a dull flush to Mark's face, but failed to sting him into making a defensive reply. He didn't have to say aloud what he was thinking. Rita could read his thoughts in his eyes as he looked at her with hurt disbelief: *The girl he had thought he was marrying wouldn't have said those words to him, wouldn't have looked at him with contempt in her face. This new Rita from a totally unsuspected background was a stranger to him.*

The distrust and uncertainty were still there in Mark's eyes the next day when Rita met him during her lunch hour. She went with little hope of salvaging her carefully planned future with him, and yet to have her fears confirmed at once by his telltale uneasiness jolted her with a sickening disappointment. She wanted to get the painful business over with and manage to conduct herself with dignity and pride, but her bitterness was her undoing. It kept welling up, causing her to lash out and deal death blows to an already injured relationship.

At the outset Mark only wanted to buy time, but his approach, intended to be diplomatic, came across as condescending, and Rita's hurt response to it succeeded in totally destroying her former image in Mark's eyes and convincing him that he'd been misled. Rita wasn't the woman he had thought he was marrying. She wasn't even tempered and reasonable, and, most upsetting of all, it didn't seem to Mark that she had a very high opinion of him. Because Rita was too proud to open up to him and explain the craving for respectability that had been her driving force, he was left at the end wondering why she had wanted to marry him.

"Mother drove back to Athens first thing this morning," Mark began evenly and thought he managed fairly well to make it simply a statement, not a recrimination for what he'd been through nor an expression of his enormous relief that his mother was gone. The previous night ranked as the most hellish of his life. He'd wished a thousand times that Rita's sister could have chosen a time to appear when his mother wasn't present. It wasn't that his mother wasn't justified in her shocked reaction to the disclosure of Rita's past, but that she'd had to keep hashing everything over and over and repeating herself.

"She wants to know as soon as possible what we decide about the wedding," Mark went on, carefully picking his words. "She and I discussed the possibility over dinner last night that your sister's visit might lead to a reconciliation with your family. You might want to include them in the wedding plans and there's hardly time to change anything.'' Mark shrugged to emphasize his logic and left a hopeful little pause for her concurrence, but Rita's answering silence accompanied by a bleak, knowing smile forced him to continue.

"We thought, too, that you might have some thoughts of taking Edna under your wing, perhaps encouraging her to finish her high school education and go on to college. If so, that could have some effect upon our marriage plans.'' Mark's pause this time wasn't nearly so hopeful. The contempt in Rita's face prepared him for a sarcastic reply.

"I'm sure you and your mother did a thorough job of discussing all the possibilities, Mark," she said cuttingly. "I can just bet that the thought of my family coming to the wedding gave both of you nightmares. As for my sister, she left Atlanta this morning with her lover, who'd spent a sleepless night worrying about her on her own in a big city. He's promised to marry her as soon as his job allows him to be in one place long enough to satisfy the marriage requirements. Be sure to pass along that romantic tidbit to your mother when you get back to your office and call to make your report.''

Mark flushed a dark angry shade of red. "I've had about enough of these cracks about my mother. All this time I thought the two of you got along so well. Frankly, my mother was upset about what happened last night, and so was I. We both had good reason. I left your apartment feeling like I was about to marry somebody I didn't know. Postponing the wedding at this late stage is awkward for everybody concerned, but I think we need to get to know each other better before—'' Rita's mirthless laugh made him break off and stare at her.

"Surely you aren't about to say 'before we rush into anything,' Mark?" Rita mocked bitterly. "We've been engaged for two years. Why don't you be honest and admit the truth. You and your mother were shocked to learn about the kind of background I come from, and you no longer consider me worthy of being a Pendleton."

"For God's sake, leave my mother out of it!" Mark banged his fist on the table in exasperation. "You have to admit that what you did isn't normal, Rita. You not only cut off all communication with your family, but you didn't even tell the man you were going to marry of their existence. Can't you see the situation from my point of view?"

"There has never been any doubt in my mind about your point of view—on anything, Mark," Rita said wearily. "I knew what your reaction would be if you knew the truth about me, and I was foolish enough to think you'd never have to know. Right now I'd have a lot more respect for you if you were man enough to face the issue head on. You know our wedding isn't just to be postponed—it's to be *canceled*. Your mother will never allow you to marry me now. Well, as far as I'm concerned, it takes place on schedule or not at all. Ever." Her smile was bitterly knowing, but in her dark eyes there lurked a faint pleading. Mark's frustration over the whole deplorable situation was deepened by the knowledge that he had to deny the unspoken plea.

"You're not being reasonable, Rita!"

His protest extinguished the tiny flickering hope that had burned despite all reason. With its death came several seconds of blackest despair that Rita had to dispel somehow or else she would wail and keen her grief. In desperation she reached for anger and hatred. She despised Mark for being weak and predictable. She despised herself for having been a fool, clinging to hope when hope was obviously gone. She hated life itself for being so damnably unfair. The powerful negative emotions burned inside her, providing a painful kind of relief. She was quite oblivious to the fact that the strong feelings that consumed her also ignited her beauty, bringing color to her fine pale skin and splendid passion to her dark eyes. Mark stared in utter fascination and waited in dread for the explosion of words that never came.

The change in her appearance excited and frightened him. It was unnerving to have the composed, subdued woman he had been on the verge of marrying disappear before his eyes and become transformed with blazing, scornful beauty. She was a book he thought he had perused and found thoroughly to his liking, only to discover that it was a story of intrigue that he lacked the courage to read. Mark wasn't man enough to confront the kind of challenge that this changed Rita presented him. He couldn't cope with her complexity, with her dark passion. His insight into his own inadequacies caused him regret, which Rita mistook as pity.

"Rita, please, I'm truly sorry—"

"Don't be, Mark," Rita cut in proudly, her anger deflating in the presence of her hardening resolve. "Believe me, I'll manage. I always have. Please inform your mother that the wedding's off, forever. I'm sure she'll want to take care of all the details of canceling it herself. After all, she decided everything herself, including the most convenient date. Her instincts must have told her that her future daughter-in-law didn't have the right kind of background to plan her own wedding." Rita paused scornfully to give Mark an opportunity to rise to some defense of his mother, but when he just shook his head in resigned dismay, she continued the painful summation of the necessary steps in severing their ties.

"We'll have to go down to the bank together and close out the money fund account, since it's in both our names. Then there's the honeymoon trip to cancel. At this late date there won't be much of a refund, but whatever there is, we can divide it—''

Rita's voice broke and her hard composure deserted her with the mention of the honeymoon trip, which, unlike her wedding, she had planned herself, with considerable effort. It had been a challenge to plan a wonderful honeymoon idyll within the budget they'd set for themselves. She'd spent many hours talking to travel agents and reading brochures and had found a honeymoon package trip to Hawaii that included air fare and luxury hotel accommodations for a price within their limit. Rita had been looking forward eagerly to the trip, which would actually be her first real vacation. She'd never even flown on a jet. With the realization that the wonderful trip was going to be denied her, like all her other hard-won dreams, suddenly everything together was more than she could bear.

"I just don't think I can stand facing everybody," she whispered despairingly, looking beyond Mark into nothingness. "My friends, everyone down at the store. I wish I could go somewhere far away where nobody knows me and hide until it's all over and everybody forgets." She swallowed and blinked her eyes furiously to clear away the painful smarting of tears. Bringing her gaze back to Mark's somber, uncomfortable face, she smiled a bitter, humorless smile. "Here we both are with two weeks' vacation time scheduled and nowhere to go. Maybe we should flip a coin for the Hawaiian trip. That way one of us would still get to see paradise."

Mark's disapproving expression told her that he thought her black humor was in bad taste at such a time as this. It was the perverse urge to shock him further that led Rita to pursue what hadn't been a serious suggestion at all.

"I can see the idea doesn't have much appeal for you," she said flippantly, "but then you were never as excited about going to Hawaii as I was. In that case, it won't be necessary to flip a coin. We can just agree that the trip's all mine. I can pay you half of whatever the refund would have been—''

"Come on, Rita, enough's enough!" Mark broke in nervously, uneasy with the note of hysteria that was creeping into her voice. On top of everything else, he didn't want a scene. "You know good and well that you're not going by yourself on our honeymoon trip!"

"I wouldn't be so sure of that, Mark," Rita returned defiantly. Suddenly she seemed to be looking inward and examining with a touch of fright the improbable course of action that was fast emerging in her mind as an actual possibility. Her voice was awed and sad as she spoke aloud her mental passage to decision.

"I wouldn't have to do a thing except finish packing all those clothes I've bought into my new luggage, get on the airplane and go. I have all the travel documents at home. It would be so easy, and it would be somewhere far, far away where nobody would know."

Mark stared at her unbelievingly. "But, Rita, what on earth will people *say*! Our honeymoon trip!" His voice was that of a man who doesn't really expect to get through with reason.

"Not *our* honeymoon trip, Mark," Rita corrected him sadly. "It's only *my* honeymoon trip now, and I'm taking it without you. It may well be the only one I ever have. As for people talking, I've had practice with that growing up, when I hadn't done a thing to cause gossip. This time at least I'll be the cause of it myself."

"Rita, you never told me—"

"No, Mark, I never did tell you," Rita said quietly, rising to her feet. "Whether I was right or wrong in not doing so is a dead issue now, don't you agree?"

Rita waited only a moment, and her pause was purely for emphasis. Her hope had died minutes earlier and wasn't ever to be exhumed. Mark Pendleton sat with slumped shoulders and regret on his face as he watched her walk away from him, out of his life. Once, when there was still time to call out and stop her, he opened his mouth to speak and then closed it again.

Chapter Two

With the announcement of the last call for boarding Flight 555, bound nonstop for San Francisco, Jack Adams folded his newspaper, tucked it under his arm, and stepped up to the check-in counter at the gate.

"Well, what's the verdict?" he inquired and drew a sympathetic smile from the airline agent behind the counter by slitting his throat with an imaginary knife. Jack had been up at the counter several times during the past twenty minutes, but he was the type who could be persistent without annoying people. It was an invaluable personality trait that he had fine-honed during a short but highly successful career in automobile sales and then used to advantage as a young business entrepreneur.

"Keep your fingers crossed, Mr. Adams. We have two unoccupied seats at this time." The airline agent touched keys on his computer terminal and read the information on the monitor as he called it up. "A party of two with the same last name, Pendleton, with a connecting flight in San Francisco to Honolulu. Of course, they still have a couple of minutes to show."

Jack groaned in quick understanding of the man's reasoned guess that the missing passengers were man and wife and would make a belated appearance together or not at all.

"I don't have a prayer if this trip is the big once-in-a-lifetime vacation in Hawaii. They'll make this flight if Mrs. Pendleton has to grab onto a wing and keep the plane from clearing the ground while poor old Pendleton catches up with all the suitcases." Jack grinned in appreciation of his own good-natured pessimism. "Better a business trip with the missus going along. That way there's always a chance one of the kids could get the sniffles and keep Mrs. P. home."

He watched the agent pick up the phone and knew immediately from the man's commiserative glance in his direction that the call was an alert to the Pendletons' late arrival at the airport. The agent was being instructed not to let the plane leave without them. Now Jack would have to wait another two hours for the flight to which he'd been reassigned when his own flight was canceled for "operational difficulties," a catchall term in airport jargon that could mean anything from engine difficulties to an underbooked flight.

Jack was about to turn away when he heard the agent inquire, "Did I understand you to say *passenger*, singular? Male or female? I see." As he hung up, the man's face offered cautious encouragement. "That was a message from our check-in station in the main terminal that a passenger for this flight is on the way." The agent lifted his eyebrows. "A lady passenger. Her husband may still be along."

Jack digested the information with surprised interest. "Mrs. P. going to Hawaii by herself? Guess it won't hurt to stick around a couple of minutes more and see what's up."

He moved around to the side of the counter where he could see the busy concourse with passengers of every description coming and going. Dressed in lightweight slacks, a V-neck pullover sweater that revealed an open-throat knit shirt, and worn, comfortable loafers, with his newspaper folded under one arm and his jacket hooked over the other shoulder, Jack was recognizable in both his dress and his manner as being a seasoned, casual traveler thoroughly at home in airports. Since the age of twelve, when his mismatched parents had divorced, he'd been traversing the country on visits to his mother, and he'd learned long ago to put impatience on hold, take delays with calm, and use the time to mentally breach the distance between point of departure and destination.

As a youth he'd had to make the transition between the widely disparate worlds of his parents. The trip from east to west took him from his father's Boston house with all its unbending rules to Taos or Sante Fe, Sausalito or Maui, wherever his freewheeling artist mother was currently in residence. He went from rigid discipline to no discipline at all, from the pressure of paternal expectations to an atmosphere where conventional notions of success were nonexistent.

It had been confusing to have parents who were opposite poles of life-style and philosophy. Jack had wished that he could please his exacting father, and yet he'd inherited too much imaginative energy from his mother to submit to dull regimen. Test scores showed he was bright, but his academic performance had been highly inconsistent. He made A's in courses that challenged him and D's and F's in those he found insufferably boring.

When in his third year he'd dropped out of the ivy league university where he had been admitted solely as the result of his father's pulling strings and joined the navy as an enlisted man, his father had washed his hands of him, declaring that Jack was his mother's child. But that wasn't true. Jack had his New England father's shrewd business acumen and money sense as well as his drive. He simply had to find his own challenges, set his own goals and reach them, live his own life.

He'd been doing that in the midwest since his discharge from the navy, settling in St. Louis first, not because it was a geographical compromise between rocky New England and the warm Pacific climate but because a navy buddy lived there. The buddy's uncle had a car dealership, and Jack went to work for him as a salesman because there wasn't anything else he particularly wanted to do. His first year he was top salesman for the dealership, the next year tops in the state for all dealerships selling the same make of car, and the third year tops in the whole midwest.

By the end of that third year, Jack was tired of selling cars. The challenge was gone, and he wanted to move on to something different. With the savings he had accumulated, he joined with two other young investors in buying a tract of land in rural Illinois and developing it into a subdivision for young couples building first homes. Jack's selling skills had come in handy in negotiating with bankers for financing. The venture had been a success and had opened up his next business opportunity, a combination gas station and convenience store in an ideal location near the subdivision.

It had made an impressive profit almost from the first day it was open, and now, a year later, Jack had sold out his interest and had every reason to be proud of his financial accomplishment at the age of thirty. He wondered how many of his university classmates had done as well with their prestigious degrees. But Jack wasn't the kind to sit for long and bask in his success. He knew that soon he'd be involved one hundred per cent in whatever new opportunity showed itself.

It felt good to be confident of his entrepreneurial instincts. He was going to test them next in a different geographical location, somewhere with a kinder climate and a more fun loving attitude toward life than either staid, rocky New England or the stolid midwest. That's why he was flying out of Atlanta. He'd spent the past two weeks in the Sunbelt, exploring the possibility that he should go south.

He had spent most of the time driving, picking up a rental car in Charleston, South Carolina, and returning it in Miami. The weather had been disappointing, unusually cold and rainy for November everyone said. Jack had looked up several contacts, talked to numerous people along the way, and hadn't once felt his personal radar go off. But, then, it hadn't been turned on. That was what he'd learned from his trip. Before he could open himself to any other place, he had to go to Hawaii and find out if all the signs pointing him there were trustworthy.

First there had been the eagerness when he made his plans to visit his mother. It was more than the usual anticipation of seeing her, enjoying her company and being amused by her wacky friends and unconventional life-style. Somewhat to his mystification, Jack felt oddly as if he were going *home*, and he'd never lived in Hawaii. He and his sister Beth had visited Lillian Adams at the Maui beach house numerous times during holidays and summer vacations and had had wonderful times there, but Jack was hard put to explain why it was more special to him than any other house in his memory, even his father's Boston house, where Jack had grown up.

Yet it wasn't just the house that called up pangs of nostalgia, but the island of Maui itself. When Jack would think about his favorite haunts, he was surprised to find just how indelibly the special beauty of mountain, plain and sea was imprinted in his memory. He remembered the sentiments if not the exact words of Mark Twain and other famous people who'd visited the Hawaiian islands and fallen under the spell of their allure, which was almost magical, defying analysis.

Despite this kindling of emotion over his visit to Hawaii, it had still been just that, a visit, until he picked up a financial magazine with an article extolling the Hawaiian islands as a business frontier. The content of the article jibed with his mother's complaints that Maui was becoming so commercialized that she was thinking strongly of moving over to more rural Kauai. Suddenly Jack had felt a light bulb clicking on over his head and the idea of moving to Hawaii was born.

It had taken some discipline not to cancel his southern reconnaissance and go rushing out to Maui two weeks early, but, contrary to the opinion Jack's father held of him, Jack had that discipline. He didn't intend to make any snap decisions. He would keep his same travel plans. Once he'd arrived on Hawaiian soil, he would look into the financial climate, decide if there was any substance to his nostalgia, and make the right decision for himself.

Now that it was only a matter of hours before he could begin making all those discoveries, Jack's eagerness was difficult to curb. He was finding it more difficult than usual not to be impatient with travel delays, but when he realized that he was standing there in the Atlanta airport wishing some mishap upon a stranger in order to get his seat, Jack reprimanded himself for his selfishness. What were an extra two hours in his life?

In this philosophical state of mind, he awaited the appearance of the woman he had already labeled in his mind as Mrs. Pendleton. When an austerely beautiful auburn-haired young woman dressed to the hilt came rushing along the concourse, Jack eyed her in idle appreciation, but wasn't prepared for her headlong rush straight for the counter beside which he lounged. He came to attention and studied her with surprised interest. While he hadn't taken the trouble to imagine in any detail what Mrs. Pendleton would look like, the name had brought to mind a matronly dignified type.

At first sight this young woman was wrong for either of the two possible travel scenarios in which Jack had placed her: vacationing with her husband or accompanying him on a business trip. The intuition that had seldom failed Jack in sizing up people told him that she was a solitary traveler. Something about her state of agitation at being late suggested that she wasn't depending on the support of a husband who would appear momentarily, and Jack feared somewhat guiltily that the circumstances weren't happy ones. He got the impression that making the flight had been a matter of life and death, and no pleasure was involved. Feeling like an unintentional culprit in having coveted her husband's seat, he watched and eavesdropped on her transaction with the airline agent.

"Here's my ticket," Rita gasped, thrusting the packet of travel documents at the uniformed man behind the counter. While he opened it with an experienced hand and took out the booklet of airline tickets, she grasped the edge of the counter to help her trembling legs hold her upright. "I would be so lucky as to take a taxi that would have an accident on the way to the airport," she said bitterly, confirming for Jack with her voice more than the comment itself his perception of her as an unhappy young woman.

The airline man looked up with professional sympathy from his perusal of the tickets for two and then glanced beyond her to determine that her missing traveling companion wasn't headed that way.

"Pendleton, party of two," he stated with a note of inquiry and didn't have time to say more before Rita was correcting him tersely.

"My name is Jones, not Pendleton. There won't be anyone using the extra ticket. I'm traveling alone."

If her nerves hadn't been so jangled and she hadn't been a rank novice in airline travel, she wouldn't have bothered to make the name correction, nor would she have added a curt explanation in response to the polite flicker of expression on the airline official's face. "Don't worry, I didn't steal somebody's tickets. Whenever they were bought, I thought my name would be Pendleton by the time I was taking this trip, but things didn't work out that way. It's still Jones and isn't likely to change any time soon."

From his listening station, Jack absorbed the explanation behind his own good luck with some incredulity. What an unlikely situation! It seemed that the Pendletons were to have been a newly married couple, and the trip to Hawaii their honeymoon trip. The wedding hadn't taken place, but the bride was going ahead with the trip minus the bridegroom, whose seat Jack would be occupying on the plane! At least he didn't have to feel guilty. It stood to reason that the wedding hadn't been canceled in the last thirty minutes, when Jack had first requested to go on standby for the flight.

Whatever normal curiosity he felt was quickly doused by caution. He'd do well not to encourage Miss Jones to tell her story. Judging from the way she'd dealt with the airline man, Jack suspected she'd welcome the opportunity to give a detailed and heavily biased account of her romantic tragedy. It would be like uncapping a gusher, he feared. There was that hint of tightly controlled hysteria in her manner that made him wary. He could spend the several hours to San Francisco being lectured on poor Pendleton's faults. Without knowing any of the facts, his sympathy rested instinctively with a fellow male who'd undoubtedly been given the boot at the last minute. Jack assumed that Miss Jones had called off the wedding. A woman gutsy enough to take her honeymoon trip alone wouldn't tolerate being left at the altar.

Cool it, Adams, don't get friendly, he told himself as he moved around to take Rita's vacated place at the front of the counter.

Rita had been a bundle of nerves on the way to the airport, even before the taxi accident. She'd been full of doubts about what she was doing and apprehensive about flying. The accident had seemed like the last straw, a chuckle of mean fate. Now as she made a turn in the mazelike boarding tunnel and saw ahead of her the open hatchway of the jet, it was like a maw about to swallow her up. Nervousness intensified into panic, and she wished with all her heart that she hadn't been able to make it to the airport on time.

Even if the jet didn't crash, sending her to her death along with all the other passengers, she was still leaving everything that was familiar and going far away to a strange place where she'd be totally alone, totally on her own. She had been mentally unbalanced to do something so crazy as this. Who in her right mind would take her honeymoon trip alone?

For all Rita's qualms, there seemed no stopping the forward momentum. An airline attendant was beckoning her to hurry, greeting her and then directing her on to the main cabin, where Rita was struck with dizziness at the sea of strange faces. She avoided the eyes of all the strangers and concentrated on the seat numbers at a level above their heads.

When she found her seats, they were in the right-hand row of two abreast along the outside of the aisle. Confronted with the choice of sitting next to the window or next to the aisle, she chose the aisle, afraid that looking down on the takeoff would only frighten her more. The aisle seat also had the advantage of being one step closer to the lavatories she'd passed on her way to the seats. If air sickness struck, she might have to bolt for one of them.

Placing her handbag and her small piece of carry-on luggage on the empty seat by the window, Rita fastened her seat belt and took deep, slow breaths, trying to calm her nerves. She wished those passengers who were getting up and retrieving items from overhead bins or going in search of magazines would settle down in their places so that the plane could take off. Once they were in the air, she hoped her fears would abate with the realization that there was no turning back.

Glancing nervously at her watch, she saw that it was time for the scheduled departure, but she still couldn't hear the engines running. What was the cause for delay? Looking up her aisle, she was able to answer the question herself. A late passenger had come on board, looking cheerfully unconcerned about the fact that he might be causing several hundred people to wait.

Rita summed him up with a glance as the type who couldn't be bothered with punctuality along with a lot of other rules of consideration. He was used to getting by on his casual good looks and charm. That was obvious from the confident way he carried himself and made smiling eye contact with his fellow passengers. She couldn't deny that he was good-looking. His squared jawline gave strength to a face with nicely modeled features, including a mouth women would definitely find sexy. As far as she was concerned, she thought his blond hair could have done with a trim and a combing, and his clothes were more appropriate for lounging around and watching TV on a Saturday afternoon at home than traveling on an airplane.

As the object of her disapproval came closer, Rita looked away toward the window in a private display of her own immunity to his brand of male charisma. She admired a man with more dignity and reserve. This fellow was the handsome wheeling and dealing sort her mother had always fallen for. That was probably why he looked vaguely familiar.

When the late arrival stopped next to Rita, she shot him a coolly questioning glance. His easy bland smile did nothing to change her brief critical assessment of his personality and character. The smile was designed to cope with a multiple of unfriendly attitudes that he might encounter in his amble through life. When he addressed her, his attractive well-modulated voice came as no surprise, but his question brought momentary puzzlement as to his meaning, if not his motive, which was simply to get her attention and win her over to admiring him along with the rest of the world.

"Would you like me to get that out of your way?"

"I beg your pardon?"

"Your carry-on bag." He nodded toward her unoccupied seat next to the window. "I'll be happy to find a place for that. Otherwise it'll have to go on the floor and take up foot space."

"No, thank you." The polite refusal suggested that he mind his own business, and lest it wasn't a clear enough discouragement from any other unwanted offers, Rita firmly averted her gaze toward the window again. She could sense his hesitation and was satisfied that she had put him in his place when he said nothing more.

When he didn't move on down the aisle to wherever his seat was located, Rita had to contain her irritation. Why was he searching through the overhead bins in a section where all the seats were taken? He was opening and banging them shut as though he had every right, presumably in search for a place to stow his brown leather flight bag, which looked as if it had been kicked around the world several times. Rita thought of her own beautiful new luggage and hoped fervently that it wouldn't be all dirty and scraped when it arrived in Hawaii. She had hated checking it.

"Excuse me, please—"

The pleasantly determined words brought her to startled attention. She looked up to find an expression on his face that matched his steely undertone. The squared jaw was resolute. The smile on the attractive mouth had taken on a businesslike cast and the clear gray eyes issued no friendly invitation. More than anything else, Rita was taken aback by the suggestion of authority in his manner.

"Could I get past to my seat, please?" It was more an announcement than a request, polite but firm.

Rita's eyes widened with her comprehension of his obvious error, which made her see his behavior in a new, less offensive light. No wonder he had offered to stow her small case, which he thought was sitting in his own seat. He'd also assumed that he was stowing his own bag in a convenient place. Now he'd have to go through the trouble of retrieving it and stowing it again, closer to his actual seat.

"This isn't your seat. It's *my* seat—I paid for it, too," she explained with a wan smile that mingled apology with private sadness.

With his insight into Rita's situation, Jack had been able to surmise fairly quickly her assumption that the seat next to her would be unoccupied. Her cold-shoulder treatment of him strengthened his initial impressions of her as a bitchy type and killed whatever sympathy he might have felt on her behalf. He was prepared to do battle for his seat. If she wanted to create a scene that would broadcast her romantic plight to everyone in earshot, that was up to her. But then Rita spoke to him in that gentle, apologetic tone and smiled her pathetic little effort at a smile, letting him look into her incredibly beautiful dark eyes and see her unhappiness. Jack's sympathies abruptly changed, and he found himself wondering what kind of bastard Pendleton must have been to hurt her like this.

With one of the airline attendants bearing down upon him, coming to hurry him up and get him seated, he had to act fast.

"Would you look at this?" he said disgustedly, holding his boarding pass so that Rita could read the seat assignment scrawled in bold black ink. "The guy at the gate told me this was the only empty seat on the whole plane. Now I find out it's taken."

"It's not exactly *taken*. Nobody else is sitting here—" Rita stopped, aware of several heads turned in their direction. She didn't want everyone on the plane feeling sorry for her.

Jack let relief flood his face. "That's great news. Would you mind if I sat there then?" Right on cue the jet's engines came to life. The airline attendant reached Jack and asked him to please take his seat and fasten his seat belt.

"Seats in an upright position and all carry-on items under the seat in front of you," she reminded, eyeing Rita's things in Jack's seat, and then swept on down the aisle.

"Are you sure you wouldn't rather sit by the window?" Jack asked when Rita had cleared his seat, unclipped her seat belt and stood up. "It doesn't matter to me."

The polite inquiry brought on a fresh bout of Rita's earlier indecision and with it a renewal of her nervousness.

"I don't know," she said, biting her lip. She looked undecidedly at the window and then at Jack. "I'd better not."

Jack noted her agitation and guessed that she was a nervous air traveler. The urge to touch her on the shoulder and make some reassuring comment was stronger than it should have been. Instead he stepped quickly to one side and gave her room to move into the aisle.

"If you change your mind, just let me know," he told her cheerfully as he took the window seat. "We can swap places any time." Mentally he gave himself some stern words of warning: *Keep in mind, Adams, you're just sitting in the absent bridegroom's seat, not taking his place.*

From past experience, Jack knew that it was wise when traveling by plane to establish early on one's own space and privacy. Conversation with seatmates could follow, but there was always a retreat. In this particular instance, such a strategy seemed more necessary than ever before. As soon as he had fastened his seat belt, he immediately unfolded his newspaper to the crossword puzzle he'd already partially worked and reached inside the vee of his sweater for the pencil stub in the pocket of his knit shirt.

Normally he could shut out distractions in almost any environment ranging from noisy turmoil to nerve-racking quiet, but today his concentration failed him, through no fault of his chance companion. Or at least through no *conscious* fault, but she was the reason Jack couldn't think of the word for a single clue. After one glance over in his direction, she had seemed to cancel out his very existence. He didn't need to partition off his portion of space. She had him walled in over by the window, and he didn't like the feeling.

Jack watched her covertly. As he'd suspected, she was definitely apprehensive about flying. She sat tense in her seat, her hands showing white at the knuckles with the force of her grip upon her leather handbag. Her attention was fixed upon the screen at the front of the large cabin where the safety film was playing, and from time to time she swallowed and took a deep breath.

Thinking that he would do her a favor by distracting her from the terrifying prospects of airborne disaster that the mention of escape hatches and life vests could excite in even a calm traveler, Jack tapped his pencil against his newspaper and made a little throat-clearing sound.

"You wouldn't happen to know—"

Rita cut him off with a sibilant "Shh" that would have done a librarian proud. Jack stared disbelievingly at her profile for several seconds, but she steadfastly ignored him, listening to every word of the safety routine that Jack could have recited for her himself. Feeling rebuffed, he turned his attention back to his crossword puzzle or at least tried to. It was impossible not to feel her nervous vibrations build into panic as the big plane taxied into takeoff position and then began rolling down the runway, gathering speed. A glance over at her showed him that her eyes were tightly closed and her face contorted in a silent cry of terror. Jack acted out of simple human compassion, knowing that he would probably be met with rebuff once again.

"Relax. Everything's okay," he said soothingly, covering one of her clenched hands with his.

Her reaction took him totally by surprise, but he didn't hesitate, slipping his arm around her when she turned blindly toward him and buried her face in his shoulder. He held her tight against him and murmured words of reassurance in the same tone he would have used with a frightened child. He was doing exactly what he'd told himself earlier that he had no intention of doing: standing in for the man who should have been there in this seat, holding her and calming her fears, and yet he couldn't feel a single regret on his own behalf. He liked being where he was at that moment. With the fragrance of her perfume in his nostrils and the tremors in her slender body making her seem feminine and vulnerable, Jack dispensed with his caution. He had to know the story behind this empty seat he was occupying. He had to know what kind of man she had trusted and given herself to. Gone was any unwillingness to hear the missing Pendleton's shortcomings.

When Rita first came to her senses, she didn't want to pull away. She felt blessedly safe and comforted. The arm encircling her was so strong and yet so gentle that she wished that she could stay there, with her face against the warm, solid wall of his chest, listening to the low soothing tones of his voice. She had to remind herself of the circumstances. She'd flung herself into the arms of this complete stranger, who was sitting where Mark should have been. Apparently Rita's handsome seat neighbor thought nothing of such occurrences.

"I'm terribly embarrassed," she murmured, sitting up and smoothing escaped tendrils of hair.

"Don't be. I didn't mind." Jack hadn't meant to sound intimate, but he found her flustered state appealing. With the pink color in her cheeks and her severe hairstyle mussed a bit, she was even more a knockout than before. He had a fleeting urge to pull out all her hairpins and see the rich auburn locks tumble down. The picture he imagined was highly provocative.

Rita read the sexual message in his admiring regard and was appalled at her own answering response. Instant physical attraction between total strangers was the stuff of cheap paperbacks and grade B movies. It didn't happen between nice people.

"I hope I didn't get lipstick on your sweater," she said stiffly, avoiding his eyes by examining the place on his sweater where she'd burrowed her face. "It's cashmere, isn't it?" The discovery had come from the contact of her cheek against the softness.

"It wouldn't matter if you had gotten lipstick on this old sweater," Jack told her with cheerful unconcern. "It's seen better days." He grinned. "I don't dare throw it away now, though. I'll have to keep wearing it on the chance that it'll bring me luck again. From now on, whenever I fly, I'll be hoping for a seat next to a beautiful woman in need of a strong shoulder on takeoffs. Can I expect the same reaction on landing?" It was light banter intended to help her relax. He hoped to draw at least a smile and hopefully a laugh. He'd like to hear her laugh. But she looked startled at his mock eager question and then deeply worried.

"I don't know. I hope not." She wound the strap of her handbag around one hand. "Actually I've never landed before. This is the first time I've ever flown."

Jack tried not to look surprised, but he knew he wasn't very successful. The revelation added to his curiosity about her. Judging from her appearance, she could afford air travel. If her fear of flying had kept her from it in the past, how had she worked up the nerve to head off to Hawaii alone on her honeymoon trip?

Rita was sensitive to his surprise and his curiosity, both of which were quite normal. She wasn't offended, but she shrank from the thought of further questions that would probe deeper into the circumstances surrounding this first flight experience. No longer nervous now that the plane had leveled off and there was no sensation of forward rushing movement, she felt emotionally drained. She wanted to sit

here in her seat and rest, quietly suspended between yesterday and tomorrow. If possible, she wouldn't even think, not
about anything. Her psychological fatigue was in her voice
and her distant smile as she thanked Jack and closed off
communication as effectively as if she'd pulled a glass shade
between them.

"Thank you for being such a good sport," she told him.
"I think I'll take a nap now." She turned her head forward, rested it on the back of her seat, and closed her eyes.

Jack eyed her with a mixture of compassion and mild
frustration for a full thirty seconds and then bent down to
retrieve his pencil, which had fallen to the floor. Once again
he had trouble concentrating on his crossword puzzle. Co-
vert glances over at the source of his distraction revealed
that despite her closed eyes she wasn't asleep and that her
thoughts, not surprisingly, weren't happy ones. From time
to time a little sigh would lift her breasts and escape her lips.
He wondered if her sad reflections upon all that was not
right in her life included a comparison of him with the man
who should have been sitting next to her. That idea was
more palatable than what he suspected to be the truth: that
she wasn't even aware that Jack was there.

He couldn't remember being so restless on a plane flight.
When the beverage cart made its trip down the aisle, he eagerly awaited it, hoping that it might pave the way for more
conversation, but he was disappointed. She ordered a coke
and sipped it in her somber isolation. When Jack found
himself waiting for lunch with the hope that sharing a meal
would provide him a chance to break through her reserve,
he took himself to task with a reminder of the facts. He
didn't even know this woman's first name. By accident he
was privy to insight that made him curious about her, but
she quite obviously had no iota of curiosity about him, no
slightest interest in him. They were strangers on an air-

plane. Jack should stop acting like an overwhelmed adolescent with an instant crush on a pretty girl.

He went back to his crossword puzzle with iron determination and had only a few words missing by the time lunch was served. He was squeezing the packet of salad dressing on his green salad when the beverage cart arrived and with it an unforeseen opportunity to come to his seat companion's aid once again. He acted quickly, with no other motive than to protect her.

"Champagne for the honeymoon couple, compliments of the airline," the attendant announced with a too-bright smile and thinly veiled curiosity that Jack comprehended instantly. He and Miss Jones definitely hadn't been behaving like a honeymoon couple.

Rita was stunned and mortified. "Oh, goodness—I didn't stop to think—" she stammered, feeling her cheeks grow hot.

"Thank you very much," Jack broke in with a broad grin that focused the airline attendant's attention completely upon him. "That's very nice, isn't it, darling?"

Rita's gasp and startled glance over at him must have made the situation even more odd to the attendant, but she served the champagne and promised to return with refills.

Rita sat there staring in chagrin at the glass in her hand. "I never thought—" she said miserably.

"Cheers," Jack said gently, reaching his glass over and touching it to hers. "I guess you're thinking I'm some nervy bastard who'll do anything to get free champagne."

Rita looked at him reluctantly. "You certainly were quick-thinking." She frowned. "You didn't *know* somehow?"

Jack might have lied if her anxiety hadn't been so transparent. He couldn't have her think that she wore some invisible announcement of her plight. His rueful expression was advance admission that he had known.

"I was waiting on standby at the gate and heard you explain the name business to the airline fellow." He shrugged. "I put two and two together and guessed." The knowledge that this was her first airplane flight gave him a new understanding of that exchange with the airline official. She'd been nervous and hadn't known enough about airport procedure to realize that establishing her identity wasn't necessary. Her curtness had been a defense, not bitchiness.

Rita put her untasted champagne carefully on her lunch tray. She was putting together her own two and two and realizing how little he had deserved her intuitive criticism of him as a chronically late, inconsiderate type.

"You were late because you didn't get a seat until the last minute. And that really is your seat. When Mark wasn't here to claim it, it was assigned to you. You didn't want to make a scene and embarrass me. Thank you for being so considerate."

Jack could guess from her guilty tone that he hadn't made a favorable first impression. Apparently the revision of her opinion of him didn't make him any more likable in her eyes, though. He'd gladly have traded her gratitude for a friendly smile.

"Don't thank me. I just make a practice of avoiding confrontation whenever possible." He toasted her casually with his glass of champagne and took a sip.

Rita forced a smile and picked up her glass. It was halfway to her lips when she went still and stared at it and then at Jack, her face dismayed. "I should never have come on this trip," she said in an anguished voice. "Things like *this* are going to happen over and over. At the airport in Honolulu, there'll be somebody to greet all the honeymoon couples with leis and take our pictures. Then at the hotel in Maui there's a special reception with *mai tai*s and champagne and flowers in the room." Rita closed her eyes and then opened them for Jack to see her pain and her dread. "I was such a fool to come," she whispered. "Everything is set up for two people. There'll be two tickets for the *luau*, two reservations on the moonlight dinner cruise . . ."

"I'm flying on to Honolulu, too. We'll be on the same flight. I'd be happy to do another imitation bridegroom act." Jack made the offer lightly and was glad for the sake of his ego that he had when her reaction was even less flattering than he'd expected.

"Oh, no—" Rita bit off the refusal and met Jack's gaze guiltily, knowing from his rueful expression that her quick glance at his clothes had spoken volumes. Her effort to cover up for the unintentional insult only made matters worse.

"That's really very kind of you to offer, but I couldn't inconvenience you like that. Thank you anyway. I'll just have to manage." She took a gulp of champagne.

Jack was ready with a good-natured smile when she slid an anxious look over at him. "We're not exactly dressed to match, are we?" He ran his eyes appreciatively over her smart attire. She wore a soft blue-gray suit teamed with a blouse in a darker shade.

His admiration, which seemed straightforward and genuine, caused Rita to be that much more flustered that she'd been so tactless. He was such a nice man, and she hadn't meant to put him down.

"I really didn't mean to be insulting. You and Mark, my ex-fiancé, are so *different* in the way you look and dress. That's all. Actually most women would think you were much better looking—" She stopped at Jack's wincing expression, realizing too late what her tone implied.

"But you don't," he finished for her wryly.

Rita hesitated from making the admission and discovered, much to her surprise, that it might not be the truth.

Confused, she avoided his eyes and busied herself taking her cutlery out of its clear plastic casing.

"All I meant to say is that Mark is more the dignified type. He's fussy about his clothes. He wears sports jackets and suits and almost always wears a tie. He's a more 'formal' sort of man than you are." She took a bite of her chicken simply to escape the awkward conversation and found that it tasted good. Her appetite and her enjoyment of food had deserted her along with sound sleep and peace of mind since her breakup with Mark. It was reassuring to feel hunger.

Jack took her hint and began eating his lunch, but he wasn't ready to drop the subject of Mark Pendleton. He pumped her with a casual skill. She answered his questions with reluctance at first and then became less hesitant as she finished her glass of champagne and began drinking her refill. From everything that Jack could gather, the Pendleton fellow was an average guy, a dime-a-dozen lawyer working for an insurance company.

By the time lunch was over and the trays had been removed, Jack still hadn't managed to glean any explanation for the breakup. Sensing that the moment was as propitious as it was likely to be, he was about to ask her point-blank what had happened when she unclipped her seat belt and began to take off her suit jacket. Jack helped her, and by the time she'd settled back in her seat, his pulse had picked up. His fingertips had brushed the silky material of her blouse, reinforcing his sensual pleasure in her figure, which was slim and more full-breasted than he'd expected. With hair and a complexion like hers, what color would her nipples and the aureoles of her breasts be? Shell pink or rose, he thought, and the intimate speculations invested his voice with sexual messages he hadn't consciously intended to convey.

"I just realized I haven't even introduced myself," he said too softly, in too husky a tone. "I'm Jack. Jack Adams."

Rita's head turned quickly toward him. He met her wide startled eyes and read in them a recognition that thrilled him before she jerked her gaze forward again.

"I'm Rita," she said in a stifled voice. "Rita Jones."

"I'm very happy to meet you, Rita." With the damage already done, Jack frankly cajoled her with his voice to look at him again and admit that it was a mutual attraction, but she resisted his appeal.

"That champagne made me sleepy," Rita announced stiltedly, sounding anything but drowsy. She closed her eyes, willing her heart to slow its beat and her blood to stop rushing through her body bringing that warm tingling sensation. It had to be the champagne affecting her like this, making her respond like a wanton to a strange man's feather-light touch and husky tone of voice. He had only performed a routine courtesy and then introduced himself, not made a pass at her.

Jack watched her awhile in frustration and then once again summoned his good judgment and common sense. Calling them up was becoming routine on this flight. He was mooning over a woman who wasn't available, and it couldn't be expected that she would be. Chances were good to certain that she was still in love with the Pendleton fellow. Jack should get his mind back on his own life and leave her strictly alone, especially since that was so clearly her own preference.

Rita was tensely aware of Jack's scrutiny and relieved when he stopped looking at her. She knew when he quietly pulled down the window shade, turned out his overhead reading light and, after a moment's hesitation, hers, too. She waited as long as she could after he had eased his chair back before she sneaked a look at him. Cautiously she turned her face in his direction and watched him several moments while he slept. When drowsiness overcame her and her lids grew heavy and dropped, she went to sleep with Jack's image clear in her mind.

this long and hard against a love based only on sex, and if it were to come to that, which it never would, anyhow, she had told him in no uncertain terms that it would not happen, whatever the circumstances.

Chapter Three

Jack woke with a quick comprehension of the circumstances. The cabin was darkened for the in-flight movie, the shades pulled down and most of the overhead lights turned out. The warm heavy pressure on his shoulder was Rita's head. She had gone to sleep and was curled toward him.

He was careful not to tense his muscles or make a sudden move that would disturb her as he shifted slightly so that he could study her face. It gave him a sense of rare privilege to look at her so close up without having to sneak glances and pretend not to be staring. Her skin was fine and delicate. He thought it would be soft and smooth to the touch. Her features were elegant, saved from perfection by the sensual generosity of her mouth. She was beautiful and to have her accessible to him, even briefly in her unconscious state, made him feel ridiculously tender and protective.

Very gently Jack eased back a tendril of auburn hair from her cheek and then let his hand hover nearby. In sleep, her problems evidently had not deserted her. A little frown cut faint lines between her arched eyebrows. Jack touched his forefinger to the tension spot, wishing that he had the power to smooth away that frown and banish her troublesome dreams. To his surprise and delight, the lines smoothed beneath his gentle touch. She eased out a sleeping sigh and her lips relaxed into the beginning of a smile.

Jack's heartbeat quickened as his attention focused on the delicate lushness of her mouth and the impulse to kiss her in her sleep grew strong. Who was she dreaming about? he wondered and touched his fingertip to her bottom lip to feel the satin texture and softness. Probably about the man whose shoulder she'd thought she'd be using as her pillow on this flight, not about Jack. The conjecture stirred frank envy and hostility for the man occupying foremost importance in her subconscious as well as her waking thoughts. With the reckless feeling that he had nothing to lose anyway, Jack bent his face close to hers and kissed her.

At first he just touched his lips to hers to savor the taste and feel of the lovely mouth he'd observed with male appreciation. When she made a little sound in her throat, he went on alert, expecting her to awaken, but instead she moved her head on his shoulder as if seeking a more comfortable spot. Jack couldn't resist kissing her again, but this time with slightly increased pressure, letting his lips cling to hers and then move coaxingly. The sensations flooding him were devastatingly sweet.

His pulse had quickened at the outset with the sense of his daring in taking such liberties. He had expected her to awake almost instantly and was prepared to meet her surprise with a joking defense and keep it from turning to outrage. When she didn't awaken and started responding to his kiss in her sleep, he was taken off guard. What had begun as an idle impulse was suddenly simple, honest need. He could no more have kept himself from taking advantage of the un-expected intimacy than he could have sprouted wings and continued the flight outside the aircraft.

The kiss was actually of short duration, and it never passed far beyond the innocent stage of mouth pressed to mouth, but Jack's senses were in upheaval and his glib ex-cuses forgotten when Rita stiffened to shocked awareness of what was happening and pushed away from him. He felt vulnerable and incomplete, as though he'd been inter-rupted in the middle of lovemaking, not stealing a kiss.

"Oh, my God!" Rita's anguished words were spoken through the shield of her hands that she held up in front of her face. She sat very straight in her seat, facing forward.

Jack could probably have counted on one hand the num-ber of times in his life prior to this one when words had failed him. His problem now wasn't thinking of something to say. Any number of comments came to mind, but none of them seemed satisfactory. None was sincere. He just couldn't bring himself to try to smooth over the moment with a quip. Even though he'd had every reason to expect rejection from her, he was disconcertingly disappointed with her reaction.

"Please, *please*—just leave me alone from now on," Rita begged with a mixture of shame and desperation that made Jack stare at her. He stubbornly held his silence, intending to force her to meet his eyes. When she didn't, his impa-tience changed to anger.

"Leave *you* alone. I didn't pull your head over here on my shoulder. When I woke up and found you all cozy, I did what any normal man would do and took advantage of the situation. For chris'sakes, it was only a kiss. I didn't try to rape you. Don't you think you're overreacting?" Jack re-gretted his harshness when he saw her visibly flinch under the impact of his words, but he wanted confrontation if that was what it took to get through her reserve. Anything was better than being treated like a leper. Her quick, humble apology was totally unexpected, totally baffling. To his frustration, she offered it without once making eye contact.

"I'm sorry," she said with bent head, looking at her clasped hands. "It was my fault. I can see how you might have gotten the wrong impression about me. Despite what just happened, I'm not starved for sex. I'm *not* going to Hawaii with any intentions of picking up strange men. I just want *peace*. I want to *forget*."

Jack was flooded with strong emotions, among them compassion for her and contempt for himself. What an insensitive bastard he was to resent her lack of interest in him when she'd just broken off a serious relationship with another man.

"I'm the one who should be apologizing. I promise I won't bother you again." His quiet voice reflected his self-disgust and a steely determination to abide by his words.

She looked at him then and the confusion in her dark eyes made hope flare up in him, but only briefly. It died as she quickly broke the eye contact and murmured, "Thank you."

He was as good as his word. For the remainder of the flight, he said nothing to Rita. She didn't feel his glance on her. She felt none of the earlier vibrations of his interest. The withdrawal of his attention was complete, but it didn't leave her in peace. Now added to her thoughts of Mark and a future that seemed bleak was a disturbing new insight into her physical nature. She was capable of being powerfully attracted to a man when she knew not a single fact about him but his name.

She'd been dreaming about Jack Adams when he awoke her with his kiss. In her dream he'd asked her to tell him about her breakup with Mark and listened only long enough to see how painful the explanation was for her. "Don't talk any more," he'd told her with that warm, wonderful smile of his. "It's all past history anyway." Then he'd kissed her, lowering his head slowly so that she could look into his clear gray eyes and see his intent. The kiss had been tender and then gently exploratory, awakening delicious sensations.

The merging of dream and reality had come as a shock. On the one hand, she'd been appalled by her wanton response to a stranger but equally as strong was the regret that she had to wake up and take moral responsibility for her actions. She'd have liked the dream to continue what she couldn't permit herself to do in real life. Her own hypocrisy gave rise to grave reproofs and self-doubt. What kind of woman was she to be more responsive to a stranger than to the man she'd wanted to marry? Mark's kiss had never made her want to dissolve and merge herself with him.

Was she her mother's daughter in spite of everything?

These troubled reflections about her moral character served at least some purpose. Time passed quickly and when the jet landed at San Francisco, she was too preoccupied with her own thoughts to be nervous. During the brief layover, Jack left the plane with no mention of his intent and got a different seat assignment. When he returned, he sat several rows in front of Rita, on the opposite side of the aisle, clearly within her view so that she could watch his friendly exchanges with one of the airline attendants who came aboard with the replacement crew, a lovely darkhaired, olive-skinned young woman of Polynesian descent.

Rita could hear enough of their several conversations during the flight to judge that they were previous acquaintances and that Jack Adams was apparently no newcomer to Hawaii. He was full of knowledgeable questions about Oahu, the principal island where Honolulu was located, and the neighbor islands, as well. The several mentions of Maui brought to Rita's mind a new possibility she hadn't considered before. What if his destination were the island of Maui, the same as hers? What if they should encounter each other accidentally? Would he be friendly after she'd gone to such lengths to discourage any interest from him? If he were, what would she do? How would she react?

Her speculation brought such a disturbing blend of eagerness and anxiety that Rita tried her best to kill it with the commonsense reminder that the imaginary encounter was highly unlikely. She didn't even know for certain that Jack Adams would be vacationing on Maui. If he were, she doubted that he would be without female companionship for long. A man with his good looks, easy charm and sex appeal would have his pick of unattached women in a resort atmosphere, and there'd be more than one willing woman who wasn't unattached.

The latter cynical reflection brought a renewal of Rita's guilt. While she herself wasn't married and didn't wear a ring on her finger, it felt downright immoral for her to be absorbed in thoughts of any man besides Mark. If it hadn't been for circumstances, Mark would be sitting next to her this moment and she would be wearing his wedding ring. How could she be willing to speak vows of faithfulness to one man and within days of breaking up with him be attracted to another?

Despite her self-reproach, Rita didn't move over to occupy the window seat, which was now empty. She sat in the aisle seat with Jack Adams in her range of view, her attention drawn to him often. Unwillingly she took pleasure in the familiar masculine cadences of his voice as he conversed with the pretty attendant. When he laughed, the rich spontaneity of the sound brought to her breast a poignant longing. She rationalized it as the normal envy an unhappy person experiences in the presence of someone else's carefreeness. It didn't seem probable that she'd ever again feel for herself the simple joy in living that she heard in Jack Adam's laughter.

When the jet landed in Honolulu, there was confusion as passengers jostled in the aisles of the plane retrieving luggage and parcels from the overhead bins. Jack stayed calmly seated and didn't look up as Rita passed on her way out, but she felt his eyes on her back while she was in his view. Her apprehension about making her travel connections and facing whatever embarrassment awaited her counterbalanced any feeling of anticlimax at parting from him without a word.

According to plan, a representative of Great Pacific Holidays was on hand, wearing a gaily printed Hawaiian shirt and holding up a printed placard. He called out instructions for travelers with his company to please wait over to one side, out of the traffic. Rita stood in the designated area, where she was joined by one couple after another, all of them newlyweds taking the same honeymoon package trip she'd chosen for herself and Mark.

Alone and miserable, feeling more conspicuous by the moment, she gathered her reserve around her and avoided eye contact with anyone in the group by glancing off into the distance. When she caught sight of Jack Adam's back, she trained her unhappy gaze on him and watched him move away from her through the busy open-air terminal.

He'd taken off the old cashmere sweater and presumably put it in his flight bag, which he carried with the leather strap slung over his shoulder. His knit shirt fit just tight enough to emphasize the solid breadth of his shoulders and the sinewy muscles in his back. He walked with an easy, confident stride, giving the impression that the airport was old familiar territory. The spring in his step bespoke eagerness for whatever awaited him here upon his arrival, but no sense of hurry.

When his blond head and the cheery red hue of his shirt had disappeared from sight, Rita felt strangely bereft. Now she was really and truly alone. Aware of polite glances in her direction, she thought with desperation of the offer she'd so summarily declined. If by some miracle jack Adams appeared before her now, willing to pose as her bridegroom, she'd grab on to his strong arm with no pride whatever. What a fool she had been to refuse him! He would have smiled and drawn attention to himself. He would have been quick-thinking and managed everything. But it was too late for such thoughts now.

Jack Adams was gone.

Rita sighed restlessly as she laid her Maui guidebook down next to her lounge chair. She practically knew it by heart. Her problem was not knowing where to go and what she'd like to see on the island, but getting up the nerve to venture off sight-seeing on her own. She had arrived in Maui on Sunday, and it was now Wednesday. So far she'd familiarized herself with the large luxury hotel where she was staying, walked through its lovely gardens, browsed in the expensive shops, eaten, slept, and sunbathed, either here by the pool with its broad vista of the ocean, where she was today, or down on the sand beach that bordered the hotel grounds.

She was physically rested, having made the adjustment to the five-hour time difference between Hawaii and Atlanta, tired of thinking about Mark and how different this trip should have been, and bored with inactivity. An hour or two in the sun could be relaxing, but she simply wasn't a sun-worshipper at heart, and her redhead's skin required cautious exposure anyway. She had to take courage in hand and either rent a car, which was what she and Mark had intended to do, or arrange to go on some group sight-seeing excursions.

The thought of driving around the island alone gave rise to natural apprehensions. What if she should have a breakdown on a stretch of isolated road? It would be safer for her to see the Haleakala Crater and experience the thrilling road to Hana with a small tour group, and yet leaving herself open to the curiosity and questions of strangers was repugnant. She was ridiculously sensitive about being here on Maui alone, perhaps because everyone else seemed to have somebody.

It had been painful seeing honeymoon couples everywhere she looked, but somehow she was even more bothered by the happily married couples who'd long since lost the awkward newness of their nuptial bond. Wondering why that was so, she'd quickly pinpointed the likely reason. She and Mark had been more like comfortable married people than an engaged couple madly in love with each other. Rita had not thrilled to his touch. Even his more passionate kisses hadn't driven her to lose control. From the beginning, she'd wanted him as a *husband*, not a lover.

She guessed almost guiltily that what she was feeling wasn't really heartbreak, not in the accepted sense, or the intensity wouldn't have lessened so quickly. She felt empty and sad when she thought about Mark and all the wonderful plans that would never come true, but the bitter disappointment had already eased into a kind of aching acceptance. It made Rita uneasy to realize that she was having such a fast emotional recovery. She didn't like to think that she was superficial.

What she wanted desperately now was a break from thinking. Her mind needed a rest. The obvious recourse was sight-seeing. She'd see about renting a car immediately. This

afternoon she would go for a drive, look at scenery, perhaps explore some of the small villages mentioned in the
guidebook.

The decision eased some of Rita's restless tension. She felt
almost happy as she sat up with the intention of slipping on
her swimsuit cover-up and gathering up her things. But before she could swing her bare legs around and slip her feet
into her backless cork-soled sandals, a newcomer down on
the beach caught her eye and made her stare in disbelief.

Was the blond man wearing khaki shorts and no shirt,
carrying black flippers in one hand and a mask and snorkel
in the other, really who she thought he was! She'd swear he
was Jack Adams, the man who'd sat beside her on the
plane! Realizing that she was holding her breath, Rita let it
out and didn't try to pretend to herself that the emotion
making her heart pound in her breast was merely surprise.
It was excitement.

Hugging her knees, she watched closely and decided that
the man sauntering along the beach and being not too subtle about checking out all the sunbathers was either Jack
Adams or an incredible look-alike. So he was vacationing on
Maui! Evidently he'd been drawn to this particular beach
because it was a popular snorkeling spot. In Hawaii all the
beaches were public, even those adjoining the properties of
the huge luxury hotels here in the Kaanapali area. There was
little basis to Rita's automatic assumption that Jack Adams
wouldn't be staying in one of those expensive hotels, other
than the memory of his casual, well-worn attire and his aged
brown leather flight bag. The fact that his accommodations might be more modestly priced than her own didn't
quiet her pulse rate or lessen the closeness of her attention.

She watched him come to a stop and appear to be inde-
cisive as he looked up and down the beach. Dropping his
snorkeling gear to the sand, he shaded his eyes and gazed

out toward the outcropping of black lava rock where dozens of snorkelers floated facedown, giving rapt attention to the underwater world. Rita had been watching them the past two days with curiosity, thinking that she'd like to see for herself what was so fascinating beneath the blue surface of the water. If Mark had been there, she would have tried to talk him into giving snorkeling a try with her, even though he'd agreed to Hawaii as their honeymoon spot with the understanding that he'd never been the athletic type and particularly disliked water sports.

Jack Adams had evidently decided to swim out. He was unceremoniously shucking the tan shorts and tossing them carelessly to the sand along with his thick-soled thongs. Underneath he wore a close-fitting black swimsuit that was the type worn by competitive swimmers. From her vantage point, Rita could see female heads turned surreptitiously in his direction, and she could understand why. With the sun glinting off his blond hair and his sleekly muscled body golden tanned, he was definitely nice to look at, just as he'd been wearing clothes.

If he was aware of the feminine attention he'd drawn, he gave no indication of it and made his entry into the water without putting on a production. Obviously he was familiar with his snorkeling equipment, donning his flippers and mask, with the snorkeling tube attached, without any problems or fuss and then swimming out facedown with easy powerful kicks that propelled him fast through the crystal clear water. Rita noticed that he didn't move his arms at all, but kept them close to his body. He looked like a golden brown torpedo headed for target.

In no time at all, he had reached the outcropping of rock and the other snorkelers. From the way that he glided among them and raised his head up from time to time, Rita wondered if he weren't more interested in them than what there was to see beneath the water's surface. Was he looking for some particular person here on this beach? *Was it possible that he was looking for her!*

She had no more than conceived the possibility and discovered its allure than he seemed to be refuting it with his actions as he swam out farther into less protected waters where she'd noticed only a few other snorkelers venture. For periods that seemed much longer than they actually must have been, he would dive down and disappear from sight altogether. Rita found herself holding her breath each time with the suspense.

And then he was heading back to shore and not taking his time, either. Rita acted fast, without stopping to think. She picked up the guidebook and dropped it into her small tote bag along with suntan lotion and room key, already in the bottom. After a second's hesitation she decided not to take the time to slip on the cover-up and jammed it in the bag, too, thrust her feet into her sandals and made for the path that led down to the beach, knowing that it would take her a roundabout way through lush gardens that would block her view of her destination.

Running in the backless sandals would have been too hazardous, but she walked as fast as she dared and was breathless from her own sense of daring as well as the exertion when she emerged onto the sand some distance to the right of where his discarded shorts formed a khaki heap. She stopped, suddenly shy and uncertain, and watched while he reached the shallow water and stood up. He might not be Jack Adams at all, and even if he was, there was no reason to assume that he'd be glad to see her. Rita had been anything but friendly to him on the plane.

She took in several gulps of air and watched him bend to remove his flippers and then strip off the mask as he straightened. *Yes, he was Jack Adams!* She hadn't seen his blond hair wet and sleek against his head before, but there was no mistaking him, and Rita couldn't remember being so happy to see a familiar face. She waited anxiously for him to glance in her direction and notice her, but his earlier interest in the sunbathers had apparently vanished. He walked over to the spot where he'd left his shorts, picked them up, slipped his sandy feet into the thongs and started back in the same direction from which he had come, away from Rita.

She watched his rapid exit with helpless dismay, recapturing some of the same panicky aloneness she'd felt seeing him walk away from her in the airport.

"Jack! Jack Adams!" The words burst out of her, and she followed along in their wake, aware but heedless of the curious eyes turned in her direction.

At the sound of her voice hailing him, he stopped instantly and went still with a recognition that somehow eased her uncertainty even before he turned and she could see his face. He didn't make any pretense of being overwhelmed with surprise, and he was definitely pleased to see her. Rita felt relieved and flustered as she walked toward him, aware of his close scrutiny, taking in her appearance from head to toe, but focusing primarily on her face.

"I saw you from up at the pool. I could hardly believe my eyes," she said breathlessly when she'd reached him. "The sight of a familiar face was almost more excitement than I could stand. I nearly broke my neck getting down here before you could get away." She took in a deep noisy breath and smiled with self-deprecation.

"So here you are. You look good," he said approvingly. "How have you been?"

There was all the admiration and welcome she could have wanted in his voice and eyes, but also a caution that she well understood. The genuine concern in his stock inquiry into the state of her well-being made it more than a social opener.

Rita hesitated, wanting to be honest and open and yet upbeat. She didn't want to dwell on her unhappiness, but forget about it for a while, forget about the circumstances causing it.

"It's been lonely, as you would expect since I haven't known a single soul. I've had too much time to sit around and feel sorry for myself. But I'm sick and tired of doing that. I'd made up my mind just before you showed up to rent a car and do some sight-seeing on my own. So how are you?" she asked, feeling the heat of embarrassment flood her cheeks. She hadn't meant to be so blatantly inviting. "Are you enjoying your vacation on Maui? This certainly seems to be a very popular spot for snorkeling."

To avoid his perceptive gray eyes that saw right through her discomfort, she made a visor of her free hand and gazed out toward the black rocks where the strange school of human fish floated on the blue water.

His low chuckle took her pleasantly by surprise. Looking quickly back at him, she was put to ease at once by the warm confidentiality of his grin. Amusement gleamed in his eyes, and it was aimed at himself, not her.

"This is a good snorkeling spot—for rank beginners. But actually a little tame for someone like myself who's certified for deep-sea diving." Jack chuckled again, and the sound was reminiscent this time. "If my memory serves me, I must have been all of eight or nine the first time I snorkeled off this beach. I'm tempted to believe some of those fat old fish out there are the same ones I saw then. They're so used to being fed that they come right up and nibble your fingers."

His mirth all but subsided, leaving just a residue of laughter mingling with the honesty in his eyes. "I came here for one purpose only, and that was to look for you," he said simply. "The only reason I went into the water was to make sure you weren't out there." He was watching her reaction closely and picked his next words with obvious care. "I meant to give you another day or two, but then I couldn't wait. I had to see you, find out if you were all right." Memory of her the way she'd looked standing there in the airport flashed into his mind. It had been all he could do to walk off and leave her. She'd looked desperately unhappy and afraid, despite her efforts to hide her feelings, but he'd known she would scorn any show of compassion from him, mixed as it was with his attraction to her as a beautiful woman.

Rita nodded quickly, anxious to reassure him that she was all right and to stop him from continuing in that serious vein. He was making her uneasy with the suggestion that there was some serious urgency in seeking her out. He was just a handsome stranger she'd sat beside on a plane for a few hours. They knew each other superficially.

"I was delighted to look out here and see you," she said brightly, smiling at him. "How did you know I would be here? I don't remember mentioning the name of my hotel on the plane."

"You didn't. It was an easy matter to make a few phone calls. My mother's lived on Maui off and on for a number of years, which makes for good contacts." His tone was in ready compliance with her wish to keep everything between them on a light, carefree plane. Rita was relieved.

"You sound like the perfect person to show me around Maui!" she said gaily.

"Nothing would please me more." Jack made a little gallant bow. "I've borrowed my mother's car for the day. It's in your hotel parking lot. We can go this way—" he gestured toward the direction he had been taking when she hailed him. "It's shorter and there's a freshwater shower on the way. I can rinse off the salt water."

Rita's expression turned skeptical and then disbelieving as she saw that he actually meant for her to go with him now, without changing clothes.

"You don't mean go like this—in my bathing suit!" she protested, holding her arms wide and looking down at herself.

"You look great to me. Hawaii's a very casual place." The frankly male approval in his voice combined with a lingering examination made Rita's conservative navy and white one-piece suit feel skimpy. Her self-consciousness wasn't unpleasant.

"But what about you? You're all wet," she pointed out. Her glance skimmed his bare shoulders and chest. The discovery that his smoothly tanned upper torso was already about dry in the warm sun required that she drop her gaze lower in search of evidence of wetness to his swimsuit. The black nylon was plastered to his hips and molded to the shape of his groin. His wide-legged stance made the fact of his male virility even more inescapable, and as she brought her eyes back up to his face, Rita was embarrassed by her intense physical awareness of him as a man.

"You'll be much more comfortable in dry clothes," she said, feeling the heat travel through her from the roots of her hair right down to her toes. The sun had grown scorchingly hot.

"I have dry clothes in the car," Jack explained equably. "I meant to change. I thought you might have something in your bag to put on over your bathing suit." His eyes touched on the cover-up visible in her bag. "But if you'd be more comfortable wearing something else, why don't I meet you in your hotel lobby, say in about fifteen minutes? Is that enough time?"

"Plenty enough."

To Rita's surprise, he turned around and started with a brisk stride down the beach, leaving her to stand there and watch him, which she couldn't resist doing for fifteen or twenty seconds at least. He looked virile from the back, too. The thought that she was staring at him with such frankly physical appreciation made her blush with shame.

Jack was intensely aware of her eyes following him and knew when she was no longer looking at him. It might be overstating things a bit to say that his head was reeling with the encounter or that he'd been knocked for a loop, but the scene on the beach had been totally unexpected, from beginning to end. He'd visualized such a different occurrence that he felt like he was dreaming.

The fact that she'd seen him first and come running after him was astounding. He'd thought he would be the one to happen upon her. Then to have her show such open welcome. That had come as a pleasure, even with the tempering realization that she was undoubtedly lonely and his was a familiar face. What he couldn't believe was that she had come on so strong to him sexually. He'd responded to her beauty and physical appeal on the plane when she'd been unhappy and repressed. To have her smile at him flirtatiously and look at his body with a blatantly appreciative female eye was devastating, particularly when she was so obviously shy in seduction.

Her transformation disturbed Jack as much as it excited him. He didn't trust her gaiety with its announcement of quick recovery. The memory of the hurt in her spectacular dark eyes was too vivid. Underneath she was most likely still grieving over the Pendleton fellow. Jack was just a badly needed diversion, and for his own protection he needed to keep that fact in mind, at least until he was sure that this was just an uncommonly strong infatuation for him.

He hadn't been able to get her out of his mind, and he'd tried hard. Today he'd come looking for her against all his better judgment with no expectation that she'd want to see him. Actually as much as anything else, he'd thought another dose of cold shoulder from her might kill the attraction. Then to be taken so by surprise...

Jack was looking forward to showing her Maui. With every step down the beach his eagerness to spend time with her grew. But he intended to heed those red flags of caution in his head, take things slowly. Before he could afford to get any more involved with beautiful Rita Jones, he had to solve some of her mystery. For his own protection, he had to learn the details behind her canceled wedding. He had to size up Mark Pendleton, the absent bridegroom and Jack's rival for her attention.

Chapter Four

By the time she'd reached her room, Rita was having regrets for her behavior down on the beach. She blushed to think of what kind of impression she must have given Jack Adams. He knew she'd come to Hawaii alone on her honeymoon trip and must be secretly shocked at the way she'd approached him so brazenly and all but openly asked him to take her sight-seeing around Maui.

Aside from concern about what Jack must be thinking of her, she knew it couldn't be right for her to be this filled with anticipation at spending the rest of the day with him. She supposed she could expect to feel vaguely guilty, as though she were being unfaithful to Mark. After all, he'd been the only man in her life for more than two years.

But then he could have been here. It was his own choosing that he wasn't. In fact, the whole train of circumstances that had led to her meeting Jack Adams was Mark's doing. If Mark had still wanted her as his wife after hearing about her background, he would have sat next to her on the plane, not Jack. She wouldn't know Jack Adams existed. She wouldn't have turned to him on takeoff, felt his strength and kindness, been exposed to his good-natured charm, fallen asleep and wakened to find her head on his shoulder... And so on. At the risk of damaging her solid case against Mark as the culprit, Rita didn't let herself think about the dream and the kiss.

She took a quick shower and changed into one of her new outfits she'd bought for the honeymoon. Both shorts and blouse were pale aqua. The blouse had a modestly scooped neckline and cap sleeves. The shorts were pleated and stylishly blousing, coming down midway to her knees. She looked dainty and feminine, just as Mark would have liked her to look, but then Mark would never have dreamed of taking her off sight-seeing wearing her bathing suit and a cover-up.

Jack might like her in something sexier. She suspected that he would also like her to wear her hair hanging loose. He'd looked at it several times down there on the beach. But Rita didn't give more than the most fleeting consideration to taking out the hairpins and brushing her auburn hair into a more carefree style. To do so would be too much a departure from the norm and would make her self-conscious.

Jack was waiting for her in the lobby, talking with one of the management staff, a man about his own age of mixed racial background as were the majority of the Hawaiians, their ancestry having attractively blended strains of Polynesian, Oriental and Caucasian blood. Rita had a few seconds to appraise Jack's appearance as she walked toward him before he glanced around and saw her. He had on khaki shorts, which she assumed to be the same ones he was wearing earlier, and a gaily printed red and white aloha shirt worn tucked in, not hanging loose, as was common. It differed from those she'd been seeing around the hotel in that it obviously wasn't new and, like the shorts, had been through the wash more than a few times. His feet were no longer sandy, but shod still in the thick-soled thongs that were popular as beach shoes. His blond hair was neatly combed and only partially dry. He looked clean, casual, and handsome, and when he noticed Rita and immediately smiled his welcome, her heartbeat doubled its time, and she felt a strong surge of pleasure.

"I'd like you to meet one of your more charming guests, if you haven't met her already," he told the man he introduced to Rita as an assistant manager of the hotel.

"Do you know him personally?" Rita asked curiously when she and Jack were walking to the parking lot. "The two of you were having such a friendly conversation."

"Actually, I'd never met him before," Jack replied. "But as I mentioned earlier, my mother lives here and is pretty well-known. She's one of those Maui 'characters,' you might say. This automobile of hers is a good indicator of her personality. She's one of the most disorganized souls you'd ever want to meet, but a sweetheart."

He chuckled fondly, leading Rita up to perhaps the most disreputable looking vehicle in the whole parking lot, a battered red Datsun station wagon. The whole back of it was filled with an untidy assortment of odds and ends, everything from a plastic bucket to old shoes and clothing and folding chairs.

"Are you sure your mother will be able to get along without her car for a day?" Rita quipped lightly and took delight in Jack's hearty laughter. It jogged her memory of the time before when she had heard it, on the flight from San Francisco to Honolulu. He had been talking to the pretty Polynesian airline attendant. Then Rita had listened to the spontaneous joyousness of the sound with despair.

Now she found herself joining in and laughing along with him until she realized that he had suddenly gone quiet and was looking at her in a strange way.

"I'm sorry," she apologized quickly. "I didn't mean to sound as though I was making fun—"

"Don't apologize," he said softly, touching her shoulder. "I just hadn't heard you laugh before and it was, well, nice."

Rita was struck with the same uneasiness she'd felt down on the beach when he'd made looking her up seem like a matter of serious importance.

"Hopefully you'll get used to it before the day is over," she said brightly. "I meant it when I said I'm tired of gloom and doom. That's why I'm looking forward so much to this sight-seeing," she added.

His eyes flashed with his quick perception, and he hesitated just a moment before he smiled in fresh compliance with her wish to keep everything light. Once again Rita was relieved that he hadn't persisted in tugging her out of the shallows into deeper emotional waters. She didn't want depth. She didn't want seriousness. She didn't want a meeting of the minds with him or a sharing of her painful history. She wanted to move over the bright surface of this new relationship and enjoy it for what it was, casual and temporary, a first of its kind for her and a wonderful relief in its absence of any future. Jack was more attractive to her than any man she'd ever met before, but he also wasn't the type she'd ever be serious about and especially not now, when she couldn't contemplate another involvement with a man.

"Hop in, then, and let's be on our way," Jack ordered her cheerfully, opening the door he hadn't bothered to lock. "Your air conditioner's already working, by the way," he bent down to add when she'd slid into the passenger seat and he had closed the door. His grin broadened in response to her smile of understanding as she realized that the window was rolled all the way down.

"Who needs air-conditioning with air like this!" she retorted, taking in a deep breath. "I see you didn't take the key," she commented when he'd gotten into the car and was proceeding to start it. "Are people more honest here in Hawaii than in the other states?"

Jack let the engine run while he fastened his seat belt and waited while she did the same. "No," he said with deadpan seriousness. "Every time I visit my mother and borrow her car, I keep hoping somebody will come along and clean it out. There isn't the slightest chance that she ever will."

Rita glanced into the back, giggled, and then looked back to meet his smiling gaze.

"Good luck," she said and then they both were laughing uproariously. The muscles in Rita's side were aching and she had tears in her eyes by the time her mirth subsided. "God, it is so good to laugh!" she said in a marveling tone.

His silence was abstracted, introducing a new tension between them that made Rita's heartbeat quicken with the suspense as she read in his eyes his desire to kiss her. When he suppressed the impulse and put the car in gear, she wondered with a tinge of disappointment if he'd read some discouragement in her face. It seemed unlikely since she'd been holding her breath with anticipation, wanting to feel his lips on hers again so much that the laughter pain in her side had moved to the pit of her stomach.

She didn't quite trust herself to speak, but the sharp awareness faded quickly as Jack concentrated his attention upon his driving and she looked eagerly out of the windows at everything. It was only a matter of minutes before they had left Kaanapali and the small-town congestion of Lahaina behind them and were driving south on a highway that skirted the coastline, with blue ocean on the right and a purple and green mountain range immediately to their left. The air blowing through the open windows was tangy and fresh with blended scents of sea and land. Rita's exhilaration came through in her voice as she exclaimed her appreciation.

"This is so unbelievably *gorgeous*!" She inhaled deeply. "I need to have my head on a swivel, though. I want to look right and left at the same time. The ocean is beautiful, but so are the mountains. They look so close up, don't they?"

Jack smiled at her, sharing her enthusiasm. "Wait until you see where I'm taking you. It's one of my favorite places on Maui." He reached over and picked up Rita's left hand, linking his fingers loosely and companionably with hers. "I'm glad things worked out for us today. Glad you happened to be at the pool keeping a lookout on the beach and so on. This is fun seeing everything through fresh eyes." His tone was casually intimate, like his touch.

"I'm glad, too. It's great luck for me to have someone who's practically a native show me around. How often do you come here to visit your mother?"

Jack squeezed her hand and then released it, causing Rita a twinge of regret for her friendly but impersonal reply. She hadn't objected to the physical contact at all. In fact, she had enjoyed it.

"The last few years I've only managed to get here once a year, usually about this time, close to Thanksgiving. It's been hard to get away."

Jack glanced over to see her looking at him appraisingly. He raised his eyebrows quizzically to encourage her to share her thoughts.

"I was just trying to guess, before I asked you, what kind of job you have," Rita admitted somewhat hesitantly. "Men tend to give clues, but so far you haven't. I don't have the vaguest idea what you do for a living."

"That's because I don't fit into any doctor, lawyer, Indian chief category," Jack told her cheerfully.

"So what do you do?"

"Go on. Guess," Jack urged her, grinning.

Rita hesitated. "You have such an outgoing personality. You seem to be able to talk to anyone and everyone. Are you in some kind of sales?" She offered her conjecture with a hint of apology, not wanting to offend him.

"In one way or another, I guess I usually am," Jack said laughingly. "Actually I did quite well selling cars for three years after I was discharged from the navy. Since then I've been involved in some real estate development and more recently in owning and managing a combination gas station and convenience store. But I think you probably hit the nail on the head. I'm a salesman at heart."

"Sounds like you've been busy doing a lot of different things," Rita mused, with as little inflection as possible. She looked out of her window at the ocean, afraid of what he might read in her face. She wasn't surprised and shouldn't be feeling this disappointment. His words, with no mention of college, had confirmed her first impression of him three days ago when she'd looked up and seen him coming down the aisle toward her on the plane. He had no career but was a handsome, charming, wheeling and dealing type, going from one venture to the next, full of ambitions for making an easy fortune, no doubt.

Rita's mother had always been irresistibly drawn to such men, believing in their big dreams and promises to take her with them to the top, despite one disappointment after another. Apparently Rita's sister Edna was cut out of the same cloth. *And now Rita herself was strongly attracted to such a man.*

In her case, nothing would ever come of the attraction, or of any like it in the future. Rita was positive of that. She might never find another man like Mark Pendleton, with all the solid qualifications of what she required in a husband, but if she didn't, she'd rather stay single and unattached than compromise and follow in her mother's footsteps. For Rita, respecting a man was far more important than admiring his looks or being physically attracted to him.

"What about you? What sort of work do you do?"

Jack's pleasant inquiry brought Rita's attention back to him.

"Now it's your turn to guess," she told him impulsively. "What do you think I do?"

He gave her several mock thoughtful glances that made her smile with anticipation of some teasing guesses. "Hmm. I'd say you have a position of some authority," he mused. "You're used to supervising people, telling them what to do. You're probably considered a pretty hard boss, fair but with a high standard of perfection." He smiled at her wide-eyed amazement. "I'll just make a wild guess and say you're an office manager. Would you like to know what kind of car I'd try to sell you if you walked onto the floor of the dealership where I worked for three years?" he added teasingly.

"It's probably the same one I have parked at my apartment building in Atlanta," Rita declared dryly.

In response to his questioning, she told him about her job heading a department in one of Atlanta's best known clothing stores, explaining that she'd worked herself up from a sales clerk's position. "But I was never good at selling," she admitted. "I didn't have a knack for it like you probably do. I was just always at work on time and very conscientious. Regular customers got to know me by name and would wait for me if I was busy when they came in. But

I probably don't even have to tell you all this. You've probably guessed it for yourself!''

Jack smiled and didn't deny her laughing accusation. Rita was working up her nerve to ask him what other insights he had into her character and personality when they arrived at an intersection.

"If we kept going along the coast instead of turning inland, we'd be in Kihei very shortly," Jack told her. "My mother lives south of Kihei. I'll take you to meet her another day."

After that he turned guide, and the conversation centered around the countryside through which they were driving. On both sides were huge sugarcane fields. Jack told her a little of the history and importance of sugarcane farming in the Hawaiian economy and explained that the sweet scent she was smelling was from the burning of the fields, prior to harvesting.

Rita listened with interest to the information and enjoyed the sound of his voice and his ready wit. She quizzed him on the pronunciation of names of streets and highways and towns and practiced the sounds aloud, finding them liquid and pleasant on the tongue.

"It's like being in grammar school and sounding out all the letters of words!" she exclaimed. "Wait. Let me see if I can figure this one out myself," she said as they approached a small town that looked for all the world like a western hamlet in a cowboy film. The name on a small sign was Paia. "*Pah-ee-ah*—right? Since every single letter is sounded individually. The Hawaiian language is so much fun. I love it! That's a Buddhist temple, isn't it?" she was demanding excitedly in the next breath. "I think I read about it in my guidebook. That big gong outside is rung or struck, or whatever they do to gongs, every morning and every evening. And right across the street a Protestant church!''

Jack smiled over at her with no hint of derision for her enthusiasm. ''Kind of hard to believe you're in the good old U.S.A., isn't it? Wait until you see the scenery just up ahead.''

He sounded proud and expectant. Seconds later the coastline came into view again, but it was much more rugged here on the northern shore and instead of a peaceful blue expanse, the ocean came thundering ashore in great tiers of white surf. The roaring sound added to the majesty of the sight.

''My, but it's beautiful,'' Rita marveled, shivering. ''But kind of overpowering and scary.''

''It is that,'' Jack agreed softly.

''Do people actually surf out there?'' she asked incredulously as they passed a small park area high on the bluff and she noticed the array of cars and vans with surf boards affixed to the tops.

''They do when the conditions are right. Today the north wind is blowing too hard. You notice nobody's out there.''

They had been driving along slowly. Jack put on the turn signal and pulled across the highway onto a rutted dirt road that led out to a grassy bluff overlooking the ocean. They drove right to the end of the road and parked on the grass, no more than twenty yards away from the edge. Jack killed the engine, swung open his door and got out. Rita followed his example and came around to meet him at the front of the car.

· ''I love this place,'' Jack said, slipping his arm around her shoulders. He smiled at her and the smile stayed on his lips as he gazed outward.

"Do you surf out there yourself when the conditions are 'right'?" Rita asked after a while. She sounded both fascinated and horrified at the notion.

"I used to, in my younger macho days. I haven't surfed in seven or eight years. It's not a casual sport, but something you have to practice regularly."

Jack took his arm from around her shoulders and walked several steps closer to the edge of the bluff, leading her by the hand. Rita lagged behind until he dropped down onto the grass and then she sat down next to him and made herself comfortable, curling her legs sideways. The sun was brilliant overhead and probably would have felt hot without the brisk, steady breeze that lifted tendrils of hair and blew them around her face. Idly she pushed the escaped strands away from her face and looked out to sea while she talked.

"I didn't realize until I started reading about Hawaii that surfing was originated by the Polynesians who settled these islands," she mused. "Supposedly they were great swimmers and loved water sports. Apparently they were also giants—what are you *doing*?" she asked in surprise as without any warning of his intention, Jack reached over and plucked out a hairpin.

"Taking your hair down," he answered matter-of-factly and pulled out another hairpin before she could stop him. "I've wanted to do that from the first time I saw you."

"Don't!" she protested and tried to scoot away from him, but he came after her, a determined, reckless smile on his face. Gently but firmly he took her hands away from her head, held both of them in one of his and made short work of pulling out the rest of the hairpins. "Sorry," he apologized contritely when she muttered, "Ouch! That pulls!" "If I didn't have to hold you, I could use both hands and be more careful."

"There," he said when he'd gotten them all out. He released Rita's hands so that he could use both sets of his fingers to comb gingerly through her thick auburn locks and fluff them around her face. He concentrated upon his task with an abstracted intensity that made her feel strange. She waited, holding her breath.

"Well?" she finally demanded, not looking at him. Her voice was breathy and defensive. "What's the verdict? How do you like the complete mess you've made of my hair?"

Jack worked his fingers deep into the soft brilliance and tilted her face to make her meet his gaze. "The verdict is 'beautiful,' 'gorgeous,' and any number of other superlatives."

"I'll bet." The retort was as scornful as she could make it with the weakness seeping through her limbs.

"You were beautiful the other way, too, but not like this—" Jack's voice was husky and abstracted. With the last word he was lowering his face to hers and kissing her.

He encountered no resistance from Rita. She closed her eyes and reveled in the touch of his mouth against hers, feeling once again the delicious sensations of that waking-sleeping kiss on the plane. His lips were firm and subtly exploratory, eager for the rediscovery of hers and yet patient, coaxing a response. She gave it for her own pleasure. In the background of her consciousness, the steady shoreward surge of the surf formed a mesmerizing rhythm that seemed to become more urgent and immediate as he kissed her harder, more demandingly. The sound became a part of her, rushing through her veins as she put her arms up around his neck and kissed him back, opening her mouth to the passionate exploration of his tongue and submitting to its conquering sweetness.

Rita had no thought of stopping him as he took her with him down on the grass. It seemed the natural order of things for him to go on kissing her forever as long as the ocean pounded the rocky shore. To object to the intimate exploration of his hands was as senseless as trying to harness the frenetic energy of the sea. His progression was inevitable. He cupped her breasts and felt their resilient fullness through her blouse, became impatient of the separating layers of cloth, and pulled the blouse free of the waistband of her shorts.

Rita sucked in her breath as he slipped his hand underneath her blouse. Her breasts ached with their expectant fullness as he took the time to rub his palm back and forth across the satiny flesh of her midriff. She moaned when he finally worked his way upward and took a breast in his hand, squeezing and kneading it. Her lacy bra couldn't keep him from feeling the hard peak of her nipple against his palm. He seemed to be penetrating her inchoate need as he took it between thumb and forefinger, rolling and pinching it to unleash fresh tides of warm, wonderful weakness. His name came from her lips like a whispered supplication.

"Jack!"

She wished she had managed somehow not to speak when he stopped kissing her and took his hand abruptly from beneath her blouse. Opening her eyes dazedly, she frowned against the brightness of the sun and murmured a protesting sound as he sat up and pulled her up, too.

"It looks like we have company," he warned, and the sound of car doors slamming brought her abruptly to her senses.

He had heard the approach of an automobile, but she had been oblivious to everything but the touch of his lips and his hands and the sound of the ocean. She wouldn't have lifted a finger to stop him if he had wanted to strip her clothes from her body and make love to her, right here on the grass for the world to see! Rita was ashamed and appalled. She avoided looking at Jack while she hurriedly tucked in her blouse and did what she could to make herself presentable.

"I'm sorry. I didn't mean for that to happen," he apologized softly, slipping his arm protectively around her shoulders. "I just got carried away and forgot about privacy." He gave her shoulders a squeeze, and when she didn't relax or look any less embarrassed, he glanced over at the newcomers and spoke with the obvious intention of reassuring her. "Don't worry about them. They don't know anybody else is in the world anyway. From the looks of them, they're another honeymoon couple."

He didn't falter, but Rita could tell he'd remembered too late that his words would cause her discomfort and possibly pain. It was a horribly awkward moment for her. She could imagine what he was thinking of her, so recently engaged to one man and allowing a virtual stranger such intimacies as she'd allowed him.

Jack cursed under his breath. "Honest to God, Rita, I forgot. Good. They're leaving." He took his arm from around her stiffly unresponsive shoulders and leaned back on his hands in an attitude of waiting. "They're gone," he announced unnecessarily moments later. She could hear for herself the sounds of the car's departure.

Rita was keenly aware of his gaze on her. Its sober thoughtfulness was unnerving. She guessed that he was trying to figure her out and finding her a puzzle, which she could well understand. She dreaded his questions, which he seemed to be having trouble formulating.

"I don't suppose there's any chance of finding my hairpins," she said, shoving her hair back from her face and twisting it into what she knew had to be an untidy version of her usual severely neat French twist. "Oh, here's one. Here's another." She let her hair go and concentrated on searching the grass as though it was of the greatest importance to locate all the missing hairpins.

"Why do you wear your hair the way you do?"

The question was such a welcome one compared to others he could have asked that Rita looked at him in startled relief.

"Why? Because I like to wear it that way." She played with the hairpins she had found instead of resuming the search.

"But you have to know that your hair is gorgeous. The color is so rich and alive. And it's just dying to wave and curl, in spite of the way you treat it, twisting it all tight and keeping it pinned down. Why do you want to hide the fact that you have beautiful hair?" His puzzled glance rested on her hair a moment longer, probed her defensive face and then slid over her slowly. He didn't have to tell her the rest of what he was wondering: Why also did she dress to hide her figure?

"I think you're making a case out of nothing," Rita informed him crisply. She tossed the pins to the grass and used both hands to flip the ends of her hair in scornful demonstration. "I can't wear my hair like this and expect anyone to take me seriously. I'm a working woman. I want to be respected for my intelligence and ability, not be whistle bait for men who think a woman's place is in the bedroom and the kitchen."

"You're not a working woman twenty-four hours a day," Jack pointed out quietly. "You were going off on vacation the first time I saw you. This morning you were lying by the pool, sunbathing. And today we're just out for some relaxed sight-seeing."

Rita felt her face flame with embarrassed color to match her brilliant hair. "I think I know what you're getting around to," she said, lifting her chin and looking him straight in the eye. "You're thinking that the way I wear my hair and dress doesn't fit the way I acted with you just now. Well, what happened a minute ago isn't something I'm in the habit of doing. I don't make love with men I hardly know. Sex isn't really that important in my life. I was engaged to the man I almost married for two years and didn't live with him."

"Two years?" Jack was quietly skeptical. "But you did sleep with him?"

"Yes, but not often. Because that was the way I wanted it, and he respected my wishes," she added forcefully when his expression turned frankly disbelieving.

Jack held her eyes while he reached over for her hand. He smoothed out her fingers on his palm and then linked them with his. "The man had something wrong with him," he said bluntly, and raised Rita's hand to his lips. While he brushed them across her knuckles, he watched her face closely. Rita was sure when his eyes narrowed with satisfaction that she had given some telltale sign of the tightening deep in her stomach.

"I've known you now for four days," he went on softly. "Of those four days, I've been around you less than twenty-four hours, and I have one hell of a time keeping my hands off you. If we were in love with each other and engaged to be married, I'd make love to you morning, noon, and night."

"But that's *you*—" Rita jerked her hand to free it of his grasp, afraid that he would feel the hot pulsing of her blood. He held it only a moment against her will, and then he released it. "My relationship with Mark was based on a lot more than sex!" she told him defiantly.

"So I would expect. A man and a woman don't have to get married for sex."

Rita watched him as he changed positions, drawing his muscular tanned legs up and sitting cross-legged, with his broad shoulders comfortably sloped. The sun glinted off his blond hair, which was ruffled by the brisk breeze. The discussion, putting them at odds, hadn't done anything to lessen his physical appeal for her. In fact, quite the contrary was true. She wanted him to touch her, kiss her again. She knew that he read that information in her eyes, but he made no move to initiate the intimacy that was easily in his power. His restraint introduced an aching suspense.

"Rita, would you mind telling me what happened between you and Mark?" He made it sound like the most distasteful kind of favor. "I really do need to know."

Rita moved restlessly, taken unaware not so much by the turn of the conversation itself as with his manner of asking, which made her deeply uncomfortable. Why did he have to keep suggesting that there was something potentially serious between them when there wasn't? Why had he said he *needed* to know?

"No, I don't mind telling you. It's perfectly natural for you to be curious. I'm sure I would be, in your place." She tossed her head, and pushed away a flyaway strand of hair. "It's all quite simple and yet difficult to explain to someone who doesn't know the people involved. I wasn't honest with Mark about my background, which is completely different from his. When he found out at the last minute, completely by accident, he was very upset that I hadn't been open with him. Actually he just wanted to postpone the wedding."

"Then you were the one who actually broke it off with him?" Jack's question was quick and incisive.

Rita sighed, finding the explanation difficult and painful. "Yes and no. I just realized at that point that there wouldn't ever be a wedding. I was terribly hurt, but deep down I knew Mark was right in having doubts about us. All the statistics say that people from the same background, raised with the same values, have the best chance of staying married." She gazed bleakly out to sea. "That would have been the worst thing that could have happened—to have gone ahead with it and had it not work. I couldn't bear to be like my mother and go through one marriage and divorce after another." She looked back at Jack, seeing his frowning expression and reading it as consternation on her behalf and pity. "Basically, that's what happened. There was too big a chance that I wouldn't fit in with Mark's family, and Mark could never be happy with a wife his family couldn't accept."

It was the most baffling damned thing Jack had ever heard. She obviously considered the matter explained, and he didn't feel like he knew much more than he had before. The pain in her voice and eyes hurt him like hell, but he had to try to make a little more sense of what had put it there.

"You were engaged for two years, and everything was fine until Pendleton discovered that the two of you weren't from the same kind of background. How are your backgrounds different? Does it have something to do with your mother's being married a number of times?"

Rita nodded reluctantly. There seemed so little point in dredging up her unfortunate family history. "It has a lot to do with my mother, period. She isn't the kind of person Mark and his family, especially his mother, would approve of. They would consider her, well, low class. And I really can't blame them. Mark's father has a doctorate degree and is a university professor. He and Mark's mother have been happily married for thirty-odd years. She's a leader in the community, involved with all sorts of civic and church projects. All three of their children have college degrees.

They're a wonderful family. Everyone in the town where they live knows them and respects them.''

Jack didn't comment because his thoughts were almost guaranteed to offend her. Mark Pendleton sounded like a stuff-shirted fool to him. Jack couldn't imagine breaking up with the woman he loved and wanted to marry because of irregularities in her family tree. The notion was absurd.

"You don't understand, do you." Rita's words were more statement than question. "That's probably because you're not from the same kind of family as Mark's, either."

Jack's eyebrows shot up at the implied slight. "Fortunately not, if being from Mark's kind of family would mean I couldn't marry the woman of my choice and live my own life the way I wanted to," he said dryly.

Rita felt her face grow flushed with her mingled resentment and apology. "I didn't mean that the way it sounded," she said defensively. "Of course, I don't know anything about your family."

Jack was getting to his feet. "Except that my mother owns the messiest car on Maui. I'm all for driving it to the nearest restaurant and having some lunch. How does that idea strike you?"

Smiling, he held a hand down to Rita. She took it and got to her feet, glad to abandon the conversation and relieved that she apparently hadn't offended him.

"It sounds wonderful to me. I'm starving," she declared lightly.

Still holding her hand, Jack stepped up so close to her that their bodies were touching. Rita's eyes widened with her surprise and uncertainty as she looked up and saw hardness and contempt in his face and eyes.

"I have one thing to say on the subject of Mark Pendleton, and then as far as I'm concerned he can never be mentioned again. The man sounds like a stupid bastard to me.

But his loss is my gain. If he shows up here tomorrow, I have no intention of stepping aside. He'll have to fight for what he gave up with so little apparent reason.'' He watched her expression narrowly, and Rita realized that he had spoken with deliberate calculation.

"Show up here!" she echoed, and smiled with bitter mockery at the notion of staid, conservative Mark doing something so impetuous. "Believe me, there isn't the slightest possibility. Mark and I are finished."

"Good. That was exactly what I was hoping to hear." Jack sounded satisfied and relieved. Dropping a light kiss on the tip of Rita's nose, he reverted back to his easygoing self. "Come on. Let's go. I know a great restaurant just down the road a piece."

Rita pulled back as he started for the car, holding on to her hand.

"Wait, Jack. Please."

He stopped and looked back at her, quizzical and yet on the alert. When she tugged at her hand to free it, and he wouldn't let her go, his grasp gentle but unrelenting, somehow what she had to tell him was twice as difficult to say.

"Jack, you and I can only be friends. I like you an awful lot. I'm sure that's obvious. You're good-looking and fun, and I enjoy your company, but I don't intend to be serious about any man for a long, long time, maybe years. I mean that!" she added desperately as he smiled and pulled her to him.

"Okay," he said cheerfully, and the smile broadened into a grin as she stared at him, disgruntled that he was making a joke of what she'd spoken in utter seriousness. "Now that we have that all straightened out, we can go and have some lunch. Afterward, if you haven't changed your mind, I'll come back and jump off the cliff." He kissed her on the lips, lightly at first and then with more depth when her lips clung to his.

"Sweetheart, your warning might have come too late," he said huskily. "I think I'm head over heels in love with you, and I haven't even taken you to bed yet. But not to worry." He grazed his knuckles lightly across her nose. "I'm a big boy. And, I have to warn you, one hell of a good salesman."

He winked and grinned so engagingly that Rita had no choice but to smile at him, and then, magically, there seemed no basis for her worries. The world was suffused with sunshine too brilliant to allow for shadows. All was lightheartedness and fun and she the luckiest of women to have Jack Adams as her companion for a few carefree days, after which she would return to the real world.

Chapter Five

Out on the highway Jack headed the car back toward Paia, but before they reached the outskirts of the small village, he turned off to the right onto a street that made a sharp descent down to a cluster of buildings on the same level with the seashore. Rita had noticed the small sign announcing The Fish House up on the highway earlier. A similar sign was tacked onto the white picket fence bordering the grounds of a gaily painted blue and white building that looked like a house with a glassed-in porch overlooking the sea. The parking area was crowded with cars.

"It looks like The Fish House is very popular," Rita commented as Jack edged the red station wagon into a slot just barely big enough.

"It is, for good reason. The menu's one of the best on the island. Without a reservation, you might as well not come here in the evening."

"Do you think we'll get a table now?"

Jack grinned. "You can count on it. I'm a crack sales-man, remember. Actually I called from your hotel while I was waiting for you and asked them to be sure and hold us a good table with a view."

"Do you know the owners?" she asked him as they walked from the car to the side entrance of the restaurant.

"Owner," he corrected. "He's an old friend of my mother's."

The interior of the restaurant was as cheerful and neat as the outside, but it wasn't as informal a place as Rita had expected and it was indeed crowded. She took in with a glance the fact that the tables were draped handsomely with crisp blue tablecloths, each had a small vase of real flowers and the tableware and stemmed goblets were quality restau-rant ware. There were wineglasses in evidence everywhere and wine bottles nestled in ice-filled buckets.

Her first thought was that she and Jack were not suitably dressed for a nice restaurant, but then she noticed sun-tanned bare legs here and there and numerous aloha shirts and summery casual blouses. The question of dress seemed a needless consideration anyway since all the tables in sight were taken, both in the room they'd entered and the ad-joining one visible through two open doorways.

Jack seemed undaunted by any possibility that they wouldn't be able to get a table. "Adams, table for two," he told the waiter who approached them. To her surprise the young man's air of polite apology turned immediately to friendly deference.

"Right this way, sir. We have the table you requested on the *lanai*."

He led them through the two dining rooms out onto the enclosed porch overlooking the ocean and seated them at a choice corner table. On the way Jack was hailed several times. He made friendly responses to the greetings, but didn't stop, explaining that he'd just arrived in Maui a few days ago and planned to be there awhile. Hearing the remark, Rita wondered if he had a job at the moment. Thinking back to their conversation about work, she recalled that he hadn't actually said he was presently employed.

After they'd sat down, the waiter asked them if they'd like a drink from the bar. Rita refused, partly because she wasn't used to drinking during the day and partly because she knew that in a place like this one, the bar tab could easily double the price of a midday meal.

"Why don't we have a bottle of wine?" Jack suggested. "No, I don't want to see a list," he told the waiter, who was excusing himself to go and get one. "I've seen your wine list, and it's more like a book. Just tell Bailey to send us something light and on the dry side, maybe a nice California chardonnay. He's around here somewhere, isn't he?"

The waiter answered that Mr. McIntosh was indeed there and paused before leaving to ask Jack if he preferred to have the wine served at once or with the meal.

"Bring it right away," Jack replied. "You can even save yourself some trouble and have the bartender open it. If Bailey recommends it, I'm sure it's fine."

"This is nice," Rita commented, glancing at the impeccably set table and then out at the ocean. "It's not what I expected. I thought you were taking me to some little place where the local people eat." She opened her menu and wasn't surprised to see that the choices were varied and suited to a sophisticated palate. The prices were high, comparable to those in a fine Atlanta restaurant. She wondered if Jack, who was perusing his menu casually, could afford to take her to an expensive place like this.

"The local people do eat here, but you can't keep a place like this a secret. The tourists find out about it, too. It has the reputation of serving the best seafood on Maui. Everything brought out of the kitchen is fresh.'' Jack closed his menu and laid it to one side.

"Have you decided already?" Rita was looking for some hint of how she could order. If he was opting for a less expensive dish, she would claim she wasn't very hungry and choose one of the appetizers.

"I'm having the Chef's Catch of the Day Medley, sautéed in a lemon butter sauce. It's always excellent. I'd recommend that for you, too, if you haven't tried some of our Hawaiian fish like *opakapaka* and *mahimahi*. But have whatever you want. The deep-water prawns are a specialty, too, and very good."

He'd mentioned two of the most expensive selections on the menu. "The appetizers look good," Rita ventured.

"Have one of them, too, or several, if you'd prefer them to an entrée. Along with a salad or soup."

Rita hesitated, working up her nerve. She decided to be direct since the issue of expense was likely to reoccur, assuming that they would spend more time together during the remaining week and a half of her Hawaiian vacation.

"Jack, isn't this going to be an awfully expensive lunch? Since I practically asked you outright to take me sight-seeing today, could I pay for it? Or at least split the bill with you?"

Her offer took him utterly by surprise, but she was relieved to see that he didn't appear insulted. His expression was ruefully questioning as he spread his hands in a helpless gesture and looked down at himself.

"Do I have the look of an insolvent person?" He looked back at her and smiled reassuringly when he saw that she was seriously concerned about possibly having hurt his feelings. "Believe me, my bank account has never been healthier. I can easily afford to buy you lunch. And even if I couldn't, I could probably strike a deal here. Bailey Mc-

Intosh is an ex-boyfriend of my mother's. They were the talk of Maui for years, not just because they had an ongoing affair but because they fought like cat and dog and staged some horrendous scenes. Now they're just friends, which is safer for everyone concerned." Jack chuckled and then noticed the expression of shock and disapproval on Rita's face.

"You shouldn't talk about your *mother* that way," she protested.

Comprehension flashed in Jack's eyes. "I haven't mentioned that my parents are divorced, have I? They split up when I was twelve. My father remarried, but my mother never did, and my sister and I were just as glad not to have another stepparent in the picture. Don't get the wrong idea. My mother wasn't promiscuous, but there were several important men in her life, and she never bothered to try to hide her relationships with them, especially after I was older and well acquainted with the birds and bees myself." Jack broke off as an enormous man bearing an open wine bottle in one beefy hand and two stemmed goblets in the other came to a halt at their table.

"Jack, it's good to see you, boy," he boomed in a deep resonant voice. Setting the wine bottle and glasses on the table with a surprising delicacy, he slapped Jack on the shoulder and pushed him down when Jack made a move to rise. "Don't get up. Sit," he commanded and beamed a warm smile at Rita, who was taking in his larger than life appearance with awed interest, having made a reasoned guess as to his identity. He must be Bailey McIntosh, Jack's mother's ex-lover. Weighing at least three hundred pounds, he looked like a retired wrestler. His walrus-style mustache was iron gray, matching the color of the fringe of hair on his head, circling a shiny bald pate.

"Rita, I'd like you to meet Bailey McIntosh, who owns this fine establishment. Bailey, a very special lady, Rita

Jones.'' Jack made the introduction in a friendly tone that matched his expression.

The huge man bowed from the waist. His shrewd blue eyes were warmly welcoming.

''My pleasure to meet such a pretty lady. I have a nice little wine here that I think you'll both enjoy.'' He poured the two wineglasses slightly more than half-full and served Rita and Jack with that deftness Rita found so surprising in a man of his enormous build. He looked on indulgently while they tasted and approved the wine, exchanged a few personal comments with Jack, and made several food recommendations that included the two Jack had mentioned, commanding them to let him know if everything wasn't to their satisfaction.

''On the house, Jack,'' he declared heartily, taking his leave. ''No argument. Good to see you, boy. Glad you came by and brought such a pretty lady.'' He clapped Jack on the shoulder again. ''Be sure and tell Lil I said hello and for her not to be such a stranger.''

''Sure thing, Bailey. And thanks.'' Jack made another move to rise and got shoved back into his chair. He sat there grinning at Rita and shaking his head, listening as Bailey McIntosh moved off behind him, calling first-name greetings to people who were obviously regular patrons of his restaurant.

''You can't argue with Bailey, once he's made up his mind,'' he mused. ''My mother claims she might have married him if he wasn't so bullheaded. Now at least you and I don't have to fight over the bill.''

Rita took a sip of her wine. ''Speaking of fighting, when you said that Bailey and your mother fought like cat and dog, I hope you don't mean literally. He looks like an exwrestler.''

"He is. But like a lot of big men, Bailey's gentle as a lamb, unless you get him really riled. He never abused my mother, but he did smash up some furniture a time or two. I can see I've shocked you again," Jack declared cheerfully, giving his own interpretation to the reaction Rita was trying to keep screened from her face. "It's not surprising since my guess is that you're from a prim and proper kind of background and not used to unconventional people like my mother. What the rest of the world does or thinks has no bearing on her, as far as she is concerned. It hasn't helped that she's an artist and tends to associate with people as wacky as she is. But you'll like her, I think. Most people do, as long as they don't depend on her for anything practical."

"I don't mean to come across as a prude," Rita protested, uncomfortable with his totally wrong assumption about her own background, which from years of habit she didn't find easy to discuss. "I'm the last person to be critical of someone else's mother, believe me. It's your attitude that surprises me. You seem so broad-minded and tolerant." She hesitated. "Weren't you ever, well, embarrassed or ashamed?"

"No, I can't say that I ever was." Jack's reply was gently sympathetic because of what he was reading between the lines. Her mother must have dragged her through some unsavory publicity with her multiple marriages and divorces. Jack suspected that big alimony and property settlements had been involved. Divorce could be a nasty business when large sums of money were at stake.

In his parents' case, there hadn't been any such disputes, since his mother was an only child and heiress to a large fortune held in trust and doled out to her in a generous annual income. Among the properties she'd inherited was the Maui beach house, located on a choice oceanfront site. Of course, anyone meeting his mother and not knowing her story wouldn't suspect her of being wealthy because she was so totally nonmaterialistic. Money meant nothing to her since she'd never had to work for a living.

"Probably I wouldn't have been so tolerant of her eccentricities if I'd lived with her," Jack mused. "But my sister and I lived with our father, who was very strict on us both, but especially on me, hoping to stamp out the bad genes, I suppose. I always looked forward to escaping all the rules and regulations when it came time to visit my mother. But enough talk of my family tree."

As if on cue, their waiter arrived to take their order. After he had gone, Jack turned the conversation to talk of places he intended to take her on Maui. Rita didn't argue with his assumption that he'd be monopolizing her time. That morning lying beside the pool, she had looked upon her remaining time in Maui as interminable and now, just hours later, ten days seemed all too short and promised to be filled with pleasant diversion.

In a corner of her mind, she mulled over what she'd learned about Jack's background, which sounded no more desirable than her own. No wonder he hadn't been able to comprehend her breakup with Mark. He was from a broken home and had a pragmatic sense of values as evidenced by his acceptance of his mother's extramarital relationships with men. Ironically he seemed as close to his mother as Mark was to Katherine Pendleton, and yet how different were those two mother-and-son relationships! As different as the sons themselves.

Rita's perception of the contrast between her ex-fiancé and her present companion caused her a pang of guilt. She respected and admired Mark for his high moral standards and traditional sense of values, but he wasn't as much fun as Jack. He was predictable and inclined to be a bit pompous, whereas Jack constantly surprised her. Jack was refreshingly spontaneous and quick to laugh at anything and everything, including himself. But then such judgments were hardly fair, Rita rebuked herself. She'd known Mark for over two years and she had just met Jack, whose charisma would undoubtedly lose its potency very quickly. And being a delightful companion was no serious recommendation of a man anyway.

Guilt over her superficial preference for Jack's company didn't keep her from thoroughly enjoying herself. The wine relaxed her and made her a little light-headed. She found herself laughing so often that she wondered if she was acting intoxicated until Jack stopped midway of some whimsical remark and said, "You bring out the comedian in me because I love to hear you laugh," and then she didn't worry about it any more.

The meal was outstanding, the food deliciously cooked and beautifully presented. The service was perfect. Rita could well understand the popularity of the restaurant by the time they'd finished eating.

"I'm glad you brought me here," she told Jack, sitting back with a contented sigh when the table had been cleared and they were waiting for their coffee to be served. "Mark and I—" She stopped abruptly, realizing what she had been about to say. It came as a shock that mentioning Mark in Jack's presence could be so casual and that speaking his name could cause her not the slightest twinge of pain. It wasn't right that she could refer to Mark already as though he were an old friend!

Jack leaned forward and touched one of her flushed cheeks with gentle fingertips. "It's okay. Don't be embarrassed. Go ahead and finish what you were saying," he ordered her gently. "I'd rather know what you're thinking, even if I don't like it."

"I was only going to say that Mark and I would probably never have found this place. That's all," she added defensively when Jack seemed to be waiting for more. He was too perceptive where she was concerned. She didn't like the feeling that he was able to read her, whether she wanted him to or not.

Their waiter's arrival with the coffee was a most welcome interruption for Rita. It was the Kona coffee grown in Hawaii and was fragrant and strong. During the time it took her to add cream and sugar to hers, taste it and pronounce it very good, she was casting around in her mind for a safe change of subject. A party of three getting up from their table a short distance away provided her inspiration with their informal attire.

"It's hard for me to believe that people dress so casually to come to a good restaurant like this and sit down to a gourmet meal with wine. Is it the same at night?"

"In the evening you'll see most of the women in Hawaiian-style dresses and the men in slacks, but on the whole people dress for comfort in Hawaii. There are few places where a coat and tie are required. It's common for businessmen in Honolulu to wear aloha shirts to their offices." Jack grinned in response to Rita's startled glance at the red and white print of the shirt he was wearing. "Not all aloha shirts are gaudy, I might add. Some are quite conservative."

Jack sipped his coffee thoughtfully, apparently following his own train of thought. "I like the casual life-style here. That's one of the reasons I'm thinking of settling down in Hawaii. There are other considerations, too, of course."

"You're thinking of *living* in Hawaii?"

"You sound amazed. People do live and work here, just like in all the other American states. Bailey McIntosh has lived on Maui for twenty years and has no intention of ever leaving. He's made a good living out of this restaurant.''

"But I assume that he came here with money to invest. You said he'd been a wrestler.''

Jack was greatly taken aback at her clearly implied assumption that he himself wouldn't have money to invest, although he realized quickly that he shouldn't have been. She'd given him a strong enough clue with her offer to pay for lunch.

"I gather I haven't exactly impressed you as someone who's been lucratively employed,'' he mused ruefully. "What makes you think I'm a failure? Is it the way I dress? The way I talk?''

"I'm sorry. I didn't mean to be insulting.'' Rita laid her hand on his bare tanned arm resting along the edge of the table and left it there for her own pleasure as well as for purposes of consolation. "I'm sure you've had good-paying jobs. You're obviously intelligent and very personable. It's just difficult to get anywhere without a college degree.'' She could tell from his chagrined expression that she'd guessed right. He hadn't attended college. "I can sympathize since I'm in the same position,'' she said gently. "You have to be the kind of person who can stick to a boring job in order to be promoted, and then there's a limit to how high you can go.''

Jack was momentarily at a loss as to what to say. His male ego was definitely bruised at her perception of him as a loser and yet how was he to correct her impression? Trot out his checkbook? Tell her about his sales awards? Brag about the money he'd made? In all fairness, he couldn't fault her for her error. He didn't wear a Rolex or drive a Mercedes. It irked and amused him to realize that this was the first time he'd ever regretted dropping out of college simply because a degree from a top eastern university would have impressed her!

"College degrees are fine for people who need them," he said finally, when he'd recovered from the worst of the injury to his pride. He covered her hand with his and squeezed it. "I'm not one of those people. I didn't want to be a doctor or a lawyer or an engineer, and I still don't. For me, staying in college would have been wasting my time just to get a piece of paper. Too often I think a college degree is just an excuse for being mediocre. It allows a man to put a professional label on himself and fit into a tidy slot instead of figuring out by trial and error what he's good at doing. That just wasn't for me."

Rita thought immediately of Mark and her guilt for seeing him as the perfect illustration of Jack's theory required her to challenge it.

"So you did go to college and drop out?"

Jack nodded. Rita was sure for a second that he was about to add something but then he didn't.

"And you've found out for yourself what you're good at?"

He smiled at her politely skeptical tone. "Usually I'm very good at selling myself, but right now I don't seem to be doing too well. Seriously, I've proven myself to have a good instinct for recognizing a business opportunity, and my talent for sales and public relations combines very well with that." He shrugged. "Surely some luck has been involved, but it's been more than that. When you have a couple of ventures work out exactly the way you predict, it builds confidence in your judgment. Right now I'm keeping my eyes and ears open, telling myself not to be in a big hurry. Something will turn up here in Hawaii, and I have to do my homework and wait for the signal to go off in my head." He gave her hand another squeeze and then caressed her knuckles with his fingertips. "Who knows? Maybe you'll decide to stay here and be my partner?"

"That's not likely." Rita forced a smile to alleviate the bite from her quick reply and then, to avoid his gaze, watched the movement of his hand on hers while she felt his touch. His hands were attractive, like everything else about him. He had so much going for him in looks, personality and charm, but not for a moment did she buy the entrepreneur success story. It just didn't ring true, and yet she didn't want to be honest and let him see her doubt. There was simply no point in hurting his feelings more than she already had. "But I do wish you lots of luck," she told him sincerely and was depressed at the thought of his growing older and becoming more and more desperate, trying one scheme after another to make money.

Jack didn't know exactly what path her private thoughts had taken to trigger sadness, but it was almost certain that she was sitting there thinking about Pendleton. Perhaps the talk of college and professions had brought him to mind. Jack remembered from her conversation on the plane that her ex-fiancé was an attorney with an insurance company and thus a prime candidate for being the type of mediocre professional Jack had disparaged. That possibility made Jack resent even more the man's ability to claim her attention from thousands of miles away while Jack was telling her about himself.

"Shall we go?" he inquired abruptly. When she readily agreed, her vaguely apologetic manner seemed a confirmation of his irritable assumption that she had been miles away from him in her thoughts.

Rita was left to conclude regretfully that her failure to believe in Jack's success had indeed come through to him and hurt his pride. Since an apology could only make matters worse, she kept her silence as they walked out to the car.

He seemed deep in his own sober thoughts and still hadn't said anything by the time they'd driven to the main highway and had to stop to check for traffic.

"Where to now?" she asked with forced cheer, thinking glumly that he probably intended to take her back to her hotel and deposit her there for keeps.

Jack looked over at her, scowling. "I'm trying to make up my mind," he said heavily. "I don't know whether to go back and jump off the cliff and be done with it or look for a jewelry store."

"A jewelry store?" Rita's smile was uncertain. He had to be joking and yet he looked so gravely serious.

"That's what I said—a jewelry store. I was thinking of buying a half a dozen Rolexes and stringing them up to my elbow. Then maybe I could convince you I'm not a vagrant."

Her laughter came in a surprised burst and then continued in delighted peals that harmonized pleasantly with his own deeper tones of merriment.

"You have the most amazing mind," she marveled, chuckling and wiping her eyes. "I never know what you're going to say next. I think I've laughed more today than I've ever laughed in my life."

"Well, that's something," he reflected dryly. "At least I tickle your funny bone, even if you don't take me seriously."

"Why do I have to take you seriously?" she demanded pleadingly. "Let's don't be serious, about anything. Let's just laugh and have a good time."

He didn't answer, but when he leaned over and kissed her on the lips, Rita took his action for agreement. Impulsively she caught his face between her hands and held him so that she could reciprocate with a grateful little kiss in return. It took her totally by surprise that pressing her lips to his could act upon him as it did.

"Oh, sweetheart," he murmured and took over, kissing her hungrily, with an urgency that erased from Rita's mind any thought of sealing a pact, any thought at all. She kissed him back, returning pressure for pressure and meeting the ardor of his tongue with her own and inflaming her need as well as his. She was as breathless as he was and her heart was pounding wildly when he pulled his lips free and rested his cheek against hers, taking deep gulps of air. When he reached up and took Rita's hands down from around his neck and sat back, holding them, she met his eyes reluctantly and read with embarrassment the question in them.

"You must really have a low opinion of me," she ventured in a shamed voice, looking away from him. "I really can't believe I'm acting like this myself. I've never turned on this way to a man before."

"Never?"

The combination of eagerness and hesitancy in the single word question drew Rita's startled gaze. Jack looked as vulnerable as he had sounded. Suddenly she was angry at him, not just for making an issue of what she'd already admitted, but for letting her answer assume such deep significance when she'd just implored him to help her keep their relationship casual. For her it couldn't be anything else, not without inviting disaster. She couldn't become emotionally involved with a man like Jack, no matter how strongly he attracted her.

"Yes, never!" she said hotly. "How many times do I have to tell you that sex is not important to me!" She stared at him in surprise and then resentment as he looked pleased and smiled.

"You look absolutely gorgeous when you're mad. Has anyone ever told you that before?" He looked in both directions for oncoming traffic and pulled out onto the highway as though the conversation had been most satisfactorily completed and there was no need to say more.

Rita glared at him in growing frustration. "You're the most *irritating* man!" she muttered.

He peaked his eyebrows, but kept his eyes on the road. "Irritating as well as funny? Hmm. Well, I suppose that's better than nothing," he mused cheerfully. "For the time being I'll postpone jumping off the cliff and hold off on the Rolexes, too. How would you like to take a look at the Iao Needle this afternoon? There's plenty of time for that, but rather late in the day to think about driving to Hana or up to the crater. I don't know about you, but I'm feeling a little lazy after that big meal. A walk would probably do us both good. There's a nice little park. The history behind the place is rather grim, though."

Rita's irritation ebbed as he began recounting the story of the culminating battle between King Kamehameha I, the famous king who had united the Hawaiian islands under single rule, and the chieftains of Maui who resisted giving up their power and made their last, bloody stand in the Iao Valley. She found herself caught up in the narrative and unable to hold onto her feelings of grievance. Jack was a natural storyteller, with an instinct for creating drama, including just enough historical detail but not too much. He also had a pleasant speaking voice, well-modulated and crisp. Rita enjoyed the sound of it and found herself thinking that she could probably listen to him talk about almost anything.

The reflection made her guilty when she recalled her tendency to tune Mark out any time he talked at length, but then Mark had been inclined to pontificate, to go on and on with an explanation or anecdote until the original point was lost in all the mass of detail. She'd wondered more than once how he could ever keep a trial jury's attention. But she wasn't going to think about Mark now. Of his own choosing, he wasn't here.

"You're right. That is a grim story," she told Jack when he'd finished. "Where are you from? I was trying to figure out your accent while you were talking. You have a strong hint of a Boston *a*."

"You're not going to be able to pass the quiz if you don't pay close attention," he chided her, but he didn't sound at all displeased as he reached over to pick up her hand and held it in a warm clasp. "There's good reason for a Boston *a* in my speech, since I grew up there. It's probably not as strong now as it was when I quit college and joined the navy. I was thrown in with guys from all over the country and traveled around the world on ships. The last few years I've been listening to the midwestern twang in Missouri and Illinois. That has surely had some effect. As to where I'm actually *from*, I was born in California, where my parents met each other."

"You've been all over the place," Rita reflected a little enviously. "This is my first time out of the South. And speaking of the South, how did you happen to be in Atlanta? Were you just routed through there?"

Jack was ridiculously pleased with her idle show of interest, belated as it was. She was asking questions she should have asked him four days ago on the plane.

"No, I'd wound up my business in Illinois earlier than expected and had some time on my hands before this trip to Hawaii. I'd never been down in the Sunbelt and decided to use the time looking up some contacts and checking into a couple of land development opportunities I'd heard about." Jack glanced over at her, curious at the little convulsive tightening of her hand in his. She was looking fixedly out of the window on her side. "But none of them interested me," he added, finding her behavior puzzling. Why ask him a question and then not listen to the answer?

"So now you're considering Hawaii instead." The comment politely concluded the conversation.

"Now I'm considering Hawaii." Jack gave her hand a little squeeze and released it. "Here we are in Wailuku. There you see the name on the sign and—if you've remembered our lesson on the Hawaiian language—you could have figured out the pronunciation for yourself."

"Of course, I remember!" Rita abandoned her unseeing scrutiny of the passing landscape to make the spirited claim. Jack couldn't miss her note of relief. "The Hawaiian language has the shortest alphabet in the world, only twelve letters, five vowels and seven consonants. Every letter is sounded. Right?"

"Right. Wailuku's quite an interesting little town for history buffs. We'll drive past some of the old churches and buildings on our way and stop by any of them you're interested in seeing on the way back. The Iao Valley's not far from here, and there's only one road in and out of it."

Jack filed away in the back of his mind her reaction to his explanation for being in the Atlanta airport and her obvious relief when it was ended. It was frustrating to him to have her show some interest in him and then quickly withdraw it. He guessed the key to her behavior was the point she kept making, that she was interested in a relationship with him based purely on the here and now. She didn't care to know what he'd done yesterday or planned to do tomorrow.

She wanted him to be her fun-loving, entertaining escort, and that was all. At least it was a role he didn't have to pretend to enjoy.

Chapter Six

The Iao Valley had a brooding, somber beauty that gave Rita goose bumps. The afternoon shadows turned the thick vegetation on the mountains a dense, dark green, and the pervasive sense of quiet and deep tranquility seemed to swallow up the sounds of laughter and conversation as other visitors besides themselves parked in the paved parking lot, spilled out of cars, climbed the steep stairs to the lookout and back down again. The quiet was especially noticeable on the path that wound beside a mountain brook through shaded natural garden, where varieties of plants Rita recognized as potted houseplants back home thrived in the wild and grew to huge size.

The Iao Needle rock formation itself might have been a monument erected by nature in memory of the Hawaiian soldiers who'd given their lives fighting either in support of their chieftains and an ancient way of life or for the powerful leader with a vision of solidarity, who won and brought the Hawaiian islands a giant step toward the present. The sense of history was oppressive to Rita as she stood on a small sunlit rock terrace gazing up at the monolithic shaft silhouetted against the sky.

"Why so serious?" Jack asked her and listened without comment while she tried to explain her feelings. When she'd finished, he gazed up at the rock formation and then, of all things, grinned a most irreverent grin. Rita stared at him, at first surprised and then disapproving. His humor seemed out of place.

Jack glanced back at her and saw her expression. "Sorry, sweetheart," he apologized, managing neither to look nor sound very regretful. His arm had been lightly around her waist, and when she stiffened away from him, he tightened it and brought her closer. "Please, don't be mad at me," he cajoled. "It's just that I've been to this place any number of times, and—" He broke off and made a conscious, unsuccessful effort to erase the humor from his face. He shook his head. "There's a big difference, I suppose, between the way a man and a woman can look at the same object." He glanced up at the shaft of rock. "The same *shape*."

"*Jack!* Shame on you!" she cried, comprehending his ribald comparison.

He grinned at her, catching the shocked amusement mingled with her reproach. "It never occurred to me that anybody could look at that rock and not see a phal—"

Rita put her hand quickly over his mouth. "Shh. People will hear you," she warned in a whisper, a reluctant smile breaking out over her face.

Jack nipped at her fingers with his teeth and then ran the tip of his tongue along one of them, making her draw her hand quickly back with a little gasp of pleasure. Before she could stop him, he had bent his head and taken a quick, deep taste of her parted lips and made her go weak against him.

"Anybody looking probably saw that, too," he teased, rubbing her nose with his and then pulling back a few inches to smile into her bemused face. "The men are all jealous because they've been looking at that rock the same way I have."

"You're terrible," she accused with no real conviction. Then her eyes went wide and she stared up at him, her face flooding with embarrassed color as she listened along with him to a low conversation drifting behind them down the steps.

"Aren't they a good-looking couple, Harry! So much in love! Remember our honeymoon? We were the same way." A deep sigh. "We didn't know other people were around then, either."

"Give 'em another thirty years, Blanche, and they'll know," came Harry's rumbling male reply. "Believe me, they'll know."

Rita bit her lip. "They were talking about us," she murmured, shocked. "They thought we were—were *married*."

"So what if they did?" Jack held her tight and wouldn't let her move away. "I don't mind. Now what were we talking about when Harry and Blanche interrupted us? Oh, yes, about the world's biggest—"

"Jack!" Rita covered his mouth again and felt his grin spread against her palm. "You really are bad!" she scolded in an undertone, waging an unsuccessful fight against a giggle that welled up in her chest.

"Go on! Let it out!" he urged her, chuckling, and the sound of his merriment was catching. They stood at the railing, leaning together and laughing, attracting curious, interested glances. But suddenly Rita couldn't bring herself to worry about the attention of strangers.

When the funny moment had subsided, it left them feeling intimate. They walked side by side down the steps, their arms around each other. There were other audible comments on the stroll out to the parking lot, compliments on Rita's brilliant auburn hair and remarks about the handsome couple they made together and their obvious state of being honeymooners in love.

Rita knew that the physical compatibility between herself and Jack was responsible for giving the false impression that they were newlyweds. There was no arguing that Jack would answer most women's dreams of the perfect bridegroom on a honeymoon. He was handsome, companionable, attentive, and, even to the straitlaced female eye, virile. Those traits weren't enough over the long haul to qualify a man as a husband, but Rita's lighthearted mood wasn't dampened by such thoughts.

She hadn't come to Hawaii looking for a husband. She hadn't come with even the remotest thought of finding a lover to substitute for her missing bridegroom. But she and Jack had found each other, and he would be her lover. Strolling with him down the pathway that led to the parking lot, leaving wrong impressions that she was a happy bride behind her, Rita was aware of that new certainty and could find in herself no resistance to it. It seemed as immutable a fact as the history behind the Iao Valley, which no longer seemed gloomy but just peaceful.

Perhaps she would have been stricken with guilt if the way she was feeling was even in the same category as what she'd expected her honeymoon to be like, but it wasn't. She had anticipated the time alone with Mark in a beautiful tropical setting, but a day like this one, full of laughter with passion always just below the surface and threatening to break through, would never have happened. She took it for what it was, fleeting diversion, and recognized that what she felt for Jack was transient, giddy infatuation, the kind that most girls get out of their system in high school with crushes on boyfriends. Climbing into the passenger side of the mud-spattered red station wagon that belonged to Jack's mother, Rita was as happy as the girl she'd never been, getting into a seventeen-year-old date's jalopy.

Jack had heard the same comments Rita had heard and was surprised at her lack of concern. He sensed that she had crossed over some borderline of reserve where the two of them were concerned because she was so relaxed and open in her physical response to him. When he reached over for her hand as they were driving away from the valley, she met his hand halfway and nestled hers contentedly in his warm clasp on the center console. To control his surge of delight, Jack had to warn himself not to take too much for granted. This could be a passing mood with her.

"Did you want to stop here in Wailuku and look around?" he asked as they drove into the outskirts of the town.

"No, maybe we can come back another day," she replied, turning her arm so that she could see her wristwatch.

"Do you have a date?" Jack asked her teasingly.

Rita smiled at him. "I hope I will. I have tickets for the *luau* at the hotel tonight and wondered if you'd go with me." She spoke confidently, expecting him to accept at once. When he didn't, she didn't know whether he was teasing her with his hesitation or just not enthusiastic at the prospect of a *luau*, which was surely old hat to him.

"I know that there's probably nothing authentic about these affairs, especially the ones at the big hotels," she went on, still quite confidently. "They're just shows staged for tourists, but I really would like to go and see what it's like, and I'm not sure I'll have nerve enough to go alone. If nothing else, it would be a free dinner," she added cajolingly. He glanced over at her then, and she could see from the direct glimpse into his gray eyes that he wasn't teasing her with his delay in accepting her invitation. He had some serious objection.

"You didn't buy those tickets after you arrived here, did you? They came with the honeymoon package."

"Why, yes, but what does that matter?" Rita was surprised at his evident distaste. "You said you didn't mind today when people thought we were honeymooners. Why should you mind using Mark's ticket to a *luau*?"

Jack grimaced. "It's not using his ticket that I mind. I just don't want him to come along." His glance was ruefully apologetic. "We managed to lose him this afternoon. I didn't look at you once and see you thinking about him. Frankly, I'd rather leave him lost." Jack sighed. "I guess I'm asking for too much to want all your attention, but it's more than selfishness. I don't want that jerk to have any more power to hurt you. I get resentful and plain jealous when you get that sad, faraway look, and I know damned well you're with me and thinking of him. So that's why I'm not crazy about using his ticket to the *luau*."

Rita pulled her hand out of his. "I can't promise you that I'm not going to think about Mark during the evening, whether we go to the *luau* or not. That is definitely asking too much." She was not only annoyed but defensive. There had been so few thoughts of Mark in Jack's company, and none that Mark would have appreciated.

"I'll take you to the *luau*," Jack said in quick capitulation.

"You don't have to," Rita said stubbornly.

"But I want to." He reached over and squeezed her tightly clasped hands. "Now that you've offered me a free dinner, you can't change your mind," he chided her lightly. "Actually I haven't been to that many *luau*s, especially the big hotel productions, and they're fun. The food is usually good, too.''

He smiled and when he couldn't cajole a smile in return, turned his attention back to the road with an air of resignation. It had been stupid of him not to accept her offer of taking her to the *luau* with no questions asked. Now he'd have to be patient and gradually ease her guard down again. Why couldn't he just take things slower?

They rode along in silence for several miles, and when Rita didn't relax, Jack steeled himself for dealing with whatever was bothering her. He just hoped he hadn't totally undermined his own position to the extent that she was having second thoughts not only about the *luau* but about having any more to do with him.

''Okay. Out with it,'' he prompted.

Rita took a deep breath and summoned her courage. ''I hope you won't take this the wrong way,'' she began reluctantly, and drew a quick probing glance that temporarily dismembered her nerve.

''Until I hear what's on your mind, I won't be able to take it any way, will I?'' he prodded gently.

''It's nothing much, really. I was wondering, well, how 'dressy' these things are. I don't know what clothes you've brought to Hawaii with you—'' She broke off, color flooding her cheeks under his astonished gaze.

''Is that *it*? That's what has you all uptight? You're afraid I'll show up tonight in something similar to what I have on and embarrass you?'' Jack sounded relieved and amused.

With her fears about insulting him laid to rest, Rita was slightly piqued at his whole attitude, which had been the basis of her concern in the first place. In his mind, proper attire wasn't important, and it was to her.

"I'm sorry, but I'm not as 'laid back' about dress as you are," she said evenly with her chin set at an uncompromising angle.

"Actually, I'm glad you brought the subject up," Jack countered cheerfully. "I was trying to figure out a tactful way of asking if you had something suitable to wear to a *luau*. Of course, you probably did your homework and wouldn't show up in an ordinary dress or—heaven forbid—pants."

He met the startled question in Rita's quick glance with a bland smile. She was almost sure, but not quite, that he was teasing her.

"I was going to wear a nice dress," she ventured, and let her voice drift off when Jack nodded discreetly and said nothing. "Well. What should I wear?" she asked him when several seconds had passed in circumspect silence. "One of those Hawaiian print dresses like I've seen in the shops? They're awfully high-priced to buy and wear just a time or two. I doubt I'd have the occasion to wear one in Atlanta."

Jack reached over and patted her hand. "Not to worry. When we get to your hotel, we'll do some shopping and get ourselves both something to wear. We might as well do this thing up right." He grinned at whatever he envisioned, making Rita both curious and doubtful that he was serious. "Now that you've mentioned a *luau*, I'm starting to think of *kalua* pig and *lomi* salmon and all sorts of good foods I haven't eaten in a long time. Are you sure you're ready for the *imu* ceremony?"

"That's when they cook the pig?"

"No, the pig's been cooking for hours in the *imu*, or earth pit, when the *luau* starts. The *imu* ceremony is when it's dug out and uncovered by all the layers of leaves so that it can be carved up and served. Everybody stands around and watches."

"How embarrassing for the poor pig. Tell me about the *lomi* salmon," Rita urged, grimacing.

Jack laughed and assured her that she would get into the spirit of things at the *luau*. Then he described the popular native foods that would be served, such as the *lomi* salmon, which was salted salmon shredded and mixed with finely chopped tomato and onion and served chilled. "Chicken *luau*" was another dish she could expect to be served. The chicken was cooked with coconut milk and leaves from the taro plant, which tasted much like spinach. There was sure to be fish, probably *mahimahi*, and, of course, fresh papayas and pineapple, plus dozens of other easily recognizable dishes, vegetables and salads and rich desserts.

"What about *poi*?" Rita wanted to know. "Exactly what is it? I just know it's a food staple—or was—and that it's made from the root of the taro plant."

"You'll want to try it at the *luau*, but you probably won't like it," Jack warned. "It's an acquired taste like some of our other ethnic foods, take sauerkraut, for example. Or maybe a better comparison is your Southern hominy grits, which to me has a bland taste. *Poi* has even more of a paste consistency and almost no taste. The Hawaiians eat it along with a highly flavored food, like *lomi* salmon."

Rita's anticipation was heightened by the conversation, which returned them to an easy, casual basis. She was looking forward unreservedly to attending the *luau* with Jack as they entered the immaculate grounds of the Kaanapali resort area and would soon be arriving at her hotel. "I'm really glad you're going with me," she told Jack warmly, thinking that he would drop her at the entrance. "It's been a delightful day. Thanks for the lunch and for being such a good guide."

"It's too early for your farewell speech," he replied cheerfully. "Remember, we have our shopping still to do."

"You were serious?"

"Absolutely."

He parked the red station wagon in the hotel parking lot and walked with her to the front entrance, lightly holding her hand. In the lobby he seemed totally at ease with the ambiance of casual tropical luxury and unconcerned about the fact that he was strolling across the highly polished tile floor in his thick-soled beach thongs. Rita noticed ruefully that the women giving him second glances weren't finding fault with the way he was dressed, as she had done. She appreciated the fact that he wasn't sending out interested signals and wished suddenly that she hadn't made a critical issue of clothes. He had taken the matter more good-naturedly than she deserved. Now he was probably going to buy an overpriced outfit he really didn't need just to humor her.

"Jack, you can help me pick out one of those Hawaiian dresses, but I'm sure you already have something that will be fine to wear," she told him earnestly as they entered the mall lined on both sides with expensive shops displaying clothing, jewelry, and gift items.

He brought her hand that he was holding up to his chest and patted it reassuringly. "Don't worry," he soothed. "We'll pick out something quiet and conservative. You'll be proud to have me by your side. I promise. This looks like a good place to start, right here." He opened the door of a clothing boutique and ushered her inside.

Rita had browsed in the shop already and was familiar with its merchandise and its high prices, but she didn't raise any objection. This whole shopping expedition was her fault, and the dresses in the shop were lovely.

"We're looking for a pretty *muumuu* for the lady and a matching aloha shirt for myself," Jack informed the saleslady with a smile that sent her hand up to touch her hair.

The woman led them over to a freestanding rack of ankle-length dresses that Rita had admired on her other visit to the shop but looked through only briefly once she'd checked the price tags. None of the dresses was less than a hundred dollars and some of the more elaborate ones were as much as two hundred. That was far more than Rita could justify spending on a garment she wasn't likely to wear back home in Atlanta. But now, in the spirit of cooperation, she decided she wouldn't balk at buying one of the lower-priced ones to please Jack.

"I'm sure you'll find something you like among these," the saleswoman said, addressing Jack. She looked at Rita to assess her size and coloring and took out a dress made of a delicate purple and blue floral print. The deep rounded yoke was edged by a ruffle of exquisite lace, and just inside that was a band of islet threaded with narrow purple ribbon. The same ruffled lace and islet trim graced the wrists of the long sleeves. The folds of material fell softly from the yoke, gracefully full but not voluminous.

Jack studied the dress a moment or two and then took it from the saleswoman's hand and held it up against Rita. He whistled appreciatively.

"I think you should try this one on," he urged and then turned back to the rack and looked through the dresses with a businesslike air, pulling out two others. Rita noticed that he hadn't once checked a price tag. "Do you have the aloha shirts to match all of these?" he inquired of the saleswoman and was assured that she did.

Rita found herself being shown to a dressing cubicle to try on the dresses Jack had selected, all of which were flattering colors for her. Before she slipped on each of the dresses and walked out into the shop to model it for him, she checked the price tag to confirm what she already suspected. He'd picked out three of the higher-priced dresses.

Rather than risk hurting his feelings, she decided she'd go ahead and buy one of them anyway.

"You decide," she told him, turning and examining her reflection in the mirror as she modeled the last one. "I like all three of them. They're all so elegant. I feel like Hawaiian royalty."

"You look like an *alii*, too," he praised warmly. "Although I don't know if there were any redheaded Polynesian princesses." He adopted a thoughtful pose, standing with a wide stance, one arm across his chest and his chin cupped in the other hand. Rita was fully appreciative of his easy masculinity as she waited for his decision, glad now that he'd insisted upon the shopping. It had turned out to be such fun, as she might have known.

"I think I like the first one we picked out the best," he announced. "The purple and blue one."

"Are you sure you're not thinking of which shirt will look best on you?" she asked him teasingly and laughed outright when the startled expression on his face showed that he hadn't selected the dress with any thought of wearing the same fabric himself. He shrugged philosophically.

"I still like the purple."

"I like it best, too," Rita confided.

Thinking that he would be several minutes finding his right size in a shirt and trying it on, she took her time changing back into her own clothes and combing her hair, which surprisingly didn't worry her being down loose as much as she would have expected. It had settled naturally into waves and soft curls that disguised the lack of styling. While she wouldn't seriously consider wearing her hair in casual disarray when she returned to work, perhaps she might go to a softer style in place of the severe French twist.

The thought of making what would be a noticeable change in her appearance somehow added to her reckless sense of adventure as she draped her beautiful new *muu-muu* carefully over her arm and went to join Jack outside and pay for it. She'd use her credit card. Gone was any remaining compunction about spending two hundred dollars for a dress she might wear only once or twice. It would be fun to dress up native-style for the *luau*.

Jack was waiting for her, leaning one elbow on the counter near the cash register. He smiled welcomingly, giving no sign of impatience.

"I've already taken care of that," Jack told her when she laid the dress on the counter and started to take out her wallet. "The dress is a present."

"You've *paid* for my dress?" Rita murmured protestingly, aware of the saleswoman's discreet attention as she folded the dress and slipped it into a bag. "But I didn't mean for you to do that. I meant to pay for it myself."

Jack folded his arms across his chest and shrugged. "It's worth the money to know you'll be dressed properly tonight and won't embarrass me," he told her with deadpan seriousness, and then winked and straightened with a teasing smile as he took the bag the saleswoman was handing across the counter.

Rita had to swallow all her arguments as he and the woman thanked each other and expressed their satisfaction with the transaction. "I'm definitely going to pay you for that dress," Rita announced when they were outside and safely beyond the woman's curious eyesight. "I'd feel terrible knowing you had spent that much money on me."

Jack was carrying a bag in either hand. He transferred one so that he could put an arm loosely around her shoulders as he guided her in the direction of the elevators.

"If you don't accept my present, you'll hurt my feelings," he pointed out reasonably. "There are no strings attached, I promise. Just wear the dress tonight and look pretty. That's all I ask.''

Rita stopped and looked up into his face. "I didn't think there would be strings attached!" she protested. "That's not the reason I objected.''

"Then it's settled.''

At the elevators, which were busy with hotel guests coming and going, Jack kissed her on the lips and handed her the dress bag. "What time should I come tonight?''

Rita took the bag reluctantly, thanked him without managing to sound very grateful, and settled with him upon the time that she would meet him in the lobby to go to the *luau*.

On the way to her room, she reasoned with herself that she wouldn't have accomplished anything by being stubborn and insisting upon reimbursing him. She'd only have hurt his feelings, and not changed the realities of the situation. He had acted out of a generous impulse that didn't fit his pocketbook, not knowing that he was jogging her memory unpleasantly. Her mother's husbands had always been fond of extravagant gestures, turning up with expensive gifts they couldn't afford when money was so lean there was scarcely enough to pay for necessities. Here was another parallel between Jack and the type of man with whom she could never let herself become involved. Being forced to recognize it made her angry and sad.

When she realized how depressed she was over the incident, Rita was shocked. She shouldn't be feeling quite that deeply distressed over evidence of weakness in a man she'd known such a short time and regarded solely as a charming, temporary companion. The only explanation was that she liked Jack a lot and wanted the best for him. He was a nice, warm, generous guy with lovable traits. It was a shame that he was destined to disappoint himself and any woman foolish enough to hitch her wagon to his star.

Rita could never be that woman.

Chapter Seven

Rita looked lovely. She glowed with an inner excitement that lighted her dark eyes and curved her lips into a smile. There was such a Cinderella element to the evening. The pretty *muumuu* added to the sense of make-believe. It was more like a costume than a real dress and told a history lesson. The modest style had been introduced to Hawaiian women by missionary wives to cover pagan nakedness and adapted to the Hawaiian love of color and beauty with the use of vivid silks and fabrics brought into the islands from the Orient by traders.

This modern version was very becoming to Rita. The graceful silhouette gave just a suggestion of the shapeliness of her slender form. The dominant violet hue of the print fabric was rich and yet muted, offsetting her exotic coloring. All that was needed as a final touch was a flower for her hair or a lei. Jack provided her with both and added more magic to the evening.

He was devastatingly handsome in the aloha shirt that matched her dress and white slacks. The two of them together made a stunning couple and attracted so much admiring attention that Rita would have been self-conscious if she hadn't been so distracted by her pleasure in the beautiful hyacinth lei Jack placed carefully over her head and the matching sprig of flowers he made a production of pinning in her hair in just the right place to suit him.

"Now for the real reason behind this native tradition," he said, smiling, and kissed her on the lips. "Hmm," he murmured. "Nice tradition." And kissed her again.

"They're beautiful, Jack!" Rita touched a delicate deep pink petal and then looked up with an expectant smile when he whistled his appreciation of the picture she made.

Jack had expected her to look pretty, but with her cheeks flushed with radiant color and her dark eyes velvety soft and yet shiny, she was incredibly beautiful in the Hawaiian get-up. What caused the lurching sensation in his chest was the happiness in her face, and the realization that he wasn't sharing her with anyone else at that moment. Her attention was solely upon him and the time and place. But whatever he did, he had to keep such thoughts hidden. He'd learned his lesson that afternoon and was determined to keep things light, as she insisted.

"The Hawaii tourist commission is missing a good bet not getting you on film tonight for one of their TV commercials," he declared admiringly. "You definitely are something to look at in that outfit."

"So are you," Rita returned, looking him over with open appreciation. The white slacks and leather dress shoes were of good quality and not new, belated proof that it probably hadn't been necessary for her to make an issue of tonight's attire, but the fact that she had didn't matter now.

"Now that we've decided that we'll be the best looking people at the *luau*, what do you say we go and sample the *mai tais*," Jack suggested, gallantly offering her his arm.

The *luau* was held on a sloping expanse of green lawn overlooking the ocean. The setting sun provided ample natural light to reveal a setting so civilized that the hotel might have picked up the furnishings from an inside banquet room and transferred them all outside. Only the smoking *imu* hinted that anything other than a typically lavish hotel buffet was about to happen.

Flanking the *imu* was a long, white-draped serving table already laden with both cold and hot foods, the latter in huge chafing pans under stainless steel covers. The elaborate centerpiece of native fruits and vegetables had a professional touch. The tables for the *luau* diners were draped in starched tablecloths and set with water goblets and standard tableware. Each table had a fresh flower arrangement and a lighted patio candle. The waitresses, busy serving *mai tais* to the guests who'd already arrived, wore gaily printed sarongs and sprigs of flowers in their hair. A musical group stationed up on a bandstand played the type of melodic music people tended to associate with the Hawaiian islands.

Rita barely had time to take all this in before she spotted the photography station set up over to one side, where arriving parties were being channeled to have their pictures taken. Twice now she'd endured the keepsake picture routine, which seemed prevalent in Hawaii, first at the airport when the honeymoon couples were officially welcomed to Hawaii and then here at the hotel where she'd been ushered immediately upon arrival, along with the other honeymooners, to a reception cocktail party. Both those times she hadn't had an escort, and her first reaction now was gratitude that Jack was at her side. She wouldn't be embarrassed again. Then immediately she liked the idea of having a picture of the two of them, dressed in their native splendor for the *luau*. She hadn't purchased either of the other pictures, which would have served no purpose but to be unhappy reminders, but she'd like to have this one.

"Good! They're going to take our picture," she told Jack in a pleased voice and then blushed as she realized that she'd spoken loud enough to draw indulgent, knowing looks from people around them, who were making the same wrong assumption about her and Jack that Harry and Blanche and nameless others had made that afternoon at the Iao Valley park. Dressed as the two of them were in new coordinating outfits and holding hands, they must look like newlyweds.

Jack took amused note of her embarrassment and squeezed her hand. His mischievous smile should have served warning for her as they waited their turn until they were next in line to be photographed.

"Could I have your name, please?" inquired the photographer's assistant, a pretty young woman in a sarong. She had Japanese features and long, straight black hair.

"Adams," Jack replied promptly, putting his arm around Rita's shoulders and smiling a proud new bridegroom's smile as he looked down into Rita's startled face.

The young woman obviously saw nothing unusual in Rita's loss of poise, finding it typical behavior for a new bride not yet adjusted to the change of her last name. She smiled wisely while she jotted briefly on the tablet she held in her hand.

"Please take your wife right over there, Mr. Adams, and the two of you look romantic for our camera," she instructed, suggesting with her tone that they wouldn't have any problem carrying out her assignment. She gestured toward the spot where the camera was pointed, next to a clump of giant blooming poinsettias that put to shame the potted variety sold at Christmas in the other states.

Rita let him lead her over to the indicated place, prepared by now for Jack to put on a big act and not really minding. Since the pretense of being newlyweds had been rather forced upon them, what was the harm in enjoying it?

"You know you're really a terrible ham," she accused him as he took her into his arms and assumed a phony adoring smile.

"Smile, darling, look happy," he prodded, not moving his lips. "It's no time to start nagging, here in front of all these people."

She smiled because he looked so funny she couldn't help herself and because his eyes were alight with laughter. He grinned back, dropping the pose, and the camera snapped, followed by a rippling of applause that brought a fresh tide of color to Rita's face.

"That's really doing it up right," Jack praised teasingly. "You look more like a blushing bride than a blushing bride does." He pleased everyone looking on by hugging her tight and kissing her on the lips, hard enough so that Rita knew she looked kissed as they made their exit amid much attention.

When they had found a table for two located at the outskirts of the seating area and giving them an unobstructed view of the sea, Rita sat down and pressed her hands to cheeks that still felt warm. "That was terribly embarrassing!" she exclaimed and then ruined her case by giggling. "You looked so ridiculous."

"I beg your pardon." Jack assumed a hurt expression. "I thought my rendition of a proud new husband went over very well."

"You overplayed it a bit, don't you think?" Rita teased him and then sighed with her sense of well-being as she looked out at the ocean and the western sky, tinted peach and rose by the fading sunset. "Isn't this wonderful, just being outside like this in this beautiful place?" she mused and underwent a gradual, sobering change of mood that made Jack go on the alert immediately.

"Uh-uh," he said, reaching over to cup her chin and gently force her to look at him. "None of that faraway, sad stuff tonight."

"I'm not sad at all," Rita replied honestly. "I was about to thank you for coming with me and about to ask you something I want you to answer truthfully and not spare my feelings." She hesitated, meeting his gaze with troubled eyes. "Don't you honestly think I should be feeling *worse* than this? I mean, how can I break up with a man I wanted to marry more than anything, go away on our honeymoon without him and have *fun*? It doesn't seem right."

Jack took both her hands and held them in his, aware of the hazards in giving her the honest opinion she'd requested. He didn't think she was ready to hear his answer or his deeply biased reasons for hoping that it was true: she hadn't ever loved Mark Pendleton, not the way she was capable of loving, with all her body and soul or she wouldn't have recovered this fast. She wouldn't be laughing and having fun with Jack and responding to him physically the way she was doing, with no apparent inkling that the attraction burning between them was no ordinary happening and was far more than a matter of sex. No, she wouldn't want to hear any of that, and Jack couldn't risk telling her just yet.

"If you'd stayed in Atlanta, you'd still be miserable right now," he told her quietly. "You'd be surrounded by people and places that would constantly jog your memory. But here you're in a totally new environment among strangers, where there's so much to divert your attention." He squeezed her hands. "Stop feeling guilty about having fun. Just enjoy yourself while you can. When you get back home to Atlanta, it'll all be waiting for you." *But not if I can help it,* he added to himself and was shaken by the depth of his resolutions.

"You're right." Rita drew in a deep relieved breath. "It's probably the change in scene that's responsible." She looked up with a smile at the waitress stopping at their table with a tray of *mai tai* cocktails, each one gaily decorated with a slice of pineapple and a cherry. She picked hers up at once and sampled it. "This is good," she approved after taking a sip. "But I'm no expert. What do you think?"

Jack sampled his cocktail and pretended to deliberate, needing a moment or two to curb his strong inner dissatisfaction. He'd been less than honest, saying what she wanted to hear. It disappointed him that she had settled so eagerly for the partial truth and wanted to go on now to safe, superficial territory. *Patience, Adams, patience,* he had to tell himself.

Rita might have noticed the hint of strain in Jack's manner if her attention hadn't been diverted. A wave of excitement was moving through the assembly of *luau* guests and then there was the announcement over the loudspeaker. It was time for the *imu* ceremony.

Because they were seated at the farthest point away from the *imu*, Rita and Jack were not among those forming the inside of the circle of watchers, but Rita was just as glad. The step-by-step description of what was happening provided by a young Hawaiian woman employed by the hotel was graphic enough for Rita's liking. She could see in her mind's eye the shovels tossing aside the hot earth covering the cooked pig and then the layers of leaves and protecting wire mesh being removed.

"I'm afraid I like my pork to come wrapped in cellophane and cut in unidentifiable portions," she confessed to Jack.

Once the pig had been revealed to open view and the flashing of cameras had diminished, those standing closest were asked to please move away and give the guests toward the back an opportunity for a close-up look. When Rita stood a second in indecision, Jack didn't try to make up her mind for her.

"I suppose I really should look at it," she said, glancing up at him for some direction.

Jack shrugged. "That's up to you. You don't have to look at it if you don't want to. I would like for you to taste it, when it's served. *Kalua* pig is really delicious."

Rita took in a deep breath as quietly as possible and eased forward. Jack was close beside her. She was glad for the supportive clasp of his hand at her waist. Bracing herself for a grisly sight, she took a quick glance down into the pit and saw not the whole animal she expected to see but two halves of a carcass minus the head. It wasn't as repulsive as she'd feared, but still that one glance was sufficient.

"Why don't we go back to our table and finish our drinks," Jack suggested as they moved away. "There's more than enough food for everybody and plenty of time to eat it. No sense in standing in line."

Rita was grateful for the suggestion, since the *imu* ceremony hadn't done anything to stimulate her appetite. She also appreciated his tactful introduction of a light subject of conversation that was totally unrelated to food. By the time they'd finished their *mai tai*s her faint disgust at the thought of eating had passed and the line at the serving table had thinned away. She was eager now to try some of the dishes Jack had described to her that afternoon.

They were able to take their time serving themselves, and Jack made sure she didn't pass by anything he wanted her to sample, but urged her to take other dishes that appealed to her as well. By the time they'd arrived at the end of the long table, their plates were heaped.

"I've taken far too much food," Rita lamented. "I'll never be able to eat all this."

She didn't eat all of it, since some of the food preparations, as Jack had cautioned, weren't to her liking, such as the *lomi* salmon and the *poi*, but what she didn't eat wasn't wasted because Jack finished it up, off of her plate, and gave her free range to help herself to what she did like from his. The whole meal, like everything she did with Jack, turned out to be great fun. *Unlike it would have been with anyone else*, she found herself thinking numerous times.

They ate off each other's plates, drank more *mai tai*s, talked and laughed while the evening grew fully dark so that the torches along the perimeters of the *luau* grounds and the candles on the individual tables cast flickering shadows and the atmosphere became magical for Rita. Perhaps the alcohol in the *mai tai*s was partly responsible for her sharpened perceptions, but she felt as though she were aware of her larger environment in a way she'd never been before and yet keenly, pleasurably attuned to every nuance of what was happening within the circle of candlelight at her own table. Her pleasure range seemed huge and comprehensive.

Overhead was the dark sky and a luminous partial moon in the company of countless brilliant stars. To her left was the ocean, dimly visible now, with the sound of its waves on the shore drowned out by the music and the voices and laughter except for brief unexpected lapses in the noise of revelry. When the dance revue began, it was a powerful onslaught on the senses, with beautiful smiling girls in brilliant costumes performing not just to the slumberous strains of the typical Hawaiian music but to wild pulsating rhythms from Tahiti and other parent islands as well.

Watching the uninhibited flash of supple honey-brown limbs, and movement of shapely hips, Rita felt the excitement ferment in her own blood and envied the dancers their frenetic freedom of movement. It must be wonderful, she thought, to let loose like that, to express wild, passionate emotion so openly with one's body.

Many dances dealt with everyday experiences and simple poetic perceptions of the physical world. The graceful movements of the dancer's hands and body mimed out the story or sentiment. Whether the intent was sexual or not, the visual impact was invariably highly sensual and, in Rita's case, stimulating. By the time the revue had ended and the *luau* was over, she felt incredibly charged up, all of her nerve endings wonderfully alive. She could still hear the music in her head, still feel the rhythm of the dancers' movements and regretted that it all had to end.

But then, as everyone got up and began to leave, making pleased comments about the revue and the *luau* as a whole, Rita's brief sense of letdown was quickly dissipated, and her heart beat faster with a new stimulation as Jack got up, came around to stand behind her and hold her upper arms in a strong, warm clasp while he leaned down to kiss her on the cheek.

"It's over, sweetheart." His voice came from so close that she could feel the warmth of his breath and shivered with the combined pleasures of his nearness and the intimate tone of his voice. The unspoken message in its low timbre was inevitable and thrilling. *The show's over, but not the evening. That's just beginning for you and me, sweetheart,* he was telling her. "We have to go now or they'll fold us up with the tables."

Rita got up, her heart pounding with her intense awareness of him. Turning around to face him, she felt as though her whole being constituted the most obvious kind of invitation. Surely he could clearly perceive how powerfully he attracted her, and how she yearned to yield to that attraction completely. She was a human neon sign with Take Me flashing on and off in garish colors. When he took her into his arms, she went willingly and tilted her head back for his kiss, which was passionate and yet restrained, like his voice when he released her and suggested, "Would you like to walk for a while? I don't know about you, but I'm feeling all those *mai tais*."

"I think I must be," Rita murmured dreamily and couldn't stir herself to move until Jack had caught up her hand and pulled on it gently to lead her down toward the ocean. This languid, agreeable state must be what posthypnotic suggestion was like. Her mind felt clear. Her body felt totally and wonderfully alive. She was ready to do whatever Jack suggested in that husky passionate tone of voice. All he had to do was mention it and keep walking straight, and she'd walk right into the sea with him.

"Jack, this has been the most wonderful evening," she told him and stumbled over some unseen obstruction. "I didn't see that boulder or whatever it was!" she protested gaily, happy about the fact that Jack had quickly slipped his arm around her to keep her from falling and was keeping it there. Without any self-consciousness, she circled his waist with her arm and leaned into him as they walked, continuing in the same dreamy, confidential voice.

"I wouldn't have missed this evening for anything. It's been fun and educational. And several times I found myself thinking that it wouldn't have been the same with any other man but you." She smiled up at him and giggled unconcernedly when she stumbled again and his arm around her waist tightened to steady her, making her momentary loss of balance seem a fortunate circumstance. "There wasn't any boulder that time. My right foot got tangled up with my left. Maybe I am a little drunk on all those *mai tais*," she confided cheerfully, finding the possibility of her inebriation only mildly interesting, certainly no cause for concern. Nothing was any cause for concern.

"Maybe a little."

"If I am, I'd like to be that way more often. I feel absolutely wonderful, better than I've ever felt before in my life." She drew in a deep breath and expelled it happily. "Oh, here we are down to the sand. I'm afraid you'll really have to hold on to me now."

"I don't mind, sweetheart." Jack squeezed her tight against him. "Believe me, I don't mind at all."

"That's good. I'm glad. I don't mind, either." Rita put her other arm around his waist and hugged him, making it well nigh impossible for them to continue walking.

"This is nice, sweetheart, but not the easiest way of walking in the sand," Jack pointed out with tender humor. "Had you noticed that?"

Rita came to a complete stop, throwing back her head and laughing delightedly.

"You have the most marvelous sense of humor!" she declared. "I love the way you make me laugh! In fact, you're the most fun of any man I've ever known." She slipped her arms from his waist up around his neck and was deeply satisfied to feel his arms closing around her. "Now you can kiss me," she told him, sighing with anticipation. "Isn't that why you brought me out here on the beach?"

"I suppose it is," Jack replied softly. "And even if I didn't have that in mind, God knows I don't have the power to turn down the invitation."

He kissed her with a tender thoroughness that made Rita's heart ache and hunger gnaw inside her. He gave her all the warm firmness of his lips and the intimate pleasure of his tongue, but he was holding himself in check, taking his enjoyment and giving her hers with careful restraint. Rita wanted more. She wanted the passion and wildness of the pagan dances she'd seen performed tonight. The secret yearning that had made her wish that she were a dancer up on the stage becoming as one with the music, which had been rousingly sensuous whether its tempo was rapid or hauntingly slow, now made her act with impulsive boldness to shake Jack's control, without giving any thought to their immediate circumstances.

Moving her body closer against his so that she was pressed against him from breasts to thighs, she interrupted the kiss with a little sideways movement of her head, and before Jack could recover from his momentary surprise, she took his upper lip between her teeth and nipped sharply, feeling his instant reaction in the quick tension of his body.

"Kiss me, Jack, like this," she whispered against his suddenly passive lips, and, holding his face with her hands, she moved her mouth hard against his, meshing the firmness of his lips almost painfully with the softness of hers, and then, with heart pounding wildly at her own shedding of inhibitions, she sent her tongue boldly inside his mouth, found his tongue and courted it seductively.

She could feel his resistance gather strength, only to quickly give way into a shudder that signaled her victory. His mouth took over the ravishment she had begun. He kissed her hard and deep, coupling his tongue with hers roughly in bold sexual symbolism of how his man's body could conquer her feminine softness. While he kissed her, his hands moved over her, roughly and possessively, exploring and establishing claim and inflaming her dormant need. Every plane and curve that he touched came singing to life and was his for the taking.

Rita gave herself over to the palms of his hands and thrilled in letting him create her and form her figure. With hard strokes he delineated the delicate arch of her back, the rounded shape of her buttocks, the tender inner curve of waist and sensuous flare of her hips. When he cupped her breasts, they became full and heavy and contracted into hard peaks that were solely his handiwork, existing for his pleasure of pinching them through the separating layers of material.

Weak with the joy of coming to life under his hands, Rita arched her back and clung to him, murmuring his name with bruised lips and discovering in her helplessness a sense of power as he reacted to the sound of her voice with a low groan. Releasing her breasts, he slipped his hands down to her buttocks, sinking his fingers into the supple, sensitive flesh and lifting her so that he could join their hips together and share with her his hard arousal.

The contact was primitively satisfying to Rita and not the awakening to reality that it apparently was to Jack, who eased her slowly down and enveloped her in a great bear hug that squeezed the air from her lungs before he gently but firmly released her, back in control again. Rita experienced the same deep, illogical disappointment she'd felt when the *luau* was over. Roused by the music and motion and color, her imagination fired by the glimpse into a prehistoric past, she hadn't wanted the entertainment to come to an end. Now she didn't want this to end, either. She didn't want her blood to cool and her body to return to normal when every cell felt incandescent and glowing.

"If this were hundreds of years ago, and we were Polynesians, we'd make love right here on the sand," she grumbled wistfully.

"But it's not, and we aren't," Jack pointed out indulgently. He tucked her hand in his arm. "We're twentieth-century Americans who've had one *mai tai* too many at a *luau* in the most densely populated spot on Maui. One of these days, I'll make love to you on the beach by the ocean, I promise, but not tonight and not here. Now why don't we walk some more before I take you back to the hotel and tuck you in. I need to clear my head a little before I drive home."

Rita trudged along beside him in grudging silence, her sandaled feet sinking into the sand. He'd made her heart leap with that promise spoken in a lover's tone and then promptly doused her nervous expectation with the indirect statement of his intention not to renew his lovemaking tonight at all, not even in a more private place, the obvious one being her room at the hotel. It hardly seemed possible that he was uncertain of her willingness, not after the way she'd kissed him and permitted him to touch her so intimately. A woman didn't behave like that and then turn a man down.

"I wouldn't want you to drive if you're feeling intoxicated," she ventured. "I'd feel responsible if you got into an accident."

Jack's heartbeat quickened at the oblique spoken invitation, which he hadn't expected. He squeezed the hand tucked into his arm.

"That's sweet of you, but I'm fine. Clearing up my head was just an excuse. It was the rest of me that needed a little recovery time."

There was another silence, filled with the crunching of their feet in the sand and the sound of the ocean caressing the shore. From the nearby hotel came the faint sounds of voices and laughter. Jack waited in suspense, hoping that she wouldn't issue a more direct invitation. He hadn't come tonight with any expectation of staying with her, and to be confronted with the possibility that he could was definitely unsettling. He didn't know if he was strong enough to resist the temptation, despite strong reasons for doing so, the most practical of which he would give her.

"It's not all that late," Rita pointed out argumentatively, as though they'd been discussing the time. "You could stay awhile and sober up."

"I'd love to, but I have a whole pile of stuff to read through tonight and an early business appointment in the morning. I'd really better go." Jack could feel her skepticism and was taken aback to realize that she plainly didn't believe him. What he was telling her was the truth, if not the entirety of his reason for not staying. "It's with a building contractor, and I don't want to talk to him without doing my homework first. I meant to spend the whole day reading up on some background information, including some state publications, but I got sidetracked, needless to say."

Rita stopped. They had come abreast of the place where she'd emerged onto the beach that morning to hail Jack. They could take the same path through the garden and up to one of the rear entrances of the hotel.

"I think I know your real reason," she told him quietly. "It's the same one that made you not want to come to the *luau* with me tonight. You're conscious of the fact that Mark and I were supposed to share the room, and you're afraid I'll think of him instead of you while we—" Rita faltered awkwardly. "You know what I mean."

"Yes, I do know what you mean." The ready confirmation rang with distaste and dispensed with the need for further elaboration. "And you're right. I don't like the idea of making love to you in the honeymoon bower one bit. But aside from that, what I've told you is true. I have work to do tonight, and I want to be sharp and on my toes early in the morning." He took Rita's shoulders in his hands and held her while he bent to kiss her on the lips. "There will be other nights," he said huskily. "Other places besides your hotel room." He kissed her again and quickly released her shoulders to grab her hands, which were on the way up to his neck. "Please," he said pleadingly. "I'll see you tomorrow."

Rita took in a deep breath to slow her quickened pulse. She felt languid and excited at the same time. It was heady knowledge that she had it in her power to overrule his decision. She could make him stay, against his wishes. And it was what she wanted to do, so badly. Pulling her hands free of Jack's grasp, she was unsure of what she would do, and her uncertainty was in her voice.

"What time tomorrow?" she asked, turning away from him toward the path. He answered, but the words hardly penetrated. It had struck her suddenly that she had undergone quite an incredible change since hurtling recklessly along that path this morning on her way to this very spot. She had been desperate to stop Jack before he left the beach, simply because his was a familiar face and she was tired of being unhappy and alone. Now, just hours later, she'd come to a level of intimacy with him that shocked her. Not only was she agreeable to having him come to her room and spend the night with her, she was contemplating forcing the issue, against his will! She must be either drunk or completely off balance mentally.

"It had better not be too early." Rita spoke the words over her shoulder as she walked rapidly across the sand. "I'll probably sleep late and wake up with a terrible hangover. I'm just now starting to sober up enough to realize that I must have gotten really high on all those *mai tai*s. You're a gentleman not to take advantage of me."

Jack took several running steps to catch up with her.

"Hey, take it easy," he cautioned, but she didn't slow down. Her arm was stiff in his protective grasp. Mentally he sorted through answers to her proud little speech and discarded each of them. This was a damned unsatisfactory conclusion to the evening, but he'd better leave things as they were. When he made love to her, he didn't want Mark Pendleton's ghost lurking in the room. He didn't want her judgment clouded with alcohol or his own mind distracted with thoughts of important obligations.

It would be different if this was in the category of a one-night stand, or even a holiday fling, but it wasn't, not for him. Far from it. Jack would curb his passion and be strong, follow his instincts and do what was best for him and, consequently, for her. Even though she didn't realize it yet, their immediate futures were linked. What they had together wasn't going to bloom to fruition and die in the space of a week and a half.

Jack didn't know how long it would last. In today's world the idea of permanent relationships between men and women was being questioned. He was a child of divorce himself and so was Rita. All he did know was that he'd never felt this deeply caring toward a woman, this cautious about not making a mistake with her, or this nakedly vulnerable. Jack wasn't sure which of those feelings was most responsible for sending him home tonight.

Chapter Eight

Rita's reflection in the mirror over the dresser in her room served as a tangible reproof, deepening her shame over her behavior following the *luau*. Her beautiful hyacinth lei was crushed. The sprig of flowers in her hair was gone, having fallen unnoticed to the sand some time during that passionate interlude on the beach that she had forced upon Jack.

Yes, literally *forced* upon him! She'd acted wantonly and showed all the evidence. Her hair was a mess. She looked bedraggled and wrinkled. Yet no amount of self-reproach or righteous scorn could keep her from being disappointed that she'd returned to her room alone.

Lifting the fragile, ruined lei from around her neck, Rita laid it tenderly on the dresser and touched her hands to the high color in her cheeks and then to her mussed hair. Slicking it back from her face, she twisted it into the tight French twist and held it, staring disapprovingly at her reflection. The change back to her old severe hairstyle didn't ease the unfamiliar turmoil inside her. She was still just as ashamed of herself, just as disappointed that the evening had ended the way it had, just as physically unsatisfied.

With a deep sigh, she released her hair and let it spring loose on its own as she undressed, thinking as she did of how it would have been if Jack had taken her up on her off-handed, but plain invitation and were here now. He would remove her clothes himself and manage to make something very special of the whole process. He had that ability to make her *feel* she was special, unique, unlike any other woman. She'd never wanted to be beautiful before and yet she liked being beautiful in Jack's eyes. That was strange.

He would think she was beautiful naked. Rita touched her bared breasts and stomach and hips and thought of Jack touching her and taking open, passionate pleasure in the sight of her body. It aroused her to think of seeing his body completely unclothed, too. With him, nakedness would be sensual and unashamed, a prelude leading naturally and inevitably to making love, which would be wonderful, she knew. It would be the kind of intense experience she knew about only secondhand from novels and movies and never really believed in before. If he could make her forget her surroundings with an embrace and a kiss, surely he could raise her to the heights of passion every woman dreamed of reaching someday in some man's arms.

But such thoughts only deepened her frustration. He wasn't here with her, and none of that was going to happen tonight.

Why wasn't he here with her now? Rita pondered that puzzling question while she slipped her nightgown over her head and prepared herself for bed, hoping that her physical dissatisfaction would be eased by the mental exercise. He certainly gave every indication of liking her and being strongly attracted to her. Was his male pride really threatened by the thought of making love to her in her honeymoon bed? She thought it needn't be. She'd only slept in the bed alone, and any thoughts and longings involving Mark hadn't been sexual in nature. Hadn't she made it clear to Jack by now that she'd never responded physically to Mark the way she did to him? Her relationship with Mark had been something else entirely.

With her teeth brushed and her face cleaned and creamed, Rita got into bed, not feeling in the least relaxed and ready for sleep, but she wasn't unhappy, either, she realized, turning off the bedside lamp. She wasn't sad. She wasn't empty. Life wasn't a tunnel narrowing at the end. She felt alive in every pore, and she'd been feeling like that all day, since that moment she'd looked out at the beach and spotted Jack. She could see him clearly in her mind as he had looked, and the picture aroused pleasure.

With a little smile on her lips, Rita curled sideways and nestled her cheek comfortably in the soft down pillow, thinking of how she'd bolted down to the beach to stop Jack before he could get away. In slow motion and brilliant color, she played it over, seeing herself, seeing him, and living it all through again. She'd become an expert at replaying scenes in her mind the past two weeks, but this was different. This was totally devoid of pain and without regret. In fact, it was so pleasant and so very leisurely that she got only as far as the parking lot and the two of them standing beside his mother's junk-filled red station wagon. Rita fell asleep with the sound of her laughter and his welling and mingling together. It was an utterly joyous sound, and there was the rich feeling of hours of recollection still to draw upon.

The next morning, sure enough, she had a slight headache and a dry mouth to remind her of the *mai tais* she'd drunk the night before at the *luau*, but after a breakfast of coffee, hot rolls, and fresh fruit, she felt fine and ready for another adventurous day with Jack. They'd discussed various sight-seeing excursions during the course of the previous day and evening, but hadn't settled on any definite plans. Rita thought he'd probably arrive with something in mind, and whatever it was, it would be fun.

To kill time, she browsed in the shops, including the one where he'd bought her *muumuu* and his aloha shirt. By eleven o'clock she was restless and impatient and by twelve downright exasperated. What could be taking him so long? He'd said he had an "early" business appointment. Half the day was gone already.

Rita had stationed herself in the hotel lobby and was grimly trying to talk herself into giving up on Jack and going sight-seeing without him when he finally appeared, looking exuberant and not at all apologetic for having kept her waiting. She was grudgingly aware of how handsome he was in trim, dark blue poplin slacks and a pale blue knit shirt open at the neck. It certainly wasn't her idea of the kind of attire for a business appointment, but she couldn't deny that he wore it well. His blond hair was windblown, but looked clean and soft to the touch. His gray eyes were alight with gladness to see her and zest for life. His step was springy and confident as he covered the distance to the rattan couch where she was sitting and dropped down beside her.

"I didn't mean to be this late. Hope you haven't had lunch already," he said cheerfully, with no discernible regret.

Rita consulted her watch, as though she didn't already know the time almost to the second, aware of his close, approving inspection of her appearance from hair to sandals.

"No, but I was just about to. How did your business appointment go? I hope you didn't stay up all night reading and then oversleep and miss it." She didn't think he looked like someone who'd burned any midnight oil reading the "piles of stuff" he'd mentioned last night. He looked healthy and fit and well rested. Despite her pique, being close to him was causing pleasant flutters in the pit of her stomach.

Jack grinned broadly. "Oh, ye of little faith," he chided. "So that's why you're annoyed at me. You think I've been sleeping in all morning. Actually, I did stay up most of the night, but I kept my appointment, and I wouldn't have missed it for anything. Damon Phillips and I hit it off well. I was impressed with him and with the construction he's done so far. He drove me around to show me some of it. That's what took so long, but it was time well spent, I think. He may be just the business partner I'm looking for."

"What sort of 'construction' has he done?"

Jack noted her faint hesitancy and excessively polite tone. Both jogged his memory of yesterday's conversation at lunch when he'd told her sketchily about his business ventures to date.

"Just about everything in the residential category. Some small apartment complexes, condominiums, single-family houses, too. Housing is a problem here in Hawaii. Land is expensive and so much of it is in the hands of big property holders and not for sale. Damon Phillips has his eye on a nice tract of land that he's heard through the grapevine can be had for a reasonable price. That's where I come in."

"You mean you'll put up the money to buy this piece of land."

Jack laughed. "When I say 'reasonable,' I'm talking of a sum in the millions. I'll put some money into the project, but the name of the game is leverage, using borrowed money, not your own. I'm the expert salesman, remember. I'll talk with interested investors and arrange for backing, but there's a lot of groundwork to be done yet. Damon has in mind a fairly clear idea of what he wants to build, but we'll need architect's plans, detailed projections on costs and profit expectations, etc.'' Jack could see from her polite, glazed expression that he had lost her attention and cut the explanation short. ''It's too soon to tell, but my gut instinct is telling me the deal could be exactly right for me. But enough talk about it for now. My mother is expecting us for lunch.''

Rita's face showed both her relief that talk of his morning's activity was ended and her surprise at his announcement. Jack was disappointed that she showed little apparent interest in what was of such great importance to him that he naturally wanted to tell her about it. He reminded himself that she was on vacation and understandably more interested in sight-seeing and enjoying herself than in sitting around in her hotel lobby listening to him talk about business.

''You'll want to take your bathing suit,'' he told her, getting to his feet and reaching for her hands to help her up. ''My mother's place is right on the ocean. We can swim and sunbathe and snorkel after lunch.'' He pulled her to her feet and held her hands while he bent down to kiss her lightly on the lips. ''By the way, hello. You look terrific.'' He kissed her again, not so lightly. ''I'll wait for you here.''

There was nothing polite or uninterested about the expression on Rita's face now as she stayed with her head tilted back for a second or two, looking into his eyes. She moved her lips together as though savoring the warm imprint of his lips and smiled at his startled attention.

''I'll go and get my bathing suit,'' she said softly. ''It won't take me five minutes.''

Jack jammed his hands into his pockets and mimed a whistle of surprise as he watched her walk away. She could turn him on with a look and a tone of voice, knew it and was all the more appealing in her shy delight in her power. He had to stifle the urge to follow right in behind her and go with her up to her room. She wouldn't be averse to the company, and the knowledge was devastating. He couldn't get used to not encountering resistance.

But, no, his mother was expecting them, and that damned room was still the same one she and Pendleton had booked for their honeymoon. Jack would wait. He wanted the time and place to be right when he made love to her. It excited him, though, and tested his control to have her come on to him so openly.

"Aren't you going to need your own car, if you intend to live here on Maui?" Rita asked him when they were walking side by side through the parking lot toward his mother's red station wagon. Before he could answer, she added smilingly, "I dreamed about your mother's car last night."

Jack's pulse took off at her tone. He ignored her lead-off question and replied on cue.

"Did you dream about me, too?"

"Hmm?" She glanced over at him with a provocative smile. "How did you guess? Yes, you were in the dream, too. It was quite a wonderful dream," she added softly.

"You're going to have to stop that!" Without breaking stride, he grabbed her arm and gave it a little admonishing shake.

"Stop what?" Rita was all exaggerated innocence. "You asked me if you were in my dream, and I said you were. That's all I said. I didn't even tell you what the dream was about."

"Don't act innocent. You know what I mean." Jack held on to her arm the last few steps to the car and didn't let her go, even after he'd opened the passenger door.

Rita smothered her smile and looked at him again with her fake innocent expression, which dissolved into an impish smile in the face of his accusation.

"Sorry," she said without any penitence.

Jack took her hands and placed them on his chest. "Feel that?" he demanded. "I know you're having fun turning the switch, but it's hard on the old heart, constantly speeding up."

Releasing her hands, he hugged her hard against him and groaned. "Soon," he said. "Soon, sweetheart. Believe me, I want you."

Rita eased her hands free and put them up around his neck. "It had better be soon." She kissed him lingeringly on the mouth and felt her own heart beat faster. "Otherwise I won't let you in my dreams." She smiled up at him, saw in his face his response to the silky promise in her voice and looked mildly apologetic. "Okay, I'll be good. I promise." She wrinkled her nose at him, pushed him away reluctantly and got into the car.

"It's just as well," she told him when he came around and slid in beside her. "I turn myself on as much as you. And I'm really not like this. That's what amazes me. There's something about you that turns me into a totally different person than I've always been—" She stopped, suddenly alerted to a change in his mood. The humor in his face was so tender and serious that she didn't want to hear whatever he was going to say and yet felt utterly powerless to cut him off.

Jack saw and felt the bloom of her panic. He put his hand on the key in the ignition, but then couldn't make himself turn it.

"There's something about 'us,' sweetheart, that lets you be yourself. Maybe you haven't realized that consciously yet. When a guy is crazy about a woman the way I'm crazy about you, she can get by with anything. Deep down you sense that, and it gives you confidence, as it should." His smile was reassuring, but his eyes were hopeful as he added,

"I love it when you play games with me because I think that's the only way right now you can tell me you're a little crazy about me, too."

Before her shock could find outlet in words of denial he didn't want to hear, Jack quickly started the car and put it in gear. He drove as though he were in a hurry and was glad that she didn't say anything at all. He needed the several minutes of agitated silence to adjust not just to what he'd said, but to the way he'd sounded. He'd never spoken to a woman in that "forever" tone of voice and empathized with the panic he'd seen in Rita's eyes and face. He'd scared himself, as well as her, with the underlying commitment. But he felt damned good, too, with every passing second, stronger, less vulnerable, until he was ready to deal with her reaction.

His declaration of affection obviously hadn't made her happy. She sat stiff and silent, looking out of her window as though the passing landscape offended her. But on the positive side, she hadn't made an immediate, scathing outburst. Jack also took some small comfort in her mental turmoil, which he could sense. It might bespeak an uncertain state of mind.

He sorted through several light openers and discarded them in favor of a rueful statement of the truth.

"I take it you're upset with me for what I said."

Braced for the first glimpse of her face and what it would tell him, Jack was deeply relieved at the mixture of reproach and dismay. He took a strange comfort in her troubled tone of voice as she answered him.

"Of course I'm upset. You and I barely know each other. We like each other a lot. We have fun together. We share a strong sexual attraction, but that's all there is, Jack. Please don't spoil everything by talking serious. I've already asked you not to."

"You mean don't say I love you."

He was saying it with his eyes and the soft resonance of his voice that very moment and exulting in the declaration.

Rita looked quickly away. "You know that's what I mean."

"And don't talk about things like the two of us living together or possibly getting married."

"Jack!" Rita looked back at him reproachfully, seeing the coaxing smile that she'd been able to hear in his voice. "This is no laughing matter," she rebuked. "I meant every word I said."

"Who's laughing?" Jack demanded cheerfully. "I just told the woman I love that I'm crazy about her and she wants to change the subject permanently. Since you don't want to live with me, can I at least hold your hand? Not even if I say 'please'?" he begged when Rita shrank away from the hand he extended toward her.

She shook her head in exasperation. "I don't know how to deal with someone like you. You treat everything as a joke."

"No, I don't. I just see the humorous side of things that hurt. That's all."

He let his rejected hand drop to her bare thigh, which went rigid under his touch. When he moved his fingers caressingly back and forth, Rita grabbed his hand, and he didn't persist. He just turned his hand upward and linked his fingers with hers, giving them a little squeeze.

"It's nice. Holding hands. Don't you think?" He grinned at her.

Rita watched their linked hands as he rested them on the console between the bucket seats. Holding hands with him was nice. Very nice, in fact. Being with him, touching him was such pleasure that it exasperated her all the more for him to spoil such a perfect status quo with serious talk.

"You're used to getting your way with women, aren't you, Jack? I hope you don't see me as some sort of challenge because I'm not available."

There was nothing humorous in the quick probing look he gave her.

"You told me yourself you're a super salesman," Rita went on defensively.

"And you see yourself as an unwilling customer?"

"Not exactly 'unwilling,'" she admitted grudgingly. The metaphor hadn't been a wise choice, but then any metaphor she'd chosen probably wouldn't have worked to her advantage. He was too quick and clever to lose a verbal contest.

"But you've wandered onto my car lot wanting to lease a car for a short period, or at least *thinking* that's what you want, and I'm trying to sell you a car. Right?"

"Something like that."

"The heart of the matter, then, is what you really need and want, isn't it? A really good salesman is able to figure that sort of thing out. That's the secret to his success. He doesn't talk anybody into buying something that person doesn't want deep down."

Rita jerked her hand free of his. "He can talk rings around someone who isn't a very good salesperson, that much is sure! I'm sorry now I started this whole discussion!" She glared at him, exasperated and resentful of his open amusement. "Don't you *dare* laugh," she told him threateningly and knew that he was smothering a grin when he looked sideways out of his window.

"First, you get upset because I'm serious, and then you get mad at me because I'm not. How can a man win?"

"I'm *not* upset, and I'm *not* mad," Rita informed him irritably. "I just want to drop this whole subject and have an enjoyable afternoon. Is that asking too much?"

"Not at all. I want us both to have a nice afternoon, and since we're almost at my mother's house, I'd probably better give you a little advance warning of what to expect. I've mentioned that she's an artist? Well, the whole place is chockablock full of her artwork. Expect to feel like you've wandered into one of those artists' co-op places, but it's all her stuff. And just in case you feel inclined to admire something, out of kindness or whatever, be prepared for having it presented to you as a gift. She's generous anyway, and I've told her you're someone very special."

"Doesn't she ever sell her artwork?" Rita inquired, pointedly not taking issue with his personal remark.

"Unfortunately not."

The good-natured regret in his reply gave rise to a natural curiosity. If his mother didn't sell her art, what was her source of income?

"Is art mainly a hobby for her, then? Does she have a job?"

Jack hooted delightedly. "A job? My mother? I'd like to see the place of business that could survive her as an employee. No, she devotes herself full-time to her art, and she's tried about every medium. Thank God she's given up on that modernistic sculpture that looks like pieces of scrap iron. I was always afraid she was going to hurt herself using the welding machine. Actually, some of her paintings aren't bad, but she really has run out of places to hang them. Now she's into native jewelry, which is healthy and relatively safe. She spends hours out on the beach searching for special little shells and bits of coral. But here we are. You'll get to meet her and see for yourself," he announced, slowing and turning into a driveway crowded on each side with luxuriant and unpruned tropical shrubbery.

"As you can see, my mother isn't much of a gardener. If this yard doesn't get some attention soon, it'll be a jungle," he predicted unconcernedly.

Rita thought personally that it was already too late to curb his mother's yard. The house was nestled in a dense tangle of vivid flowering vegetation. She couldn't tell much about the structure itself except that it was made of weathered wood and was low and rambling. House and grounds together had an unkempt charm that matched up with what Jack had led her to expect of his mother.

The interior of the house was in keeping with the outside, bizarrely cluttered and yet not without a certain appeal. There wasn't an overabundance of the well-worn rattan furniture, which looked comfortable with upholstered cushions in neutral tones. The earthen tile floor was attractively bare underfoot, not scattered with rugs. It was the haphazard display of Lillian Adam's artwork that gave the sense of crowdedness. There was hardly a space of wall that wasn't covered with oil paintings, watercolors, collages or hangings of one type or another. Every available table surface bore pottery bowls and vases, ceramic figures, clay busts, lead and copper sculptures. Large pieces sat hither and yon on the floor, looking as though someone passing through might have put them down and forgotten them.

Rita tried in vain to screen her utter incredulity from her face as she looked around, afraid that any moment Jack's mother might appear. His low, delighted chuckle was evidence of her lack of success.

"Remember, be careful what you say," he warned teasingly. "You may find yourself a proud new owner. Why don't you look around some more while I find my mother? Heaven help us, I hope she hasn't decided to surprise us and cook something up in the kitchen. I told her sandwiches and fruit would be fine for lunch. I see she has the table set out on the *lanai*."

Following his glance, Rita forgot the amazing decor of the house in her appreciation of its ocean view. Left alone while Jack went to find his mother, she wandered through the open sliding-glass door out onto a flagstone paved terrace shaded from the sun's brilliance by the projection of the roof. Forming a screen on either side of the property were tall board fences overgrown with bougainvillea and other flowering vines Rita didn't recognize. The rear lawn wasn't any more well-tended than the front, but it wasn't as over-grown. Grass grew down to a sharp drop-off, and beyond that point was sand beach and then the ocean.

Rita drew in a whiff of the fresh, salty air and gave her attention idly to an examination of the rear of the house, which rambled to her left. There were two other sheltered patios like this one, only smaller, leading off rooms that she assumed to be bedrooms. All the way at the end of the house was a covered walkway leading a short distance to a de-tached building in the same style as the house. Her guess was that it was separate guest quarters. It didn't have the look of a storage shed, and there was just a peek of a private *lanai* through the tangle of vines and shrubbery.

The house was large for just one person and had all the potential of being a showplace, with some money and care put into improvements and maintenance. Judging from the evidence, Jack's mother obviously didn't have that money, which led Rita to wonder how she'd come to acquire the house in the first place. Jack had said that his mother was a long-time resident on Maui and that he had been coming here for many years. Perhaps she'd bought the beach house with her divorce settlement. Property had probably been much cheaper back in those days before the tourist boom had spread from Oahu to the neighbor islands. Now she was probably just hanging on to it, despite her inability to keep it up.

Rita's speculations seemed right on target when Jack brought his mother out on the *lanai* to meet her. Lillian Adams didn't look like a woman of means in her knee-length floral cotton *muumuu* and Dr. Scholl's sandals. She obviously liked jewelry, yet she wore none that looked expensive. Her hands were laden with elaborate rings of silver and turquoise and mother-of-pearl, not diamonds or precious gems. The long, triple-strand shell necklace around her neck was amazingly intricate in design, made up of the tiniest little shells Rita had ever seen, but it and the dangling matching earrings weren't in the same category as heirloom pearls.

She looked like what she was, an artist, the mistress of her unusual domain. Somehow she was perfectly right to be Jack's mother, even though the only physical endowment she'd given her son was her eyes. Otherwise he must have taken after his father, because Lillian's hair was salt-and-pepper black, braided and worn in a thick coronet, whereas Jack's was blond, and she was small-boned and compact in build with tiny hands and feet, while he was at least an inch or two over six feet and rangy.

The similarities in mother and son were more in personality, Rita suspected. Lillian Adams radiated warmth and geniality. She looked Rita over with open interest and yet with no hint of the usual mother's challenge: *Is she good enough for my son?* Rita liked her on sight, just as she'd liked Jack, once she'd gotten over her initial resistance to his personal charisma. Mother and son had the same casual confidence, apparently the same cheerful disregard of outward appearance and social convention.

Jack introduced his mother fondly, but with the same indulgent tone he had used when telling Rita about her.

"Rita, I want you to meet my mother, Lillian Adams."

"I'm happy to meet you. Jack's told me so much about you." Rita responded to the introduction with a trace of awkwardness because she was uncertain as to how she should address Jack's mother. Somehow *Mrs. Adams* seemed too formal and perhaps not appropriate, considering that she had been divorced for many years, and yet using her first name would be presumptuous.

Lillian Adams recognized Rita's problem and dispensed with it cheerfully. "You can call me Lil. Everybody does. You are a beauty, just like Jack said. Such lovely hair and skin and eyes."

Rita blushed under her admiring regard, but oddly enough with more pleasure than embarrassment. Lillian Adams was the type who could get by with such artless directness.

"Mother, why don't you and Rita sit down and get acquainted while I bring out lunch," Jack instructed. He smiled teasingly at both of them. "Just be sure to say good things about me while I'm gone."

Lillian waved him off while she took a chair at the table set very simply for three.

"Who says we're desperate enough for conversation to talk about you at all. I'm constantly amazed by the male ego, aren't you, Rita? Sit down," she urged graciously.

Rita did as she was told, surprised that she felt so relaxed at being left alone with Jack's mother. The prospect of being questioned didn't bother her at all. But Lillian didn't show any of the usual mother's instincts. She didn't probe into Rita's background or seem inclined at all to discuss Jack.

"This is so nice," she said, sounding genuinely pleased. "I'm glad Jack brought you. So far, what do you think of Maui? It's always so interesting to get the newcomer's impressions. We old-timers tend to take everything so for granted.''

Rita made an enthusiastic reply and then found herself talking on, expressing her delight in the beautiful scenery and the tropical climate. She mentioned what she'd seen so far and some of the places she wanted to see. Lillian seemed thoroughly interested, making perceptive comments and asking questions. So relaxed and natural was the flow of conversation that Rita didn't realize until some minutes had passed that Jack was gone a surprisingly long time. She'd thought he was just bringing out from the kitchen a lunch that had been prepared in advance, but perhaps that wasn't the case.

''Should I go and give Jack a hand?'' she offered tentatively.

Lillian looked faintly surprised, as though Rita's offer had brought Jack to mind.

''You can, if you want. There's no point in me even offering. He always chases me out of the kitchen. But here he is now.'' Lillian smiled at Jack and inspected with pleased anticipation the large tray of food he bore. ''Hmm, that looks good, doesn't it, Rita? Rita was about to come out to the kitchen and offer to help.''

''Obviously my help wasn't needed,'' Rita remarked, feeling as impressed as she sounded. ''That salad looks wonderful.'' So did the plate of assorted cold cuts and cheese, attractively arranged, and the basket of bread and rolls.

''Didn't my mother tell you all my virtues while I was slaving out in the kitchen?'' Jack asked with exaggerated disappointment as he deftly transferred the contents of the tray to the table. ''I'm going to make some lucky woman a wonderful husband, you know. Tell her, mother, how I clean the house when I visit and cook you wonderful meals."

"He does, Rita. I always look forward to Jack's visits. He has a way of taking care of everything. Which reminds me, Jack."

Jack groaned loudly. "Wait until I sit down to tell me. What is it now? The electricity's going to be turned off in ten minutes? The garbage collection has been discontinued?"

"None of those things," Lillian denied serenely. "It's that plumber who did some work for me last . . ." She hesitated, frowning. "Anyway, he's called and threatened to sue me if I don't pay his bill. I explained that I was too busy and couldn't talk to him then. He was rude, and I hung up on him."

"Last when?" Jack prompted. "When did he work for you?"

"It's so hard to remember things that are so unimportant," she complained vaguely, picking up the bowl of tossed green salad and offering it to Rita, who was trying to look politely disinterested in the conversation. "Please, help yourself," Lillian urged pleasantly.

"It's not unimportant to a workman to be paid," Jack pointed out dryly. "That's not the same plumber who did all that work for you last summer, is it?" He shook his head as he smiled at Rita and handed her the plate of cheese and cold cuts. "The salami's terrific. I sneaked a slice in the kitchen."

"Was it that long ago? Goodness, time passes fast," Lillian declared cheerfully, busy making herself a sandwich. "You say the salami's good, Jack? It doesn't have too much garlic in it, does it? I like garlic, but it gives me heartburn."

"I'll call the fellow right after lunch." Jack sounded good-naturedly resigned. "I don't suppose you remember his name or have his phone number." He read the answer in his mother's stricken expression and sighed. "I didn't think so. There's probably not enough money in your checking account to cover the bill, either. The salami is a little heavy on the garlic," he added solicitously, seeing his mother deliberate over taking a slice.

"What's a little heartburn! It looks too good to resist." Lillian added the slice of salami to her sandwich and buttered a piece of bread for the top. "To tell you the truth, Jack, I don't know whether there's money in that checking account or not. What with these computers, you can just never tell any more. A few weeks ago I had quite an unpleasant discussion with a new young fellow who's with the local branch of the bank. I told him I've had an account with that bank for years, and I don't appreciate having them refuse to cash my checks just because the balance happens to be a little low at the time."

Lillian was righteously indignant. When she looked from Jack to Rita, evidently seeking support, Rita didn't know what to say. The discussion made her uncomfortable.

Jack shook his head, chuckling. "You're unbelievable. And you're never going to change. But let's drop this for now. I'll take care of it."

Rita was relieved. It had been an effort not to look shocked and appalled, not just at the open revelation of Lillian's financial problems, but at her attitude and Jack's toward them. Unpaid bills, lawsuits, and bad checks were no laughing matter in Rita's mind. Apparently they were nothing new in Lillian's life and of no serious concern to her or her son.

Jack had said he would "take care of it." What did that mean? Would he pay the bill himself with his own money or would he use his glib tongue and fast-thinking mind to put off the irate plumber, who'd gone for months without being paid for his work? Perhaps he'd pay him part of it and promise installments. That had been her mother's standard approach, leading to accumulated debts she couldn't hope to pay.

Rita had no intention of asking Jack how he intended to handle it. She didn't want to know.

Chapter Nine

Lillian Adams apparently didn't give the unpaid plumber and impending lawsuit—or her depleted bank account—another thought once she'd mentioned them to Jack and been told he'd take care of them. After lunch she changed into a faded old black one-piece bathing suit and came down to the beach with Jack and Rita, where she searched for shells and coral, using a small wire-rimmed net that she dug into the sand where the waves washed ashore. Patiently she would sort through the bits of coral and broken shells, crying out her triumph when she would find one of the tiny shells she was seeking or a bit of coral that met with her specifications. Finding the materials for her jewelry was apparently a painstaking process.

Rita found the situation totally relaxed and a little incredible. She wondered how many men would be so contented to spend the afternoon in this type of threesome, with a new female interest and his mother! Mark hadn't been that uninhibited and natural toward Rita in his mother's presence even after he and Rita had been engaged for two years and were soon to be married, but then Mark and Katherine Pendleton hadn't had the same kind of closeness Rita sensed between Jack and his mother. Mark revered his mother and was always anxious for her approval, whereas there was no element of judgment, on either side, in the mother-son relationship between Jack and Lillian. They were friends and enjoyed being around each other.

As Rita lay close beside Jack on a large beach towel that he'd spread next to his, overlapping the edges, she thought about the differences between the two men and the two mothers and her own conflicting attitudes. Mark and his mother were models of upper middle-class society. Rita could find no fault with them. Mark was a college graduate, a member of one of the oldest and most established professions, a man of solid character and high values. He was also pleasant and likable and attractive. Jack, on the other hand, was a college dropout and had no profession. He was highly intelligent and charismatic, true, but he was a dreamer, one of those gifted men who would never stick to any one endeavor long enough to succeed. He was also handsome, witty, sexy, and loads of fun.

Though Rita saw her preference for exactly what it was, shamefully superficial, a thing of the moment, she still couldn't bring herself to wish that Jack would disappear and Mark would be lying there in his place. She was content with a male companion she'd known less than a week rather than the man she'd been about to marry! It was awful of her to feel that way, and yet why deny the truth to herself?

Likewise, she admired Katherine Pendleton to the extent that she had tried to emulate her poise and manner and style of dress, even her way of thinking, but Rita couldn't look back and pinpoint an occasion when she'd been totally relaxed enough to truly enjoy Katherine's company. Rita had always been intimidated, always afraid that she wouldn't measure up to Katherine's high standard.

Lillian Adams, on the other hand, was an eccentric, a law unto herself with no concept of fitting any of society's roles: mother, wife, career woman, bill-payer. She dressed and lived and used her time precisely to suit herself. And yet Rita had warmed to her immediately. She could say with ease that she *liked* Lillian, and the same words didn't fit her feelings about Katherine Pendleton.

"I'm glad you and my mother like each other. I thought you would."

Jack's pleased voice broke into Rita's reflections, his words startling her by fitting into her train of thought.

"You must be reading my mind!" she exclaimed, turning her head sideways and looking at him through the screen of her lashes. The sight of his bare chest and shoulders and his profile confirmed the mental choice between him and Mark that she'd made a minute earlier. It took some effort on her part not to reach her hand over and touch him. The desire to do so awoke a little ache in her midriff.

"You're right. I do like your mother."

The telltale softness of her voice had nothing to do with his mother. It was a message sent over to him and it had an immediate effect. She felt anticipation coil inside her as he raised up and turned sideways toward her, propping himself on his elbow.

"Take it easy," he warned softly. "The sun's enough of an aphrodisiac, not to mention how sexy you look in that bikini. I've been lying here driving myself crazy thinking about taking it off." He reached lazily behind him and picked up a handful of sand. Rita drew in her breath with a little gasp as he slowly dribbled it on her bare midriff. It felt hot and silky.

"This bikini's modest compared to the ones I see here," she pointed out breathlessly.

"With your figure you'd look sexy in a sack." He began brushing off the sand with his fingertips, a few grains at a time. The effect on Rita's body was quick and devastating. She felt her nipples explode into hard nubs, and weakness wash through her.

"Don't do that!" She levered herself up and brushed away the sand with brusque movements before remaining propped on both elbows, glancing down the beach where Lillian had slowly worked her way. She was happily engrossed in her search for the ocean's bounty and seemingly oblivious to the two of them, much to Rita's relief.

Jack looked back over his shoulder, following Rita's gaze. His fond expression stayed on his face as he turned his attention back to Rita but became intense with sexual awareness as he took open note of the hard imprint of her nipples against the pale yellow nylon of her bikini top and the curves of her breasts escaping the V-shaped cups. Meeting her eyes, he smiled.

"Guess what? We're going to have the house to ourselves tonight. My mother's invited out, and then tomorrow morning early she'll be leaving, taking a flight over to Kauai to visit friends for a few days."

Rita sat up, surprised at the information disclosed in a tone that made her pulses hammer with its intimate promise.

"Your mother's leaving when you're here visiting her?"

Jack smiled at the reluctant eagerness blended with her disbelief.

"It was my idea."

"Jack! You didn't *ask* your mother to leave her own house! I mean, you didn't actually come out and *tell* her—" Rita glanced down the beach again, this time with dismay at the impropriety of the exchange she was imagining.

"Of course, I didn't spell it out with words," Jack scoffed and then undermined the reassurance by adding, "I didn't have to."

"Jack! I'm so embarrassed! What *did* you say?"

He sat up and reached over to the heap of snorkeling gear he'd brought out and dumped onto the sand. Picking up a mask and attached snorkeling tube, he shook it and handed it to her and then reached over for the other one while he answered.

"I told her that I intended to be around on a permanent basis. And since this wasn't a visit and since I was going to be spending a lot of time showing you around the island, she should go on about her life as usual." He transferred the black rubber fins over to the beach towels. "Ready to go in the water? Our food should be settled by now."

Rita ignored the casual suggestion. "That still doesn't explain why she'd *leave*. Jack, did you tell her about me, about—you know, everything?"

Jack got up on his haunches in preparation for rising. Despite her agitation, Rita was keenly aware of how male and attractive he was in the brief, black nylon swimsuit, his thighs muscled and powerful, his upper torso smooth and golden tan. Her pulse raced at the thought of going into the water with him.

"I told her you were beautiful and special and a little on the old-fashioned side. She took the hint and probably figured out for herself that you'd feel awkward sleeping here with me if she were in the house, even though the guest house, where I'm staying, isn't attached to the house. When she brought up the idea of visiting her friends on Kauai, I didn't argue. Now that she's met you, I can tell she thoroughly approves."

Rita had a sudden thought that added a sharp new element to her discomfort.

"This kind of thing hasn't happened *often*, I hope. I mean—" She broke off at the sight of his quick smile, realizing that she'd sounded not just disapproving, but *jealous*, and naturally he'd picked up on it at once.

"This 'kind of thing' hasn't happened at all," he denied in a soft, pleased voice. "When I visit, I usually spend a lot of time with my mother and her friends. I look up old acquaintances and go out with them. More than likely I'll be 'fixed up' with somebody's best friend or sister." His shrug was eloquent. "Sometimes those dates end up in bed. More often they don't." His smile placed Rita in a separate, special category all her own. "I don't make a habit of tracing down gorgeous redheads I've sat next to on the plane. Or bringing them home to meet my mother before I hustle her out of her own house."

It occurred to Rita then that he could have spared her this embarrassment if he hadn't brought her here today to meet his mother and to be confronted with the older woman's frank acceptance of a sexual intimacy between Rita and her son. He could have waited until tomorrow and presented Rita with the fact of his mother's absence from her house without explaining how it came to be. But he'd taken a riskier, more honest approach, and Rita discovered, somewhat to her surprise, that she wouldn't have wanted to change things. Although she was never likely to see Lillian Adams again after leaving Hawaii, she still wouldn't give up having met her and having gotten to know her at least a little.

"I'm pleased that you did give me this opportunity to meet your mother," she told Jack impulsively. "She is quite the character that you said she was. I haven't met anyone like her before, and I'm not likely to forget her."

Jack looked as though he were about to say something and then apparently he changed his mind. Rita hoped she hadn't been tactless in calling his mother a "character." He didn't appear upset as he rose to his feet with fluid ease and reached for her hands to help her up, and he sounded cheerful enough.

"She's one of a kind all right. At times even the people who like her the best are glad of that fact. What do you say we cool off and give you that snorkeling lesson? There's not as much to see out there as in some other places I can take you, but this is a good, safe place to learn."

Rita was excited about the opportunity to try snorkeling and willingly dropped the conversation to concentrate on Jack's instructions. He was a good teacher as she'd suspected he would be, clear and concise and infinitely patient. When she caught on to breathing through the snorkeling tube, he complimented her and made her feel like a prodigy in having learned quickly. He assured her as they swam out to deeper water that he would be close the whole time in case she had any problems. Rita felt utterly secure. She'd seen him in the water and was confident that he'd make sure she was safe.

Actually her main problem was wanting to express herself. She was enchanted with the colorful fish and the reef formations and wished that it were possible to snorkel and talk at the same time. The only way she could say to Jack, "Look at that! Isn't that the weirdest fish you've ever seen!" or "That yellow and purple striped fellow is incredibly beautiful and not at all scared of me!" was to point.

When Jack suddenly dived down, her interest in marine life instantly palled in favor of watching him. He was sleek and supple and beautifully coordinated, a sexy blond, tanned merman. It was strange and exciting to see his almost naked body gilded by the sunlight that filtered through the clear water. Rita wished that she could dive down after him. The thought of being alone with him that night, when his mother had gone out, made her heart beat faster and she suddenly felt quite short-winded.

Bobbing her head up out of the water, she jerked out the snorkel mouthpiece and sucked in a deep breath of air. Jack was almost immediately there beside her.

"You okay?" he asked concernedly and was reassured when Rita nodded quickly. "What happened? Did you suck in some water through the snorkel? Remember, when that happens, just blow hard, like this." He demonstrated and then looked at her closely. "Are you about ready to get out and warm up? I'm starting to feel cold."

"You are? You don't look cold." She brought her hand to a bare golden shoulder slick with sea water and looked surprised as she clasped it. "You are cold."

He smiled. "I'm a warm-blooded animal, not a fish. Aren't you cold?" Under the water, he stroked a hand along the curve of her waist. "Pretty cold there. Let's see. What about here?" He caressed her hip and slid his palm across her belly. "Yes, definitely chilled, but nice, and warming, too." He slipped his other hand down below the surface of the water. Using both of them, he rubbed her buttocks and squeezed them, slid his palms up her back and around to her breasts. "How's that?" he asked softly, kneading and squeezing. "Any better? I know I'm beginning to feel warmer."

"Are you? I was worried."

Rita held herself afloat with the hand clasping his shoulder and ran the other one down along his chest. Holding his gaze, she rubbed lower, across the tightened muscles of his belly, enjoying the feel of him as much as the pleasure of teasing him.

"You're getting warmer, too," she murmured and slid her hands down over the wet nylon covering his hip.

"Be careful of your hand, sweetheart," he warned softly. "You're running out of warm into hot."

"Hmm." She tipped her head back and smiled at him. "What's that play title? *Some Like It Hot*?"

"Some might as well like it hot a little later on tonight, but right now I'm going to cool us both off." He stopped treading water and wrapped his arms and legs around her. "Hold your breath. We're going und—"

Rita sucked in a gasp of air just in time. Putting her arms around his neck, she clung to him as they drifted down. Her breasts were flattened against his chest, her stomach and hips joined to his, the separating layers of nylon cloth serving as the most insubstantial barrier. They shared the intimate details of physical arousal, the hardness of her nipples, the swollen thrust of his groin, the tom-tom beating of their hearts. Held so close in his arms, feeling the shuddering power in them and in his muscled thighs, Rita wished crazily that by some miracle they could breathe underwater long enough to drift to the bottom of the sea and make love there.

But, of course, they couldn't. Before their lungs burst, they had to come back to the surface. They had to untangle their limbs and swim separately back to shore, making mental and physical adjustments necessary for curbing their passion, for postponing the satisfaction of their need, which seemed to Rita to grow stronger each time they aroused each other, so far for naught.

The afternoon passed in a haze of pleasure. Rita was careful, for her own good and his, not to be openly provocative, and so was Jack. Their mutual restraint only deepened the easy intimacy between them as they sunbathed, cooled off in the water, and swam out to the reef to snorkel another time or two.

Rita was dozing in the shade of a beach umbrella Jack had set up to protect her when Lillian Adams went in. When she awoke, she was alone on the beach. Jack was out in the water swimming. As she watched him reach a far out point and head back for shore, his rhythm became a part of her and the languid need that was diffused throughout her body sharpened and intensified until she felt as though there were strong cables running between the generalized ache in her lower abdomen and pelvis to her furthest extremities. Even her fingertips and toes were affected by the tension.

She wanted him as she'd never wanted a man before. As he neared the shore and had to stand in the shallow water, her uncontrollable yearning brought her to her feet and drew her down to the water's edge to meet him. She didn't care that she radiated it in her face and eyes and body. She was thrilled and not at all surprised when he read her urgency and responded to it, splashing fast through the shallows and enveloping her in a great hug that made her gasp with the shock of her sun-warmed body pressed against his sea-cooled hardness.

"You feel like ice!" she squealed.

"You feel fantastic." He squeezed her hard and put her down. "I think you've had enough sun for today, don't you?" He touched her nose with a gentle forefinger and then took her hand and led her over to the beach towels. "We can't have that beautiful skin turning to leather. I'll take you up to the house. You can use my shower in the guest house. Afterward you can take a rest in my bed, if you're tired, or I'm sure my mother would be happy to show you her studio and introduce you to the art of making native jewelry."

Rita watched him as he shook out the towels and gathered them into a bundle, which he tucked into the crook of one arm. He wrapped the other arm casually around her shoulders.

"What about you? What are you going to be doing?" she asked petulantly, walking beside him toward rough-hewn timbers forming steps from the sand up to the grass lawn.

"I have several matters to take care of, including some telephone calls and a trip to the supermarket to get some steaks for our dinner tonight. I hope you don't mind another home-made meal. My mother will be needing her car."

Rita didn't mind at all. She didn't care if they had sandwiches. She just wanted to be alone with Jack, to have him to herself. And though the next couple of hours passed as pleasantly as those before them, her undercurrent of impatience grew.

It felt novel and incredibly intimate to be left on her own in Jack's quarters, with his toilet articles in the bathroom and his clothes hanging in the closet. Surprisingly, he was neat. His bed might have been made by a woman, and yet Rita knew he had to have made it himself. Lillian was hardly the neat, domestic type, and she couldn't afford a housekeeper.

Rita showered and afterward dressed in her shorts and blouse and went into the main house. Lillian was in her studio with the door open, busily cleaning the little shells she'd found on the beach that day. She welcomed Rita in and didn't require any urging to talk about her jewelry making. She demonstrated the delicate process of drilling a hole in the tiny, fragile shells and showed Rita some of the jewelry she'd made. Rita forgot Jack's advice and was genuinely admiring, only to find herself the owner of a lovely, intricate shell necklace.

"I feel so bad about taking it," Rita told Jack later when they had the house to themselves. "After watching her this afternoon on the beach and then seeing her work in her studio, I hate to think of the hours she put into making this."

Jack was tending steaks on a built-in barbecue grill at the edge of the *lanai*, and Rita was sitting curled up in a comfortable chair watching him, admiring his casual expertise and the attractive male picture he made in old, soft jeans and an aloha shirt. His feet were bare. He glanced over at her smilingly, his eyes touching on the shell necklace and then making an appreciative once-over of the rest of her.

"I'd say that necklace found the perfect home," he mused. Laying down his long-handled fork, he folded his arms across his chest and looked out toward the ocean and the darkening horizon. "Just think of all those tiny little shells making their way ashore into my mother's net. They could have met with a far worse fate than to be around your pretty neck. It boggles the mind to think of how much chance is involved in life, doesn't it? What were the possibilities that I'd be standing at one particular gate in a big airport in a city where I wouldn't have been if my last business deal hadn't just happened to go through early?" He shook his head and looked back at her, his face tender and sober. "Are you cold?" he asked concernedly, seeing her shiver.

"A little," she lied. It had been his tone of voice and his seriousness that had made her flesh prickle. Getting up, she went over to stand beside him, holding her hands out toward the grill. "I didn't know you were such a philosopher." She smiled and wrinkled her nose at him.

He bent down and kissed her on the lips, but much to her disappointment, he didn't take her into his arms. Nor did he take the hint and lighten his mood. He was deeply thoughtful as he picked up the fork again and tested the steaks for firmness. "There're lots of things you don't know about me yet. Lots of things I don't know about you. Tonight's a good time to get started learning them. These steaks are done." He picked up the platter and paused, stopping to notice her shiver again. "You are cold. We'll eat inside."

The meal was delicious. The steaks were juicy and tender, cooked medium rare as they both liked them. Jack had baked potatoes in the microwave and made another mixed green salad similar to the one at lunch. He opened a bottle of wine. Everything would have been perfect if Rita hadn't sensed his underlying seriousness. Even as they chatted and joked, even when he smiled, the thoughtfulness was there in his eyes. She found herself increasingly nervous and exasperated that the evening wasn't shaping up as she had anticipated. Here they were finally alone. They finally had the freedom to indulge in the most provocative repartee, the opportunity to arouse each other to wild passion and this time not have to control it, but Jack was holding them back. He was being attentive and loving but definitely restrained. Why? It was baffling.

After they'd eaten, Rita helped him clear the table and straighten up the kitchen. It didn't take them long. His ease and efficiency provided her the inspiration for what she meant to be a playful opening.

"You are a good hand around the house," she commented teasingly as they were leaving the kitchen. "I noticed how neatly your bed was made. Did you make it yourself?"

"Do you like neat men, Rita?"

It wasn't the kind of comeback she wanted, not playful and not idle. He'd taken her opener and turned it to his own use, she realized with mild frustration. And then before she could decide how to respond, whether to ignore the serious intent or attack it head on, he was capitalizing on her uncertainty with a swift follow-up that took her breath away with its unexpectedness.

"What about Mark Pendleton? Was he the neat and tidy type? I expect that he was from what you've told me. I gather you liked the way he dressed. What else did you like about him, Rita? What made you decide to marry him? What was it that he offered you? I need to know all of that. Come over here and sit by me on the couch and tell me, please." He took her gently but firmly by the arm and led her.

"But I don't want to talk about that!" Rita protested, dragging her feet. "You *don't* need to know it. It's all over, and it has nothing to do with you and me."

"Everything that's ever happened to you has to do with you and me," he contradicted gravely. "Why did you want to marry him, Rita? Did you really love him?"

Rita plopped down on the couch and groaned. "I can't believe this! All day we've been driving each other crazy, and now that we're finally alone, what do you want to do? Talk about me and another man! Why, Jack?"

Jack sat down next to her. "It's because of the way we drive each other crazy that I have to know these things, Rita. Whether you want to hear it or not, I'm falling in love with you. Or, more likely, I already have. That's good reason for needing to know what it was that you saw in Pendleton that you don't see in me. What did the man have that made you want to marry him, even though you admit that he didn't even turn you on?"

Rita turned sideways toward him, her whole posture as well as her face imploring.

"No, you're *not* in love with me, Jack. Not any more than I'm in love with you, although I *like* you more than any man I've ever known. *Like*, I said, not love!" she added on a note of desperation as she read the hope flaring up in his

face. "And why do you have to spoil everything? Why do
you have to make me put into words things that are just
going to hurt your feelings?"

"I can take hurt feelings, Rita. What I can't take is not
knowing. Please, tell me. Why did you want to marry Pendleton? You didn't really love him, did you?"

Rita slumped back against the sofa and closed her eyes,
disappointment, irritation, and a strange hopelessness
washing through her. She was no match for Jack's determination. He was going to force her against her will to tell
him things that would kill what was between them and all
for no reason. It made her sick at heart.

"It's such a boring story," she said, sighing. "Mark and
I are both boring people, not like you. You won't find it at
all interesting."

"You're not boring. I find everything about you interesting. Come on, tell me."

Rita's long silence wasn't recalcitrant. She just didn't
know where or how to begin. It wasn't easy to overcome a
lifetime's habit of secrecy, to talk of a background she'd
never shared with anyone, to explain powerful motives and
needs that she preferred not to analyze. In the end it just
seemed easier to try to answer his specific questions, figuring out the truth as she went along. It was going to be
damning, she knew, and some of it would cut him deeply,
hurt his feelings needlessly, destroy the delight they had in
each other. But he insisted upon knowing it.

"Did I really love Mark?" she began heavily. "I was very
fond of him, but, no, I wasn't deeply and passionately in
love with him. I'd be lying if I said I was totally unaware of
that fact all along. It just wasn't important. What did he
offer me?" Rita looked at Jack apologetically. "Everything that I'd always wanted. A life that was secure and re-

spectable and stable. Mark would have been a faithful husband, a good father. But it just wasn't meant to be.''

The sad, wistful look on her face twisted Jack's guts. He had to wait a second to make sure his voice wouldn't come out sounding as jealous as he felt.

"But couldn't you have had all that with a man you loved, Rita? Did you give up on finding him and settle for Pendleton? And now that it's over with him, why are you so dead set against believing that man could be me? Is it just too soon after you've been hurt?"

Rita looked away. "Jack, please—"

"Rita, why are you fighting what's between us? What does Pendleton have that I don't? Do you admire his intelligence? Do you think he has a great future in law or politics? I can't understand why you'd marry him when he didn't even turn you on and yet you don't want to hear a serious word from me. Why don't you want me to love you?"

Rita shook her head miserably. "I doubt Mark's anywhere near as bright as you are, Jack. That's why it's such a shame that you didn't educate yourself for some profession. You could have been a brilliant lawyer. With the right connections you'd be good in politics, too."

Jack stared hard at her. "Is that it, then? You're bothered by the fact that I don't have a college degree?"

Rita nodded reluctantly. "That's part of it. But mainly, Jack, I just can't let myself become involved with the type of man that you are. I know you have big ideas, big dreams. And every intention of making them come true." She looked down at the necklace his mother had given her and touched one of the tiny shells. "You were talking earlier of the role chance plays in our lives. Heredity plays an important role, too, in making us what we are. So does environment. I'm beginning to wonder if a person can actually overcome the three of them. I've worked so hard to escape being me, Rita Jones.''

Up until now Jack had restrained himself from touching her. He reached for her hand that was toying with the shell necklace, captured it gently, and brought it to his lips.

''Tell me about Rita Jones,'' he commanded her so lovingly that Rita looked up at him, incredulous that he could sound like that after all that she had told him. He smiled reassuringly. ''Don't leave out anything and don't worry about my feelings.'' He drew her into his arms and rested his head against hers. After only a moment's resistance, Rita relaxed. She nestled against him, and the words started to come of their own accord, haltingly at first, and then they flowed.

She lost track of time. She told him all about her background, giving not just the details but confessing her sense of being low class and hopelessly excluded from the ranks of contemporaries from stable, respectable homes. She recalled names and incidents that she hadn't thought of in years, recounted the different towns where she'd lived, schools and rental homes and neighbors. Jack hugged her a little tighter now and then, and occasionally he drew in an audible breath, but he resisted any impulse he might have felt to make a comment or ask a question. He let her tell her own story. Afterward he was gentle but blunt in reflecting upon what she'd told him.

''I'd never have figured you for growing up on the wrong side of the tracks, but it explains a lot I couldn't make sense of before. So Pendleton backed out when your sister showed up and spilled the beans? The bastard. He didn't deserve you anyway. You're too good for him.''

Rita raised up her head and looked searchingly into his face for some trace that he was offended. She'd admitted openly the similarities she saw between him and her mother's ne'er-do-well husbands, and here he was defending her stoutly.

She blinked at a sudden mist of tears. "Jack, I'm sorry. Now you see why I didn't want to tell you."

He smiled into her troubled face as he framed it with his hands and lowered his lips to hers. The kiss was slow and deep. It left Rita weak and breathless.

"Don't be sorry," he said huskily. "Now I know exactly what the problem is, and it isn't a problem. It just remains for you to find that out. But I'm all out of the mood for talking." He kissed her again. "What about you?"

Rita put her arms up around his neck and smiled at him.

"I don't know if I'll ever need to talk again. I haven't ever talked this much to anyone before. You know as much about me now as I know myself." Her eyes widened with surprise as he shook his head.

"That's where you're wrong. I know *more*."

Before Rita could pursue the correction, Jack dispensed with further conversation. He kissed her again, and by the time he was finished, she didn't care who knew what about whom. All that mattered was that Jack had turned into the lover she'd wanted all day, only the waiting period seemed longer than that. It seemed that she'd wanted him forever. And the wait was well worthwhile.

Chapter Ten

They walked outside across the lawn to the guest house, their arms around each other. Rita had never felt so close to another human being, and surely not in her adult life. Jack knew everything about her and he still approved. He still made her feel that she was unique and very special to him.

The communion between them made words of appreciation unnecessary as they absorbed the beauty and pleasures of the night. Overhead was the luminous moon and millions of brilliant stars softly lighting the ocean, a presence beyond the lawn, whispering rhythmically against the sand. The sweetness of tropical flowers blended tantalizingly with the sea air. It was a magical world given specially to them to enhance their enjoyment of each other. It teased them with an invitation to be languid that was at odds with their urgency yet somehow heightened it.

Jack led Rita to the *lanai* facing the ocean off his bedroom and paused there to take her into his arms and kiss her.

Rita's response inflamed him and his voice was low and unsteady with his passion when the kiss had finally ended.

"We can go down to the beach and make love," he offered, squeezing her hard against his length and then caressing her back and shoulders with a roughness that made Rita tighten her arms around his neck and stand on tiptoes to press closer. "That's what you wanted last night, remember?"

His voice added the message that it was of tremendous importance to him to give her whatever she wanted, whatever would make her happy. The sentiment itself thrilled Rita and made her feel adored even while his words jarred her with a sense of disbelief. Could the *luau* really have been only last night? It seemed longer than that. She felt like a different woman tonight.

"But it's so far down to the beach," she whispered, nuzzling her lips against his neck and delighting in his indrawn breath and the tightening of his hands on her shoulders. "And I really did want to muss that neat bed of yours." She tasted his firm warm flesh with the tip of her tongue, thinking of the way it would look in the light, smooth and golden brown. When his whole body flinched and tightened and he sucked in his breath again, she thrilled in her power to stir him.

"Jack, I love your body," she told him, unbuttoning his shirt and smoothing her hands across his chest and up over his shoulders, feeling the ripple of muscles and nerves she awakened. When he lowered his arms and shrugged, she took the hint immediately and pushed the shirt free of his shoulders. He dropped it down on the flagstones.

"The feeling's mutual, believe me. I can't wait to see you. All of you." He pulled her blouse free of the waistband of her shorts. Rita paused in her caressing exploration of his chest and shoulders and back long enough to lift her arms for him and let him strip the blouse off. Then she waited, heart pounding, as he unfastened her bra and slipped it off. She felt his groan of satisfaction deep in her abdomen as he took her breasts in his hands.

"God, but you're luscious, sweetheart."

Rita felt her nipples prickle and harden with her anticipation as he lowered his head to her chest. She grabbed onto his shoulders for support at first as his lips and tongue made contact with an aching breast. Then as she became accustomed to the waves of weakness and the shooting pangs of pleasure he was creating with his leisurely nuzzling and licking attention to the full outer curves, she caressed his shoulders and back, murmuring compliments. But she had to clutch at him again as he focused upon the hard center of her breast, sucking and nipping at it with his teeth while he squeezed with his hand.

Rita gasped out contradictory expressions of what she was feeling. She told him what he was doing to her was incredibly wonderful, but that she couldn't bear it. When he dropped away his hands and moved over to the neglected breast and kissed it tenderly, she was briefly filled with regret that she had discouraged him until she felt him unclipping the waistband of her shorts and sliding the zipper down.

He squatted down in front of her to help her remove her shorts and stayed in the position when she was wearing just her bikini panties.

"It's too dark out here," he complained softly, running his hands over her hips and thighs and sliding them around to shape the rounded curves of her buttocks. "I want to see you. All of you. I want to feel you. Taste you." He kissed her thighs, making her tremble, and slipped his fingers under the elastic waistband of her panties.

Rita sucked in her breath and concentrated on standing upright on legs suffused with delicious weakness as he eased down her panties and caressed the intimate new territory he'd exposed for the first time. Lightly he brushed his palm across her pelvic triangle, heard her low moan, and then eased his hand between her legs to take a gentle possession. He murmured a deep, satisfied sound as Rita opened her thighs a little and then squeezed them closed around his hand, moaning softly again.

"Ah, yes, sweetheart, I want you, too."

He kissed her stomach and turned his hand sideways, making one single devastating stroke along her center as he drew his hand free and stood up, unsnapping his jeans on the way. He shed them and his briefs and then took Rita into his arms, drawing her close gently, fitting them together delicately so that she could feel the obstruction his passion had created and her body yearned to accommodate.

Then he hugged her tight against him, so tight that she could barely breathe and could feel the pulse of his hard flesh between them. She felt encompassed by his warmth and strength and yet stirred to wild dissatisfaction by his need, which prodded her own.

"Make love to me, Jack," she commanded and begged him.

"I will, my darling." His arms loosened just enough so that he could bury his face into her neck and kiss her. "I've never wanted anything more."

Inside his room he turned on the lamp next to his bed, and for several moments they blinked at each other, adjusting to the light, adjusting to being naked together, finding new stimulation in the expected pleasures of sight. They'd already seen each other in the minimum of clothing. Rita knew that his body was supple and fit and tanned. But now she was seeing the patch of white skin that had been covered by his brief black swimsuit, the intimate growth of golden hair, the tumescence that she'd stirred to swollen life.

"You're so damned beautiful I can't believe it," Jack told her softly, with a mixture of reverence and male hunger. He reached out and touched the hardened bud of her nipple with a fingertip and then circled it, tracing the shell pink aureole. "I thought you'd be delicate and pink here, the way you are." Rita felt the heat rise up in her body as his eyes dropped to her pelvic triangle, marked by a luxuriant tangle of coppery hair. "And I wondered what color your hair would be there."

"You're embarrassing me," she protested softly.

He looked back quickly at her face, saw the heightened color with surprise and tender pleasure. "Am I? I didn't mean to. I just got carried away at the sight of you." He smiled. "You seemed pretty busy with looking yourself."

The smile faded as he reached out both hands and slipped his fingertips beneath her hair so that he could shape the slender column of her neck and then follow the lines of her shoulders.

"Now I can touch you and see you at the same time. Out there I could just see you in my mind. I want to see you when you touch me, too, your face and your hands." He took her hands that dangled at her side and placed them on his chest. "Touch me, sweetheart," he begged her softly. "Touch me everywhere. I want you to know every single inch of me. I want to know every pretty inch of you."

His endurance didn't measure up to the occasion. Rita took his invitation and rapidly overcame her shyness with the sheer joy of touching him, which, as he had promised, was greatly heightened by her visual pleasure. In short order she was venturing into that intimate territory she hadn't explored before, and his reaction to her warm encompassing hand stilled her immediately. His low groan expressed agony, and he went rigid, as though with pain.

Rita gently released him and eased her body close as she put her arms around his waist.

"Let's make love, Jack," she said, hugging him tight. The feelings that welled up inside her were so powerful and good and so mixed with a great tenderness for him that she yearned to express them, but could think of only the obvious, misleading words: *I love you.* It wouldn't be fair or honest to speak them, and *I like you so much* was pitifully inadequate, so she said nothing. She let her body speak her warmth and her urge to give to him unstintingly.

Already she knew he was a knowledgeable and sensitive lover. Already he had aroused in her a level of desire and passion she'd never known before in her limited sexual experience, but she was unprepared for the total sensory devastation of his lovemaking. She'd heard the word *ecstasy* and was familiar with what it meant, but now for the first time she comprehended the knife-edged intermingling of pleasure and pain as Jack unleashed in her an abandoned response of which she hadn't dreamed herself capable and then carried her to climax.

He joined his body with hers carefully, entering her and filling her with his hardness and warmth. Rita rejoiced in the closeness, wrapping her legs around him. But as he began to move inside her with strong, rhythmical strokes, a pleasurable tension built quickly. She moved her hips in conjunction with his at first and then in opposition, to exaggerate the impact of his thrusts. As the tension became a fast-spiraling upward-and-outward sensation with the promise of unavoidable destruction when the expansion had reached its limitations, she could no longer bear a steady rhythm and thrashed and moved under him with wild abandon, urging him to spurts of frenzied speed interspersed with slow deliberate plunges into impossible depths. Toward the end she begged desperately for relief and cried out with the joy of it when it finally came.

For long moments she was hardly conscious of Jack's dead weight as he lay slumped on top of her. When he groaned and rolled off, gathering her up close against him, she was too spent to say anything or even to think. Jack was the first one to regain his power of speech. She heard his words with vague admiration for his recovery before their meaning even penetrated.

"I'm glad you don't like sex, sweetheart. You'd be more than I can handle if you did." He chuckled and rumpled her hair. "I love you. You're fantastic."

Rita took a deep breath and stirred lazily against him. "You're a very sexy man," she mumbled. "I noticed that about you right off." She yawned and snuggled closer. "I wish I didn't have to get dressed and go back to the hotel."

Jack reached down and pulled the sheet up over them and then turned out the lamp. With the room plunged into darkness, the sound of the ocean seemed to come right inside the room.

"You don't have to go. I'd like you to stay and sleep with me. Tomorrow morning I'll serve you breakfast in bed," he enticed softly.

Rita sighed longingly, struggling with her sense of propriety. "That's almost too good to pass up. It doesn't seem right, though, with your mother in the house." Her reluctant tone invited him to present arguments in favor of her staying.

"She'll be gone tomorrow night. You can take a nap, if you want. I'll stay awake and listen for the car. You can always change your mind when I wake you."

She was quiet for so long and her breathing was so slow and regular that Jack thought she'd taken his suggestion.

Judging from the drowsiness of her voice as she spoke into the silence, she might have dropped off and roused herself back to semi-wakefulness.

"Jack..."

"Yes, darling."

"I guess you might drop off and not hear your mother come in. I mean, this isn't actually a part of the house, is it? Somebody could break into it, and we'd never know back here. You did say she was catching an early plane in the morning." The last words were slurred sleepily, and immediately afterward she was sleeping soundly, having dispensed with the worry of getting up and returning to the hotel.

Jack smiled in the darkness, listening to her breathe, feeling her relaxed warmth against him. But he didn't drop off to sleep despite being released from his promise to stay awake. He heard the sound of his mother's car when she came home a half hour later and was awake for at least another hour after that, thinking.

He mulled over the background Rita had divulged to him that night and wondered how he should approach correcting her erroneous assumptions about him. How should he go about telling her, for example, that she was wrong in thinking that Mark Pendleton had any advantage over Jack in the family tree department? She was impressed with the fact that Mark Pendleton's father was a university professor. Jack's family on the New England side had a Princeton dean, a state supreme court judge, and a United States congressman, for starters. Jack's father was a major stockholder and chairman of the board of a big eastern bank whose name Rita would recognize. Any family get-together was a collection of wealthy, influential people with social register status.

His mother's side of the family, based in California, wasn't as socially prominent and steeped in tradition, but there was great wealth and behind-the-scenes political clout. His mother was the heiress of a publishing fortune. Jack realized as he thought back over his conversation with Rita about his mother that he hadn't mentioned that. It was something that he took much for granted.

On the whole Jack took his background for granted. It wasn't a source of particular pride. He seldom had reason to give it thought, as he was doing now. He supposed he was basically self-centered, living pretty much in the here and now of what he was doing. It didn't diminish his regard for Rita one iota to know that her mother hadn't finished high school and had worked in bars and nightclubs. But considering the beating Rita's pride had taken so recently at the hands of that stuff-shirted bastard Pendleton and his mother, Jack decided he'd hold off telling her about his origins and mentioning his high-powered relatives. First, he'd let her know him better, become sure of him.

It definitely hurt that she perceived him as a wheeling and dealing loser type, like the men who'd raised her mother's hopes and disappointed her time after time. Jack guessed he'd come on too strong with his salesman's manner and given the impression that he was all talk. In her eyes he obviously didn't look the part of the successful businessman that he actually was. Admittedly his style was laid back and casual. Maybe it was a legacy from his mother that his confidence didn't depend on what he was wearing, though when the situation called for it, he could wear a suit and tie with the best of them or a morning coat or tux or whatever.

If Rita wanted to dress him up, Jack would go along with her, within limitations, but meanwhile how should he go about changing his image other than telling her that she was wrong in her judgment of him? Should he go into more detail about his past business ventures? Should he show her proof of his monetary worth? The idea of having to sell himself was repugnant, hard on the pride. Jack decided that he would just play it by ear, depend upon his instincts to do and say the right thing.

After reaching that conclusion, he tabled the whole matter, savored the satisfactions of having her there in bed with him, safe and warm and vulnerable, and thought about his prospective new venture there on Maui until he went to sleep. The challenge of business and of life itself had a sweeter edge now that he'd found Rita. He wanted to succeed more than ever and share that success with her.

It didn't bother Jack that he was thinking in terms of permanency after knowing Rita for just days. Some relationships took years to nurture, some months or weeks, and others just hours or minutes. He thought he'd fallen in love with Rita sitting next to her on the plane. When she'd flung herself into his arms on takeoff, he'd wanted nothing on earth more at that moment than to protect her and take care of her. The feeling had only gotten stronger with the pleasure-filled hours in her company.

Here under the Hawaiian sun, where the attitude was held that life was good and meant to be enjoyed, she was blooming, coming into her own personality that she'd curbed trying to tailor herself to suit the standards of a man like Pendleton, who could never appreciate her, never let her be herself. Jack went into a cold sweat thinking of how close a call she'd had, almost marrying the creep.

One of these days he was going to tell Rita's sister Edna of the great service she'd done him. He was looking forward to meeting Edna and Rita's mother and even the latest husband. Rita would be shocked and appalled at the suggestion now, but he could look ahead into the future and see a time when she'd want to make up with her family, a time when she could accept them and love them for what they were. Jack himself had been working around toward that attitude. Maybe his love for Rita was having an overall mellowing influence, but he could foresee a time when he and his father would be friends.

Jack smiled again in the darkness, thinking that he'd better go to sleep and leave some conjecture for future nights like this one when he felt too brimming over with the goodness of life to let consciousness go.

When Rita awoke, she was alone in the bed. Through the glass doors opening onto the *lanai* she could see that the sun shone outside. It must be as late as nine o'clock. Jack's mother would be gone by now. Jack was probably on his way back here from the airport. The two of them would have the whole place to themselves now, the house, the beach, this wonderful guest house with its own ocean view.

Pushing herself up on her elbows, she looked out expectantly beyond the shrubbery and bougainvillea vines framing the *lanai* and saw that, sure enough, Jack had his bed positioned so that he could awaken in the morning, look out and see the ocean. She'd known he would. What pure aesthetic luxury!

Rita yawned and stretched and gave into the temptation to postpone getting out of bed just for a minute or two. She stuffed her pillow and Jack's behind her back and luxuriated in a sense of leisure as she looked out at the bright, fresh morning world awaiting her, awaiting her and Jack. Thought of him and last night made her smile dreamily, and she stretched again, feeling the tingling of life in her breasts as the sheet slid over them and fell down around her hips.

Looking down, she cupped her breasts, remembering Jack's admiring and explicit comments about them. He'd made her feel beautiful and sexy, *good* about her body in a way she hadn't felt before. Just thinking about the touch of his hands and the moist warmth of his mouth made her shiver with pleasure. The sensory memory had her nipples peeking out and then contracting into tight little buds that would tempt Jack if he walked into the room.

The possibility of having him find her like this, in the midst of fondling herself and arousing her body with recollections of his lovemaking, was embarrassing and yet highly stimulating, wrecking her lazy mood. Rita threw aside the sheet and got out of bed, deciding that she would get dressed and go out on the *lanai* and enjoy the view from there while she waited for him.

The problem with getting dressed was that her clothes had disappeared, she discovered with surprise. Why had he taken her clothes? Did he think he might come back and find her gone? Was he keeping her a naked prisoner in his private quarters? The whimsical thought entertained her as she made herself quite at home in his bathroom, using his toothbrush and comb.

Much as she'd expected, there wasn't a robe of any kind in his closet. The best available substitute would be one of his aloha shirts. She was taking her choice off the hanger when she heard quiet sounds on the *lanai* and then Jack's cheerful voice.

"Time to rise and shine, sleeping beauty."

The screen door slid open and he was standing there, looking at her, smiling at her as she buttoned up his shirt. His admiring assessment was strictly male and so warmly distracting that she didn't notice at once the garment draped over his arm.

"I couldn't find my clothes. Oh, I see you brought me something."

"It's one of my mother's *muumuu*s." He tossed it carelessly onto the bed. "But I like my shirt on you better." Rita's heart pounded pleasurably as he walked over to her and took her in his arms. "Good morning," he said softly and kissed her. "Hmm. See why I like you in my shirt? It's nice and short," he murmured, slipping his hands underneath the shirt to caress her buttocks, just barely covered by the raised level of the shirttail with her arms up around his neck. "You were so warm and cuddly this morning I started to wake you, but I didn't have the heart."

Rita was frankly disappointed when he gave the shirttail a little downward jerk and put her back from him.

"I brought you breakfast, just like I promised. Hungry?"

She smiled at his pleased, eager tone and let him draw her out onto the *lanai*.

"Jack, that's beautiful!" she exclaimed with sincere appreciation when she saw the large tray he'd set on the table, complete with a pottery bowl of fresh flowers. "That fruit looks delicious." She inhaled and eyed the napkin-covered wicker basket inquiringly. "Do I smell hot muffins?"

"You certainly do." Jack held her chair for her. After she'd sat down, he transferred the contents of the tray onto the table, setting down each item with a flourish. "We have fresh pineapple and papaya. Blueberry muffins right out of the oven. Guava jelly. Coffee. Can I pour you a cup?"

"You certainly can." Rita sniffed the rich fragrance. "Is that Kona coffee?"

"Nothing but the best for you, my love."

Jack dropped a kiss on top of her head and sat down opposite her. He opened up his arms in an expansive gesture and breathed a deep, satisfied sigh.

"Now isn't this nice, I ask you? Waking up and having breakfast served by your own personal male slave."

"This is very nice. I could get spoiled." Rita smiled at him and sipped her coffee. The taste was rich and delicious, adding to the totality of her pleasure.

Jack had done it again, turned something as routine and ordinary as eating breakfast into a delightful, special event.

"Do you always feed your lady prisoners this well?" she asked him teasingly in between bites of sweet, tangy papaya and hot buttered muffin. "I can hardly go anywhere without my clothes," she added, seeing that he found the notion of her as his prisoner novel and interesting. "What did you do with them?"

"I hope it's okay. I washed them. I thought you'd probably want a fresh changing, and I checked the instructions on the tags. They're in the dryer now—on the delicate cycle," he added, wiggling his eyebrows and making Rita blush.

"I've never had a man wash my clothes before," she mused, a little embarrassed and yet intrigued with the picture he'd raised in her mind of him as male launderer. He'd handled her personal clothing familiarly, looking for the tags in them, including her panties and bra. What a surprising man he was and how thoughtful. His apparent ease in doing domestic chores didn't diminish his masculinity in her sight, though, not one whit. That was demonstrated when after breakfast he began to stack the empty dishes and seemed ready to proceed with the day without first making love to her.

"After that nourishing breakfast, are you ready to get dressed and do some sight-seeing? I thought we'd drive the road to Hana, have a picnic lunch at the Seven Pools."

"That sounds nice." Rita made her reply polite and unenthusiastic on purpose. Just as she'd intended, Jack looked at her questioningly. Her pulse raced at her own intended boldness. "I just wondered. It's supposed to be a whole day's trip to Hana and back. Is there time to get everything done and still go? You know, washing up the dishes, making the bed..."

Jack put the dish he was holding on top of the stack with a little clatter. He didn't smile but his eyes had a wicked twinkle.

"You didn't think I meant to rush off and leave the place in a mess? I thought the two of us together could get things done in no time. One of us could take the kitchen, the other the bedroom, or..." He waggled his eyebrows as though struck by a bright thought. "We could work together!"

Rita got up from the table in a leisurely fashion and strolled toward the opening into the bedroom.

"I feel so lazy," she complained, stretching her arms high and then linking them behind her head. Stopping, she pivoted slowly and caught Jack in the act of watching the shirttail rise over her derriere. "I don't know if I can be trusted to make that bed. I might just crawl back in."

He got up with a lithe quickness that made her heart plummet and then pound with excitement as he came over to her.

"In that case, I'd better stick around and help. It's a lot easier making a bed with two people anyway."

Much to Rita's disappointment he didn't scoop her up and carry her into the bedroom. In fact, it seemed as if he actually intended to do exactly what he'd said, help her make up the bed.

"I'll make up your side, and you make up mine," he suggested, walking around to the side of the bed on which she'd slept. "That makes it more fun, don't you think?"

Rita eyed him suspiciously and then with disgruntlement as he began to straighten the sheets and plump the pillows.

"Hey this isn't going too well," he said, looking up. "You're not doing your share—" He leaned on his hands and watched her, a little smile on his face, as she unbuttoned the aloha shirt, opened it up deliberately and took it off, sliding it free of her shoulders and down her arms carefully, as though to avoid wrinkling it.

"I'll be right there," she promised softly, and walked naked over to the closet. "I want to hang this up first."

Jack had straightened when she'd finished her production of hanging the shirt in the closet. Smiling at him innocently, she sashayed over to the bed opposite him and busied herself smoothing the bottom sheet.

"I know how particular you are." She kept her head down, trying to hide her smile. He was taking off his clothes. She could hear the quiet rustle. But he didn't walk around the bed. Naturally he did the unexpected, taking her by surprise, delighting her with his impromptu answer to her seduction.

"Jack!" she squealed as he bounced full length into the bed and dragged her on top of him. "What are you *doing*! Stop that!" she shrieked as he tickled her. "I'm ticklish! I can't stand that!"

She could stand the feel of him under her, hard and warm and male. She could stand his arms closing around her wriggling nakedness as he stopped the tickling, hugging her hard. And, oh, how she could stand his palms stroking along her back and down over her buttocks and thighs.

"You turn me on, and you know it," he said accusingly, looking into her eyes as she smiled down at him complacently.

Rita tried to look innocent. "I just wanted to do something nice for you. In return for breakfast and free laundry and all." She sighed happily and kissed him on the mouth, loving the firm shape of it and his quick eager response.

"Totally unselfish of you," he mused between her kisses. "Being nice to me like this."

Rita braced her forearms on his chest and looked down at him.

"I woke up this morning thinking about you—and about *this*," she confessed wonderingly. "You're terrible for me. You have me doing and thinking things I never dreamed— Jack!" she gasped as he raised her by the waist.

"Stop talking and help me give you what you want," he ordered tenderly. "What I want, too," he added and spoke intimate encouragements as Rita hesitated and then did as she was told. He closed his eyes and groaned as he lowered her and she took him deep into her. "Have you ever felt anything better than that? Sweetheart, you're fantastic."

"I've never done this before," Rita told him, her voice conveying her sense of novelty at being on top and her shyness at being so completely visible.

Jack opened his eyes and smiled at her. "Just let me know, sweet, if you don't like it. Let me know when you don't like anything I do. Like this." He took her breasts in his hands and fondled them. "Making love to you is something I want to be perfect at."

Rita smoothed her palms across his chest and moved her hips experimentally, giving rise to delicious sensations.

"You don't have any room for improvement, Jack," she told him softly and bent down to kiss him on the lips. "You're already the perfect lover, as far as I'm concerned."

Jack hooked his arm around her neck to keep her there for a deeper, rousing kiss, and the discussion of lovemaking was discontinued. Such words as they spoke after that were an expression of their delight in each other's bodies and their growing urgency as their lovemaking became impassioned. Rita quickly lost her shyness and was as uninhibited in this new position as she'd been the night before underneath Jack. She reveled in her freedom and power, but ultimately had to depend on Jack to take over, to harness her wild movements with his hands on her hips, to soothe and urge her on with his voice when release became a desperate necessity. His words of love, filled with exhilaration and pain, touched off the need in her to express her own powerful feelings mixed with tenderness and gratitude.

"I love you, Rita!" he cried as he gave way to his climax.

"And I love you, too, Jack!" The words were out before she could stop them. Concern for having said them spoiled her peaceful aftermath, kept her from sinking into mindless oblivion as she'd done last night. She hoped he understood that it had been her passion speaking and didn't take her seriously. The last thing she wanted to do was be dishonest with Jack. She didn't want to raise false hopes and hurt him.

"Jack, that was unbelievable. It can't be like that time after time, can it?"

Jack took note of the quick recovery, heard the uneasiness and knew the reason, but his grasp of the situation couldn't kill his exultation. His answer came from the heart, not the head.

"I don't know, honey, but I hope to find out. Ask me again ten years from now." He felt tension flow into her body on top of him and opened his eyes to look into her face as she raised up.

"Jack, don't look at me like that!" Rita begged him, seeing his open, vulnerable expression. "Please. I got carried away. I didn't even know what I was saying."

Jack held her loosely around the waist, keeping her on top of him, where she could hardly avoid his gaze.

"Does that mean you don't love me at all? Not just a teensy little bit?"

Rita frowned at his lightheartedness.

"There you go again, making a laughing matter of something serious. I wonder why I even worry about you. I don't think you know the meaning of the word *love*."

"I'm not laughing. I'm just happy," he soothed, looking unchastened. "Being in love with you makes me happy. I just wished being in love with me would make you feel the same way. Come on. Be honest. Don't you love me a little? I have a lot of lovable traits, now don't I?"

Rita shook her head, smiling grudgingly. "You're hopeless. Absolutely hopeless."

"Well, if you won't tell me, I'll have to dig the information out of you. Will you at least answer my questions truthfully?"

"Jack, come on—" Rita tried to roll off of him, but he kept her where she was, using only as much force as was needed and no more.

"Just a few simple questions. Number one, do you find me physically attractive?"

"For heaven's sake! You know I do! Now this has gone far enough."

"You could make this a lot shorter, if you wanted. I'm willing to listen."

Rita sighed. "I'm getting a crick in my neck—"

"Oh, sorry, why didn't you say something?" Jack turned them with a lithe twist of his body and deposited her on her side beside him. "How's that? Better?" He dropped a tender kiss onto the tip of her nose and sighed. "I guess I'm just going to have to work a little harder to impress you."

Underneath his lightness, Rita could sense that he was hurt. She felt her resistance to him melt in her immediate sympathy.

"Jack, you know how much I like you. Okay, maybe it is *more* than 'like.' Maybe what I feel is love of a kind." She caressed his cheek and turned to warm mush inside when he nuzzled it against her hand. "You are definitely a lovable man and so much fun. Considerate too, and thoughtful. You do things other men wouldn't think of doing. I love being with you. You make me laugh." She smoothed her hand over a brown shoulder. "You already know I think you're a wonderful lover. I've told you that in more than words. Also—" She hesitated, grappling to express a thought that wasn't clear. "This sounds terribly egotistical, but you make me feel good about myself, and I like that, too." *Have I said enough?* she asked him anxiously with her concerned face, and Jack answered with a quick reassuring smile.

"Thank you, darling," he said simply. "Now I want to ask you something very important—no, it's not what you think," he added, reading the flash of panic on her face. "I realize it's a little soon for either of us to be making 'till death do us part' promises. This is the question. Consider it carefully, please. Would you be fighting just as hard against getting seriously involved with me, the way we both know you are doing, if I had a college degree and a profession? Say, medicine or law or engineering. And was established in a steady position? I want to know the truth, whether you think it will hurt or not. It'll be less painful in the long run for me to know exactly how I stand with you, don't you see?"

Rita shook her head ruefully. "I might as well answer you truthfully, Jack, because you'd get the answer out of me anyway, wouldn't you? You'd have made an incredible courtroom lawyer." She looked intrigued at the thought. "I can just see you addressing the jury."

"Right now I'm waiting for a one-woman verdict," he put in patiently.

Rita's face was slowly flooded with deep apology. "I'm sorry, Jack, but it would make a big difference," she said gently. "It's not right now that worries me. It's down the line a few years when things haven't worked out for you. I'm sorry but—" She broke off, staring at his slow, satisfied grin. "I don't understand you at all! Any other man would have hurt feelings, and you, why, you look *happy*!"

Jack gave her a loud smacking kiss on the lips, sat up and swung himself athletically over to the edge of the bed.

"I'm not any other man, sweetheart," he said cheerfully. "I'm a Princeton dropout—" He flashed her an abashed grin. "I've been waiting for just the right psychological moment to drop that on you."

"Jack! You didn't go to Princeton!"

"Did, too. If you want, I'll have them send you a transcript." His smile was roguish. "Or maybe a *partial* transcript. Wonder if they'd send selected grades?"

"Jack, did you really go to Princeton?"

He leaned back and gave her a gentle slap on her bare buttocks.

"I sure did, and I didn't flunk out, either. I quit. And I've never been sorry a day in my life until I met you and found out you like your men with university degrees. With a little foresight, I might have stuck it out for you, but it's too late now. Meanwhile, time's a wasting, woman, while you lie here in bed, naked as the day you were born. Do you think you can manage to get this bed made up while I go and get your clothes?"

He whistled happily while he dressed in his own discarded clothing under her bemused and baffled scrutiny. When he was dressed, he gave her a warm smile and an approving once-over before he left by way of the *lanai*, stopping to load up the breakfast dishes on the tray.

"I don't hear any sounds of movement in there!" he called over his shoulder before he bore the tray away. "If that bed's not made up to my standards, I'll be forced to beat you soundly when I get back.''

Rita had to smile at the notion of a brutal Jack. She kept smiling the whole time she made the bed, thinking of what a pleasure it was going to be to mess it up with him again.

Had he really gone to Princeton? No, of course not. He had only been putting her on, and consummate salesman that he was, he'd more than half convinced her he was telling the truth. What a man! What an impossible, utterly delightful man! How could any woman *not* adore him?

Chapter Eleven

Parked outside the front door was a small, powder-blue hatchback car. Rita eyed it in surprise. She'd assumed they would be using his mother's red station wagon again today.

"It's a lease car," Jack explained. "I'll be forced to squeeze in some business appointments the next few days, and I wouldn't want to leave you stranded. I usually prefer to lease a car instead of owning one. That way when it needs repairs, I just get another one in exchange."

"But when did you pick it up?"

He'd taken his mother to the airport and then come back to the house and made breakfast. The business offices would just have been opening their doors about the time he served breakfast on the *lanai*.

"I didn't. They delivered it. I called and made the arrangements yesterday afternoon. When I got back from the airport this morning, it was parked right where you see it. We'll take it today and try it out. If it doesn't suit you, we'll swap it out for another one,'' he added, seeing the skepticism on her face.

"I'm sure it's fine. I'm just a little surprised at the way people do business here. That's all. I can't imagine a car-leasing agency just dropping off a car on the basis of a telephone call and not getting some papers signed. Legally you must not even be responsible for the car.''

"Not just anybody could get the same service. The owner of the agency knows my mother, of course.''

Jack had opened the passenger door moments earlier and Rita got in quickly now, not wanting him to read her thoughts in her expression. She frankly didn't see how being the son of an eccentric woman who didn't pay her bills could get Jack business favors. If anything, she'd think just the opposite would be true.

"It's a cute little car,'' she told Jack brightly when he slid under the wheel. "And brand new.'' She sniffed. "You can always smell the new, can't you? I notice that almost all the cars are small here on Maui. Is it because the roads are narrow?''

With Jack's reply, the conversation veered away from the casual transaction behind the leasing of the car. He had been on the verge of divulging his mother's wealth, which was as well known locally as her personal eccentricities and her carelessness in her business affairs. But there would be other opportunities, he was sure.

They stopped at a general store in Paia and bought a picnic lunch. Leaving the small village behind them, Rita looked for The Fish House sign and felt like she was on familiar territory when she spotted it.

"Look! The surfers are out today!'' she exclaimed as the stretch of coast Jack had said was one of his favorite spots on the island came into view. He'd taken her there on Wednesday. They'd parked on the high bluff overlooking the rolling surf. He'd kissed her, for the second time, and made their eventual lovemaking a foregone conclusion.

Could that really be only two days ago? she marveled. How could she have come to know a man so well, so intimately, in that short a time? Or, more accurately, how could a man have come to know *her* so well? She felt as though Jack knew everything about her, not just the facts about her past but every nook and cranny of her soul, while she actually knew little about him. He was a mystery man. Part of her craved the details to fill in his personal portrait. Part of her was reluctant to know more. Before she could resolve the conflict, Jack spoke up.

"You're not nervous, are you?"

"Nervous? Why should I be nervous?" Rita countered quickly, meeting his quizzical gaze. "You mean because of the road? Should I be worried?"

"No, it's actually a safe enough road. You just have to take it slow and easy." He patted her hands, making her realize that they were linked tightly in her lap. "I've made the drive a number of times before, and I've got an excellent record as a driver, I might add. So, relax."

Rita did relax, relieved that he had made a wrong interpretation of her tension. She could hardly correct his error, tell him that deciding whether to ask him about himself had caused her anxiety because she was afraid of what she would learn, fearful that he would substantiate all her intuitions about him. Fortunately the opportunity was gone for now. All her attention was focused upon the present as the road began to ascend and wind its way along the mountainous coastline.

The ride was thrilling, the vistas breathtaking. The mountain vegetation was the most luxuriant plant growth Rita had ever seen. She lost count of the many lovely waterfalls. Several times Jack stopped the car when they would come to a natural grotto with crystal streams cascading down a sheer wall of rock into a pool below. At first he would pull over whenever possible in response to Rita's awed admiration of the spectacular scenery. They would get out and peer over precipices. Rita would take pictures, always managing to get Jack in the foreground.

But after a while it became obvious that at their current rate of progress they'd never reach Hana that same day, let alone make the return trip.

"Tell you what," Jack said as they were getting back into the car after one such stop. "Why don't we work out some signals. 'Oooh' can mean 'hey, that's nice, but keep going.' 'Aaah' will mean 'slow down and let's take a closer look.' And 'Jack, will you *look* at that!' is a definite 'pull over and stop.' Got it?"

"I don't know. Maybe we'd better run through it again. Now what was 'aaah' again?"

Practicing the code language led to so much laughter that Rita ended up with sides aching and tears in her eyes.

Since driving the road to Hana was a popular tourist attraction, they caught sight of other cars, sometimes far up the mountain or out on what looked like an impossibly treacherous ledge. Occasionally other drivers pulled up at the same spot where they'd stopped. Inevitably there were the honeymooners, easy to identify. One couple asked Jack if he'd mind taking their picture together.

"We're on our honeymoon," the young woman explained. "It would be nice to have some proof that we saw all these beautiful sights together." She smiled knowingly. "Would you like us to take your picture together, too?"

"I was just about to ask," Jack declared, throwing his arm around Rita's shoulder. "Wouldn't that be nice, sweetheart, to have a picture of the two of us here?"

Rita played right along, knowing that the pretense of also being honeymooners probably should be causing her some guilt. But it wasn't. It was just harmless good fun. She didn't know exactly when it had happened, but she no longer felt any loyalty to Mark as the absent bridegroom. He'd chosen not to come on his honeymoon with her, chosen not to marry her. He was past, sad history, and this was the here and now with Jack.

"Weren't they cute?" she mused when they were back in the car and driving again.

Jack glanced over quickly and confirmed that her expression, like her tone, wasn't sad.

"They're probably saying the same thing right this minute about us."

"Probably." She met his glance and smiled. "You'll never guess what I'm thinking."

"Will I like it?"

"You should. It should make your ego swell up like a balloon."

"Then tell me, by all means."

"I was thinking back there that of all the honeymoon couples I've seen here in Hawaii—and there've been quite a few—none of the guys measure up to you. You're every woman's idea of the perfect bridegroom. I was also thinking—"

"Yes, yes," Jack put in with humorous anxiety. "You were thinking. So far I'm crazy about your thoughts."

"This is halfway serious," she admonished. "I was thinking that this trip isn't the trip I'd planned to have with Mark, and—" Jack looked over in time to see the little face she made. "I feel a little guilty admitting this, but I never expected to have this much fun. Do you think that's awful of me to feel that way? Can you imagine a woman enjoying her honeymoon more because her bridegroom didn't come along?''

Jack assumed a mock horrified expression. "I am frankly quite shocked."

Rita punched him playfully in the arm. "Come on!"

"That's right. You said you were being halfway serious. Well, this is not halfway serious. It's serious through and through. This isn't the trip I planned to have either, but I'm having the best time of my life. And I'm glad as hell that Pendleton decided not to come along with you. Frankly, I haven't missed him."

His unspoken question, *What about you?* hung in the air between them. Cautiously Jack glanced over and intersected gazes with her. Her guilty expression spoke for itself. She hadn't missed him either—or at least not much. Jack didn't find it necessary to press her and make her speak the admission openly, but his rush of exultation made him wish there were some place to pull off the road. He wanted more than anything to take her into his arms and kiss her.

The picture-taking incident followed by the conversation established a new intimacy between them. For Rita, the admissions she'd made openly to Jack were a commitment of a kind, even if temporary. He was the companion she hadn't chosen for this trip to Hawaii but wouldn't exchange for any other for its duration—not even Mark, if he showed up within the next half hour.

Jack felt as though his unseen competition for her attention had been soundly beaten, at least for the time, and he was able to relax his inner guard against doing or saying any careless little thing that might trip off her memory and make her sad. He became even more openly possessive and attentive so that there was no doubt in the minds of anyone who saw them, even the occupants of cars who passed them when they'd pulled over and gotten out, that they were honeymooners. The key giveaway was that more often than not they were looking at each other, talking and laughing, and giving only token attention to the grand scenery.

Whatever they were doing, they were touching. If he wasn't caught in the act of kissing her, on the top of her head, her cheek or nose or lips, he had his arm around her or was holding her hand. When she was taking a picture, he was right there, patient, proud, vigilant, making sure that no careless step took her tumbling down a thickly grown ravine.

Rita felt coddled and adored. She got used to Jack telling her that he loved her and didn't bother to protest seriousness, concluding that he was just a loving, expressive man. Probably he told every girl he liked a lot the same thing, but it was definitely warm and nice to be the sole focus of his attention for now. Anything beyond "now" Rita didn't think about.

Hana turned out to be a quiet, pretty little hamlet incredibly oblivious to the stream of traffic driving through it. There was no shopping district at all, few identifiable places of business other than an inn and a combination gas station and grocery store. Just outside the village the highway deteriorated, and it was a slow, jolting ride to the Seven Pools, but they weren't the only ones by far willing to endure the discomfort. When they arrived, the grassy field designated as parking area was full of cars and vans.

Jack bypassed the parking area and took a rutted lane that led them to a huge open meadow where camping was permitted. The grass grew right to the edge of a high bluff overlooking the sea. Several dozen recreational vehicles and campers were spread wide apart for privacy, and there were other picnickers like themselves. Jack parked the car near the spot he pointed out as a good picnic place, and then they followed the marked trail to the pools.

Rita hadn't been expecting a sight quite so awesome. Years of water erosion had carved sheer rock walls on either side of a succession of large pools, each fed by a waterfall from the one up above, with the last pool feeding into the sea at a rocky mouth. Inland, forming a picturesque frame, was the small iron bridge they'd just driven across, and beyond that presumably more pools, since Rita wasn't able to count seven.

"This is really something," she marveled. "How did all those people get down there? It looks so steep and rocky on both sides."

"It is. There are several paths, but it's strictly a 'climb down at your own risk' situation. Somebody started the rumor that Hawaiian royalty bathed here. I don't know how much substance there is to it. The water's icy cold. As you can see, no one down there is actually swimming, just dipping in a foot or a hand."

"You've been down there yourself?"

"Sure. Want to try it?"

Rita pulled back, torn between her strong reticence and her wish not to appear lacking in the adventurous spirit. Making a perilous descent to do what a lot of other people were doing and then having to climb up again over wet, slick rocks frankly didn't appeal to her. "I don't think I do," she admitted apologetically. "I guess I'm a little on the cowardly side when it comes to risking broken arms and legs."

"Good. I was hoping you'd refuse. I'd rather eat lunch and lie in the sun anyway."

On the return walk to the car, Rita held Jack's hand in a firm, grateful clasp, thinking that what had just happened was a clear example of what she'd tried fumblingly to tell him that morning when she'd reeled off the reasons she liked him so much. She could be herself, not be adventurous, not be whatever didn't come natural to her, and he never made her feel that he was disappointed in her, that she hadn't measured up. Whatever she decided, he responded immediately with approval. Never had anyone made her feel so special, so perfect just the way she was.

"Thanks, Jack." She gave his hand a little squeeze and met his warm, questioning glance. "For being you. And letting me be me." She smiled at him, and he smiled back, but she could tell by the quizzical light in his eyes that he didn't follow her train of thought. "Back there, you could have made me feel like a ninny, and you didn't."

Jack nodded. "Because you didn't want to climb down to the pools." He shrugged as though to say it wasn't important. "Perhaps another time you might want to." His glance went admiringly over her white shorts and pale yellow blouse and dropped to her pretty sandals. "You're not exactly dressed for scaling wet cliffs today anyway. Those clothes are too nice and your shoes aren't safe. We can come back better prepared."

"But we probably won't," Rita pointed out reasonably. "There are too many other things we'll want to do. Too many other places to see in just a few days. I'll be catching a plane back to Atlanta Sunday week. Today's already Friday."

"I'm hoping to talk you into staying longer."

It was the first mention of her possibly lengthening her stay, and he made it so casually that she couldn't explain the sudden pounding of her heart and her own urgency in dispensing with the suggestion at once.

"I can't stay longer. I only have two weeks off from my job. I'll be expected back at the store—" Her last word ended on a surprised note as she took a longer stride and came up short. Jack had stopped in his tracks, still holding firmly to her hand. His face was full of his intention to kiss her as he drew her back to him and took her into his arms.

"Jack, someone will come along and see us!" she protested weakly as he lowered his head. He stopped a few inches above her parted lips, which were conveying a more encouraging message.

"Let them." His smile was tender and possessive. "They'll just think what everybody else does—that we're newlyweds on our honeymoon." His arms tightened as he closed the remaining distance between his lips and hers, kissing her with a lingering sweetness that filled Rita's whole insides with sharp yearning.

"Jack," she whispered when he ended the kiss as tenderly as it had begun. This time the protest in her voice was diffused and nameless, coming from deep inside her. It had nothing to do with the possibility of people walking by and seeing them. She didn't care if the whole world was looking on.

"Jack," she said again, in a stronger, more determined voice. "My life is in Atlanta. I have a good job there, my apartment, friends, everything. I can't throw all that away for extra vacation time."

"Of course you can't." He kissed her again, lightly this time, and released her. Linking her arm with his, he started them walking along the path again.

Overwhelmed with a sense of anticlimax, Rita had trouble summoning her coordination. Her feet dragged, and she stumbled over a big clump of weeds. Was that all he intended to say on the subject? If he couldn't put more effort into persuading her to extend her vacation time in Hawaii, why even mention it to begin with?

"You certainly give up easily." She watched him irritably as he tried without success to smother a grin.

"I haven't given up at all." He managed to turn the pleased grin into an inoffensive smile. "One important lesson I learned being a salesman—no, wait, hear me out," he pleaded, placing his free hand on her arm to keep her from jerking it free. "I was only going to say that the most important rule in sales is never to force a definite yes or no before the time is right. The bigger the sale, the more delicate the timing." His fingers caressed her tense forearm, coaxing the muscles to relax.

"Don't you see," he continued persuasively, "that the same rule applies in more important situations where two people are trying to come to agreement. It's human nature for us to say no when we're being pressed and don't feel ready to answer, and once we've said no, it's easier to stick by our answer, even if deep down we know it's the wrong one, than to change it."

"What you're saying doesn't apply," Rita said defiantly. She sensed that to agree with the simplest premise could undermine all resistance to him. "If I stayed, I'd be risking my livelihood and everything I've worked hard to earn just so the two of us can spend more time together playing. A week after I'm gone, if it takes that long, you'll have forgotten me. You'll have found another playmate." Her prediction made her glower at him accusingly. "It's selfish of you, Jack, to try to convince me to do something that wouldn't be in my best interest. Besides which, I resent being just some kind of selling challenge to you. We're talking about my life, my future. This isn't a game."

"No, it isn't a game," Jack agreed quietly. "And I was wrong to use the buying and selling frame of reference. I apologize. For now, why don't we just leave matters the way they are? You'll be leaving Sunday week, returning to Atlanta and your life there. I'll be staying here on Maui, starting a new business venture." He unlinked their arms and held her hand loosely instead. "Am I forgiven?"

"Yes, of course."

Never in her life had Rita experienced any less satisfaction in winning an argument. Looking up ahead, she saw that the path would shortly merge with the big meadow. In view was the little powder-blue car, looking small and familiar. The sight of it increased her emotional turmoil. She thought of Jack driving it around Maui after she was gone, alone or with some other woman. Both alternatives were unbearable. She called up the image of herself driving the congested city streets of Atlanta in her own little sporty car, on the way to work or heading home to her apartment. The vision provoked such intense loneliness that out of pure desperation she tried imagining Jack beside her in her car, walking with her through the door of her apartment, just to see if his presence was at all compatible with her real life. And, wonder of wonders, it was! The distance between Atlanta and Maui, between her world and his, could be breached, at least temporarily, at least from time to time!

With this realization Rita felt the heaviness weighing her down lift away, leaving her almost too light, almost too buoyant. Instinctively she held on tighter to Jack's hand as inspiration threatened to cancel out the earth's gravitational pull.

"You could visit me in Atlanta, you know!" Her smile was brilliant, her voice jubilant. "I have a paid vacation every year. I can come back to Hawaii and visit you. We can still see each other, Jack! It doesn't have to be over between us just because I go back to Atlanta and you stay here, does it?"

Rita thought her heart would burst with happiness when Jack's immediate and spontaneous boost of spirits seemed to match her own. His eyes lighted up with gladness and a smile broke across his face. "I love you, Rita Jones! Do you love me, too?" he shouted as he stopped and hugged her hard around the waist, lifting her off her feet and twirling her round and round until she thought they would go tumbling dizzily onto the grass.

But she didn't care. There was no sense of insecurity, no fear in his arms. "Yes! Yes! Yes! I love you, Jack!" she shouted back, hanging on for dear life and laughing along with him, high on love, high on life. Now that some workable compromise between separation and commitment had been worked out, it seemed all right to express her feelings.

"Will you visit me in Atlanta, Jack?" she pressed him eagerly when he had finally put her on her feet and they were walking across the grass to the car, her arm around his waist and his arm around her shoulders. "When do you think you could get away? Maybe Christmas? We could decorate my apartment together, put up a tree. I'm already looking forward to it. It will be more fun than any Christmas I've ever had before. Will you come, Jack?"

Looking the way she did, excited and wistful and eager, it wasn't in Jack's power to refuse her, but he couldn't make a promise that he didn't intend to keep, and the time wasn't right to divulge his own holiday picture, which coincided with hers except for one crucial difference, the location. Jack wanted to spend Christmas and every other holiday with her, but not in Atlanta.

"Spending Christmas together sounds like a definite winner to me," he declared cheerfully, giving her shoulders a little squeeze. "But right now I'm too hungry to think about anything but lunch. How about you? Hungry?" He glanced over and had to steel himself against the sight of her crestfallen features. Her puckish smile took him totally by surprise.

"I might as well warn you," she said. "I'm not giving up on the idea of Atlanta at Christmas. I'm just taking the advice of a certain expert salesman I know and not pushing the issue. I wouldn't want to pressure you into making the wrong answer.''

Jack threw back his head and laughed delightedly.

"You're too smart for me. From now on, I'm going to watch every word and not give you any more of my trade secrets.''

They ate near the edge of the high bluff, sitting cross-legged on an old bedspread Jack had brought along. Afterward they lay contentedly, side by side, basking in the sun, listening to the ocean as it crashed against the rocks below them. Rita dozed off and woke to find Jack sound asleep. Easing over on her stomach, she propped herself up on her elbows and watched him sleep, taking delight in the opportunity to study him close up at her leisure.

He was a handsome man. His bone structure was clean and angular. His features were regular, but too expressive ever to be boring, especially his mouth. His hair was golden and fine, soft to the touch. Her palms itched now with the urge to touch it, to touch his face. His eyelashes were light, golden-tipped on the ends. She watched them with mild surprise as they lifted, giving her a direct view into clear gray eyes that didn't contain any drowsiness and glinted with teasing humor.

"You big fraud, you!" she accused, drawing back. "You weren't asleep! You were just lying there, letting me admire you.''

He reached up lazily and capped the back of her head with his hand. "Was, too, asleep," he declared, pulling her face down to his. "I was having this beautiful dream about being a sleeping prince and being awakened by the kiss of a redheaded princess. Then I opened up my eyes, saw you, and knew that being awake was even better than dreaming. Come on, honey, kiss me before I turn into a frog or something. How did that story go anyway?''

"Who cares?" Rita murmured, giving in to the temptation he offered and others besides that she'd been resisting, thinking that he was asleep. Smoothing his hair back from his forehead to feel its silky texture, she put her mouth against his and savored the contact before she moved her head in little circles, easing his lips open. With the tip of her tongue she explored the soft moistness of his inner lips, top and bottom, and felt the hand on her head slip down to her neck and work its way underneath her hair.

Framing his face, she stroked his cheekbones with her fingertips while she plunged her tongue into his mouth and let it flirt seductively with his. With her elbow leaning on his chest, she was aware of the increased rate of his heartbeat and wasn't at all taken by surprise when he seized her head in both hands and kissed her hard, reversing the pursuit of tongues. Rita kissed him back, and the kiss became deep and hungry.

Jack groaned as he tore his lips away from hers, and hugged her hard, holding her against his chest. She could feel the thud of his heartbeat against her breast and knew that he was absorbing the beat of her heart, which was just as wild and rampant as his.

"Shame on you, woman," Jack growled. "Wake me up from a peaceful sleep and get me all hot and bothered."

"That's gratitude for you." Rita's voice was muffled against his shoulder. "I saved you from being turned into a frog, didn't I?"

"I'm not sure we ever got that story straight."

Jack turned on his side, rolling her over onto her back. He raised up on his elbow, looking down at her. The open passion on his face made Rita go weak with pleasure.

"I think I just remembered how it goes," she murmured. "A redheaded damsel finds a handsome man sleeping beside the sea. She kisses him and puts him completely under her spell so that he does whatever she tells him to do, especially around holidays.'' Rita tried without any success to keep from smiling in response to his ready grin.

"You persistent little witch," he accused tenderly. "Do anything to get your way, will you?"

"Anything."

Rita tightened her arms around his neck and smiled up at him.

"You will come to Atlanta for Christmas, won't you, Jack? Promise me?"

"No, I won't go to Atlanta for Christmas," he said with soft deliberation and watched her eyes widen in startled dismay. "I won't have to go to Atlanta to be with you, Rita. If things go according to my plan, you're going to be here with me."

"Oh." A little frown cut lines between her eyebrows as she considered the reversal in plans that she thought he was suggesting. "You want me to come here instead. I suppose I could. I just thought you might have more free time. I'll just have a couple of days off while you—" She looked thoughtful and then hesitant as she dealt with the new possibility that had just occurred. "If it's a matter of plane fare, Jack, I could help pay..."

"It's not a matter of plane fare, Rita," he contradicted firmly. "I can afford to fly to Atlanta. Despite the impression I've given you somehow, I am *not* down and out. It's not money I'm going to be short on, but time." He watched skepticism flicker across her face. "If Damon Phillips and I go into partnership—"

"Maybe I could manage to get more time off," Rita cut in quickly. "Christmas in Hawaii. That's kind of a strange thought. We don't always have snow for Christmas in Atlanta, but at least we usually have cold weather. Jack, I'm sorry," she added contritely as he sat up. "I really didn't mean to hurt your feelings by offering money—"

"You didn't hurt my feelings, Rita," Jack denied patiently. "Or at least not by offering to pay my plane fare." He looked over at her as she sat up next to him, her face puzzled and anxious. "What does hurt is that you don't believe in me at all. You don't take this building project with Damon Phillips seriously, do you? You think it's all some scheme in my mind."

Rita felt her guilty apology spread over her face. She opened her mouth to make a denial and then closed it. Biting her lip, she looked away.

"I'm sorry." Uncomfortable under his steady gaze, she glanced at him and then studied his face uncertainly, unable to read what he was thinking. He didn't look angry. He didn't actually look upset, but rather perplexed.

"Don't look so worried," he chided, stroking gentle fingertips along her cheek. "I still love you, in spite of the black and blue marks on my male ego."

Relief at his light tone spread across her face.

"I love you, too, Jack." She kissed him on the lips, looked anxiously into his face and then quickly kissed him again when he opened his mouth to speak.

"Is the trip back from Hana any faster?" she murmured coaxingly. "I certainly hope so."

Chapter Twelve

The return trip was faster without the frequent stops to take pictures and have a closer look at the scenery. Rita found the drive with the steep downward convoluted dips and curves just as exhilarating as it had been climbing.

"This reminds me of a roller coaster!" she cried out during one sequence of hairpin turns.

Glimpses off into deep valleys with perilous coastlines were just as awesome as before, but now there was the added pleasure of reminiscence. Rita identified the places where they had pulled over and stopped and pointed them out to Jack with a "remember when?" eagerness that made him smile.

"Look, there's where you took that couple's picture and they took ours," and "That's the place where I got so close to the edge and made you nervous. You grabbed me and pulled me back, remember?"

"Do I remember." Jack squeezed her hand, which was resting familiarly on his thigh. "You gave me heart failure."

When the highway had leveled and the road to Hana was behind them, Rita sighed wistfully.

"Someday I want to go there again."

"We'll go back, lots of times," Jack assured her warmly.

Rita didn't pursue the promise, but she reveled in his lover's tone, which said that he would do anything, give her anything in his power to make her happy. She reveled in his touch as he squeezed her hand again and thought ahead eagerly to the privacy awaiting them at his mother's house.

"I'm going to need my things," she mused reluctantly, caressing his thigh and feeling the muscles tighten under her palm. "I suppose we should go to the hotel now, shouldn't we?"

Jack positioned her hand more intimately on his groin and then stroked along her bare inner thigh.

"Why do you need more clothes? I can hop up early every morning and wash this outfit for you. I like it a lot. The shorts are nice and short to show off your pretty legs and there's plenty of room for this." He eased his fingers underneath the crotch and rubbed gently back and forth.

Rita's hand tightened on his groin in response to the rise of delicious sensations, and she could feel his hardness growing under her palm.

"If you really like the outfit that much, we'll wait until later to go to the hotel," she said softly. "But for now you'd better use both hands for driving, don't you think?"

Jack obediently took his hand from between her thighs and returned it to the wheel. He grinned over at her wickedly.

"You can use both hands, too, if you want to."

"That sounds like bragging to me!"

"You just bring out the best in me."

"Do I really?"

Her mixture of curiosity and wonder softened his grin into a tender smile.

"You do, really. But you also bring out the worst," he added with mock gravity.

"How unfortunate. Could you give me an example?"

"Certainly. The most recent example would be lunch today. I had wicked thoughts with every bite of my sandwich, wishing we were in a more private place so that I could satisfy my taste buds with you instead."

"You weren't really thinking that!" Rita sounded more intrigued than shocked. "While you were eating?"

"Yes, I was. The only way I got through the meal was to promise myself that when we got back home, I'd have you for dessert." He made a growling sound as he looked her over. "Now that we're almost there, I can hardly wait. It's going to be the sweet binge of my life."

"Sounds as though I've fallen into the clutches of a cannibal."

"And what about you? What did you have in mind for dessert?"

Rita shocked herself with the blatant provocation of her reply and then turned pink with embarrassment.

"Did I really say that? You're the one who brings out the worst in me!"

Jack stopped her hand before she could move it away from his groin. He held it hard against him.

"I love you at your worst, honey." He smiled over at her. "Hold on. We're almost there."

The sexual repartee turned out to have been përhaps too arousing. They ended up making love almost without preliminaries once they arrived at the house. It was only afterward, when their need had been satisfied and then awakened more gradually that they were able to perform all the promised intimacies.

Rita felt as though Jack carried out his stated intention of tasting every inch of her body. She had no secret place that he did not explore with his lips and his tongue, no private pleasure spot that he didn't call singing to life. He made her feel incredibly lush and beautiful and desirable. He spoke words of praise that were reverent and yet lustily male. Rita glowed under his minute inspection, bloomed into unreserved womanhood under his kisses and his touch and opened up to him, relinquishing what modesty and physical privacy remained.

When she'd succumbed to the spasms of the most intense, selfish pleasure and was left quivering and spent, her first thought was that she wanted to do for him what he had done for her. She wanted to know his body as intimately as he knew hers now. She wanted to make him feel simultaneously weak and powerful, languid and highly stimulated.

The desire to please him was foremost at first, but the sounds of his indrawn breath made her heart beat faster, his murmured words struck a chord of pleasure, and the passionate reactions of his body stirred her until at some point his enjoyment became hers. She lost her self-consciousness, became surer, bolder, more experimental and heightened her own stimulation as she raised the level of his. Her physical excitement grew along with his own. There was no repugnance, no thought of stopping until nature exploded his pleasure and granted him a solitary release.

But Jack wanted to share it with her.

"Come up here to me," he said, stopping her and drawing her up. "I want to make love to you again."

Until then Rita hadn't consciously realized how hotly aroused she was, how achingly ready for his lovemaking. Her breasts were as heavy and yearning as though he had been kissing and caressing them. Her thighs were eager to part and the folds of her womanhood moist and urgent to receive him.

The journey to climax was faster than it had ever been before for them, and the speed made it all the more exhilarating. The ascent was wild and out of control and once they'd plunged off the precipice of sensation, they defied gravity for a joyous second or two of the upward flight, disintegrated and then reassembled themselves from the pieces on the peaceful trip down.

"Jack, making love with you just *can't* get better and better, like this," Rita marveled afterward, when body and mind were together again. "Each time we've made love, I've told myself I couldn't take anything more."

"Sounds as though you don't know your own capacity," Jack mused lazily. He eased away from her and idly fondled her breasts, speaking his appreciation for their shape and fullness and satiny skin texture.

"Jack, not again?" Rita said unbelievingly as she felt a slight stirring of his body.

"No, I don't think so. I'm just being a glutton. I'm like a kid in a candy store. Stuffed but still greedy. Do you mind?" He bent his head to her chest and proceeded to feast at leisure.

Rita didn't mind. She enjoyed the warmth of his mouth, the rasping roughness of his tongue, just as she enjoyed the sensitive genius of his hands. But the mild pleasure wasn't lasting. It sharpened, became more intense, and turned into desire.

"This wasn't what I intended," Jack insisted as they made love again. "Don't expect anything more of me tonight," he warned as they hauled themselves off the bed and headed languidly for the shower, where the task of soaping her from head to toe managed to arouse him again.

"That's a false alarm. It'll go away," he told her in answer to her incredulous inspection. "Here. Let's get you rinsed off."

Rita stood obediently under the warm stream of water, her head tilted back and her eyes closed, letting it course over her hair and down her clean, tingling body. A shower had never been such total, sensory pleasure before, and part of the reason was the way he touched her and looked at her as though her body belonged to him, as though it was his own revered handiwork, which in fact it was. She'd never been a perfect female creation until he'd formed her with his unqualified approval.

"God, you're beautiful," Jack told her. "Even soaking wet."

Rita smiled as she reached up to turn the shower head and divert the spray. Then she opened her eyes, still smiling, and reached for the bar of soap.

"Your turn," she said with soft meaning, meeting his gaze. "Or my turn, rather. I think I'm going to enjoy this more than you." Her eyes moved over him as she wet the soap bar and turned it in her hands, working up a lather.

"I doubt that."

"You should be a male model," she told him teasingly as she turned him around for her and began lathering his back and shoulders. "You could model underwear or swimsuits. Or, better yet, do sexy after-shave or shampoo commercials. You've seen the kind I mean. The guy's just stepped out of the shower and is wearing nothing but a towel."

"I know the ones you mean. Usually it's a husband and wife routine, isn't it? He throws her the tube of shampoo or vice versa. Wouldn't work for me."

"No, it wouldn't. You're not the husband type. You're the kind a woman fantasizes about as her lover."

"That wasn't exactly what I meant." Rita's hands faltered at his even tone of voice and then worked more briskly. "I just meant I have the wrong color hair. Blond hair like mine looks terrible wet."

"Now that you mention it, the guys in those shampoo commercials are usually dark-haired," Rita declared too brightly. "The underwear and swimsuit ads are still a sure bet, though."

In the silence she worked her way down to his hard-muscled buttocks and massaged them with a soapy hand, knowing that more was to come.

"Why don't you see me as the husband type, Rita? You never have, have you? Not right from the first, before you knew anything about me. How can a woman just look at a guy and tell whether he has qualities that would make a good husband?"

"For heaven's sake, Jack, I was only teasing you just now! Most men would be flattered. Who's to say that one of these days you won't settle down and make some woman a good husband, but you're not the dull, dependable, *routine* kind of guy. That's all I meant." She finished giving the backs of his thighs and calves brisk, cursory attention and straightened up behind him.

"There. I've finished back here. Turn around and I'll do your front—or if you'd rather, you can do it yourself."

Her tone more than the words themselves issued the ultimatum. Either he could stop making an issue of her innocent comments and go back to their enjoyable give and take, or else he would find himself alone in the shower.

Rita was tense and irritable, waiting for him to turn around. He was much more skilled in argument than she was, better with words, faster thinking, capable of turning on the charm and melting her, but she intended to stand her ground.

"I'll finish up," Jack said with a kind of uncompromising pleasantness, sticking his hand back behind him for the soap.

Rita blinked, staring at the hand. Of all the possible reactions, this one was totally unexpected. It hadn't occurred to her that he wouldn't eventually back down.

"Didn't you like the way I was doing it?" Hurt was mixed with defiance. She braced herself, hands on hips, as he finally turned around.

"I loved the way you were doing it." He glanced down with her at the unmistakable physical evidence that she had pleased him, but when he looked back at her face, he was still inflexibly calm. He made an authoritative motion toward the soap in her hand on her right hip and kept his hand extended when she drew back in refusal.

"I love everything you do to me, Rita," he said in the same reasoned voice. "But I want more out of you than sex, and I want you to have more of me than my body. I don't want to be just your playmate and lover, but you refuse to see me as anything else. When I try to get to the bottom of your impressions of me, which I think are wrong, you put up a fight. You resist every effort I make to talk seriously about you and me. You don't seem to want to know who and what I really am." He repeated the imperious movement of his extended hand. "Give me the soap. You can get dried off while I finish showering."

"Have it your way," she said resentfully, placing the bar of soap in his hand.

"It's not my way."

"Well, it certainly isn't mine."

He didn't answer her argumentative reply. She watched him uncertainly, not knowing what to say or do, as he held the bar of soap under the water and worked it in his hands, not looking at her. The change in him struck a faint chord of remembrance. He'd shown her a glimpse of this resolute quality on the plane, when he'd been ready to demand his seat. But the insight had been fleeting, and she'd forgotten it. She'd become accustomed to his accommodating attitude toward her.

Now as he set about lathering his chest and arms and then his stomach, the possibility that he'd suddenly smile at her in the familiar way and restore the warm camaraderie died. Rita was pierced with a sharp rejection as he turned away from her, facing the spray, and then stayed with his back to her, washing the front of his body. She felt ridiculously like crying and vented her disappointment and hurt in a silent protest. *Why did you have to spoil things, Jack! Why? Why? Why? Everything was perfect. We were having such fun!*

The desire to cry was stronger than before when her appeal seemed to bounce off his smooth wet back. He was impervious, distant, and she was unbearably alone just a few inches behind him, empty, miserable. She was Cinderella at midnight, defrocked, robbed of her beauty, no longer a perfect female creation, just a disappointed naked woman. There seemed no alternative other than to do as he'd suggested, get out and dry herself off. He didn't speak, didn't seem to notice as she opened the shower door and then closed it behind her.

Rita was stationed in front of the vanity mirror, wrapped securely in her towel, when Jack finally turned off the shower. Nervously she began combing her hair again to have something to do while she waited apprehensively for him to step out. He would look at her and his expression would give her some clue as to what came next.

But he didn't even glance her way. He took one of the oversized bath towels from the big chrome bar and started toweling himself off, as though he were all alone in the bathroom. Her suspense was more than she could tolerate.

"So what happens now? Is the honeymoon over?"

He looked over then, but Rita cowardly fixed her gaze on her own reflection. With the first word of his reply, her eyes went flying to him, but he was busy toweling off again.

"As far as I'm concerned, it'll never be over," Jack replied evenly. "That's the whole problem, isn't it? That's where we differ." His voice became slightly muffled as he draped the towel over his head to blot his wet hair. "We can either go out to dinner somewhere or stay here and fix something to eat. If you want to go somewhere fancy, we can go to your hotel first. You'll want to pick up some more of your things anyway."

Rita started combing her hair again as he wrapped his towel around his waist and secured it. Her heart pounded as he came up behind her and took the comb out of her hand. She watched him as he neatly combed his wet hair and then dropped the comb down on the counter.

"See what I mean about wet blond hair," he said, meeting her eyes in the mirror.

His quiet disappointment hurt her. Protest as strong as what she'd felt in the shower welled up in Rita again, but now part of it was on Jack's behalf. For him as well as herself, she wanted to cry out, *Why? Why? Why?* Why couldn't two people as strongly attracted to each other as herself and Jack be perfectly suited to fill each other's needs and qualifications? She hadn't wanted to hurt him, hadn't even meant to love him.

"Jack, I'm sorry. Honestly, I never meant to hurt your feelings."

"It's okay."

He bolstered the reassurance with a smile that was purely for her benefit and slipped his arms around her waist, hugging her lightly against him.

"I guess I'm just an impatient type," he said reflectively, addressing himself as much as her. "Once I make up my mind, there's no doubt, just the matter of figuring out the way to get what I want." He sighed and leaned his cheek against her head. "I have to keep reminding myself that you and I are coming from such different places."

Rita swallowed to ease the sharp ache in her throat. She would give anything to undo the damage that had been done. In place of the casual, teasing intimacy was something more poignant and intense, something that frightened her with its seriousness. The warm humor had died from Jack's eyes, and the world seemed a much bleaker place for its loss.

"I guess we've had our first lover's quarrel," she said with a wan attempt at lightness. "You have no idea how upset I was just now to have you mad at me. I was afraid I might be on my own for the rest of my time here in Hawaii. I thought you might take me back to my hotel and leave me there."

Jack's arms tightened and Rita unconsciously held her breath, watching him in the mirror as he bent his head to kiss her bare shoulder.

"You didn't really think that. You know you have me wrapped around your little finger." The warm indulgence in his tone was like a familiar caress after a long period of separation. Rita shivered with the heat of his breath on her skin and tilted her head sideways for him, opening access to the curve of her neck. "You know I want you here with me. You know I'm crazy about you, no matter what."

"And I want to be here with you, Jack. I'm crazy about you, too," she whispered as he slid his mouth along her shoulder, stopping to press little kisses into her responsive flesh. "*Please*," she said feelingly, closing her eyes tight, "let's not *ever* do that again. It was so *awful*, Jack, feeling that wall between us." She smiled as she opened her eyes and waited anxiously for him to raise his head and meet her gaze in the mirror. "People have been mistaking us for newlyweds. I guess it was only to be expected that we'd have a spat, sooner or later. Making up *is* nice, though, isn't it?"

She turned in his arms, linking her hands up behind his neck and pulling herself very close to him.

"Jack?" Her voice and face were startled and then pleased. Holding his gaze, she deliberately moved her hips back and forth against his. "You said it would go away."

His smile was tender and, miracle of miracles, genuinely amused. Rita exulted in the light of humor that was rekindled in his eyes.

"Well, I was wrong. It didn't, not entirely, anyway."

"Not even when you were mad at me?"

His answer was punctuated with sweet clinging kisses on her lips. "I was never mad. Offended is more the word. And hurt. Frustrated." He stopped talking to kiss her lingeringly.

"Jack." Rita drew back a little to look into his eyes, her face softly urgent like her voice. Being back in his arms like this, being reconciled with him, had restored the world to order, but she wanted to ensure against having it fall apart again. "You said just now that you and I were 'coming from different places.' Well, maybe we are. Maybe that's the answer. For my part, I feel like I've come from a nightmare into a dream, and I don't want anything to spoil it. I don't want to wake up a second sooner than I absolutely have to. Everything that's happening to me right now is so wonderful and so perfect, so not quite real that I can't bear for anything to spoil it." Rita swallowed to alleviate some of her intensity.

"I'm having the vacation of a lifetime in a place too beautiful to be true." She smiled a warm, intimate smile. "I've met the man who is my perfect lover. I've fallen madly and romantically in love with him." The smile faded. "Please, Jack, is it wrong for me to want to enjoy all this to the hilt? To want to laugh and make love and be happy—with you? To want to float along and drift and fly. None of this was supposed to happen. I should be having a miserable time, a woman all alone on her honeymoon. But I don't want to question or analyze any of it. I don't want to think about the next hour or the next day or anything but *now*. I've never been foolishly happy like this before. Please *let me*."

Jack hugged her tight. Rita buried her face in his shoulder, spent with her effort of convincing him. She'd put everything into her plea. The knowledge that he was granting her what she begged of him made happiness gradually well up inside her, expanding her like helium filling a balloon. When his embrace slackened, the sight of his face was the needed touch to make her world perfect. His faint rueful smile said that his capitulation wasn't grudging. The Jack she adored was back, and he was about to say something that would delight her.

"What?" she prompted him eagerly.

He shook his head resignedly. "And I thought I had taken that little battle of wills in the shower. Here it turns out not even to have been a draw." He bumped his nose against hers. "You fight dirty, sweetheart. Telling a man what a great lover he is when he's wearing nothing but a towel."

"Not for long he isn't!" Rita warned gaily and without any resistance from Jack removed his towel. Her smile at him was radiantly happy. "Oh, Jack, I do love you when you're like this!"

"Only like 'this'?" Jack faked chagrin as he held her away from him and they both looked down. "That doesn't mean I have to stay this way?"

"You know what I mean! I love you when you're fun and make me laugh." Her smile wavered as she watched him reflect upon her unthinking words. "Jack, please! Don't take every single thing I say to heart! That's what I was just asking you not to do! Now, about dinner," she said, quickly changing the subject. "Why don't we just fix up something here instead of going out?" With deliberation she loosened her towel, unwound it slowly and dropped it aside.

Meeting his eyes, she blushed with the knowledge that she was completely transparent to him. But her awkwardness was fleeting, eased by his warmth, his total acceptance. He told her with his expression, with his faint smile, that he saw right through her, and he loved what he saw.

"It's all your fault," she accused softly. "You've turned me into a shameless woman."

"In that case, I'll just have to assume full blame," he said, taking her into his arms.

Instead of preparing a meal, they went out for hamburgers and French fries, brought the food back to the house to eat and afterward went for a leisurely moonlight walk on the beach. Rita was utterly content. She felt as though she could stroll along the sand forever with her arm around his waist and his wrapped warmly around her shoulders. They talked about the moonlight on the water, tried to define the alluring scent of the breeze, reminisced about the day behind them, talked of the next day's plans.

Once they'd decided to arise in the predawn hours and drive up to Haleakala Crater to see the sun rise, an experience Jack insisted she couldn't miss, it was sensible to retire early. Rita fell asleep with little delay, snug in Jack's arms. Some time later she roused up and discovered herself alone in the bed. A light was on in the room, over at the desk, and Jack was sitting there reading.

"What's wrong? Can't you sleep?" she inquired drowsily.

"I've already slept." He smiled at her over his shoulder. "Better catch your last thirty minutes. I'm going to be getting you up."

He didn't require more than three or four hours' sleep at a stretch, he explained the next day when she questioned him on the drive back from Haleakala. Going up, she'd dozed most of the way.

"I'm kind of a workaholic," he admitted, "especially when I'm starting something new. When I'm not actually gathering information, talking to people or doing something related to business, I'm still working out details in my mind. I even do a lot of subconscious problem-solving. I can go to bed thinking about something that has to be resolved and know the instant I wake up what the answer is."

He looked over at her expectantly and found her looking out of the window. They'd left the higher altitude and black volcanic rock of Haleakala behind them. On either side of the car now was green pastureland dotted incongruously with cactus plants.

"I didn't notice all those cacti on the way up," Rita commented. "It was too dark. They don't look as though they belong, do they?"

"You wouldn't have noticed if it had been light," he chided. "You were sound asleep most of the way."

"I was asleep because it was dark," she countered. "If it had been light, I'd have been awake and I'd have noticed."

There was no further mention of Jack's sleeplessness the night before, of his claimed compulsion for work, no interest expressed in what he had been reading in the early hours while she slept. When he divulged that he had a meeting with Damon Phillips that afternoon at the site of the property Phillips was interested in buying for his housing development, Rita quickly declined Jack's invitation to come along and meet his prospective partner. Instead she would take the opportunity to go to the hotel and get her things. Jack was disappointed, but he didn't try to change her mind.

That evening she subtly resisted any efforts on Jack's part to discuss his meeting. And when she woke up again that night and discovered him engrossed in paperwork at his desk, she said nothing then or the next day.

Jack had to contain his frustration at her lack of interest in his business life. He wanted to tell her about his personal impressions of Phillips, share his growing sense of certainty that the construction venture looked very good, mention some of the facts and figures he was gleaning from his reading and get her reactions. His view of his future included the general certainty that she was going to be an integral part of it. He wanted badly to deal with the specifics.

She gave every indication of loving him, or of loving the partial man she allowed him to be in her presence. The attentive, passionate lover. The clever, fun-loving companion. The knowledgeable guide and teacher. They went sightseeing, sunbathed and snorkeled, ate out or prepared meals together at the beach house, laughed and carried on conversations that were whimsical, teasing, or thoughtful in a general, philosophical vein. It bothered Jack now and again that Rita didn't question him about his background. Her lack of curiosity didn't give him any natural openings to tell her about himself, and then suddenly there was less time than he had realized.

On Wednesday morning, his sister Beth called. Jack and Rita had just breakfasted out on the *lanai* off the living room and were stacking the dishes in the dishwasher. He answered the phone, and his voice warmed with affection immediately upon learning the identity of the caller.

"Hi, Brat, how are you? It's my sister Beth," he told Rita, without bothering to cover the mouthpiece, and then included her in the telephone conversation with his smile as he continued it. "Who am I talking to? I can see you're as nosy as ever. Of course, it's not our mother. Right, she knows you're my sister. No, mother isn't here. She's gone over to Kauai for a few days. Yes, mother and I are both aware that tomorrow's Thanksgiving, but you couldn't make it this year and I plan to be around indefinitely—"

Rita could surmise that Beth had broken in and was talking at some length. Jack's face registered surprise, chagrin, and then resignation. She listened anxiously for his next words to give her a clue and understood his succession of emotions all too well. Jack's sister was flying to Maui from California, that very afternoon! She wanted Jack to pick her up at the airport and arrange for his mother's early return to Maui, too, so that they could all three spend Thanksgiving together, as was their family custom. Rita's time alone with Jack was almost over. She had just a few hours with him now, and his attention would be claimed by his family. The realization made her so sick at heart that she tuned out on the end of the conversation.

"It's not as bad as all that," Jack soothed as he hung up the phone and held out his arms for her to come to him. Rita came unhesitatingly, and the warmth and strength of his embrace only made her feel worse, as did his cheerful acceptance of the disruption of their time together. "You'll like my sister," Jack promised. "And she's dying of curiosity to meet you."

"Oh, Jack, I'm sure your sister is nice, but why couldn't she have waited another week to visit!" Rita hugged him tight around his waist and pressed her face into his shoulder, muffling her words but not her despair. "Now I'll have to go back to the hotel! We won't be able to spend the rest of the time together. And I'm leaving *Sunday*!"

Jack squeezed her tight. "No, you don't have to go back to the hotel. I've already thought of what to do. I'll give Beth and the kids the guest house—"

"The kids!" Rita pulled back to look at him, her face tragic. "I'll definitely have to go to the hotel. It would be bad enough to stay here with you and your mother and sister. But not with children!"

"Hear me out," Jack said patiently. "There are three bedrooms in the main part of the house. You and I can have separate rooms, as far as everybody else is concerned. Beth and the kids can sleep in the guest house. Joanie can sleep with her mother and we can set up a cot for Jimmy or give him a sleeping bag. There's no problem." Jack squeezed her tight again and kissed her on the lips. "Please. I want you here with me."

"Jack, I'm so *disappointed*. I know it's selfish of me, but I can't help it. I thought we had all these days left together, and now we've just got *hours* . . ."

Jack glanced at the wall clock. "Seven plus a few minutes, to be exact," he mused. "Any suggestions of what to do with them?" His tone and expression were full of broad hints.

Rita smiled reluctantly. "Before your sister arrives, we'll need to move our things into the other bedrooms and change the sheets on your bed."

"Maybe we'd better get started on all that. It could take fifteen or twenty minutes, and then it could take longer." He kissed the corner of her mouth and then nuzzled his lips against hers. "We might run into delays."

"Might," Rita murmured, teasing the inside of his upper lip with the tip of her tongue.

By noon they'd managed the transfer of her things and his to bedrooms in the main house and had the guest house tidied for its new occupants. Then they went for a swim and ate lunch out on the beach.

"Shouldn't we be going out and buying a turkey?" Rita asked. "They're usually frozen and they take hours and hours to thaw. Or don't you and your mother and sister have a traditional Thanksgiving dinner?"

"With my mother you don't have a traditional anything, no matter how hard she tries," Jack replied wryly. He grinned. "You can't imagine what a disaster she can make of cooking your ordinary turkey. It always seemed so dull and unimaginative to her to stuff one with the usual stuffings. Beth and I managed to convince her when we were very young that we hated turkey. And baked ham," he added, shaking his head at a private reminiscence.

"Well, what did you eat at holidays? And what did you do?"

He entertained her with one anecdote after another, including a hilarious story of the Christmas that his mother had invited a large group to dinner and had had the whole affair catered. She was living in San Francisco at the time. The main dish was a suckling pig, a source of offense to his mother's current man friend, who was Jewish. The two of them had argued violently and proceeded to throw the pig back and forth at each other, dismembering it and making a terrible mess of the premises.

Rita laughed along with him, enjoying his mirth as well as the amusing story itself, and kept her thoughts to herself. She wondered how on earth his mother had been able to afford the extravagance of a catered holiday meal. Or had that been another unpaid bill? Coming from a background like that, no wonder Jack was a dreamer. No wonder he seemed perfectly tranquil and unworried about the future when he didn't even have a job.

She had to admire him in a way. He had adjusted to his less-than-ideal environment far more successfully than she had done. As far as she could detect, there were no feelings of inferiority, no backlash against embarrassment, no indication even that he'd ever reacted to circumstances such as he'd mentioned with embarrassment or humiliation.

What sort of person was his father? she wondered. It was odd that Jack had had so little to say about him other than the fact that he and Beth had lived with their father and stepmother. Odd, too, now that she thought about it, that Jack didn't make casual references to relatives, as most people, unlike Rita herself, tended to do. Mark had mentioned his family often. She'd known what to expect of his father and mother and sisters before she'd ever met them, been intimidated and on her guard wanting to impress them.

There was no such pressure now as she was about to meet Jack's sister, no feeling of being up for approval. The difference between the two situations was obvious. Jack's family and Mark's were on different social and financial levels. Rita didn't have to feel so defensive with Jack's family about her low-class background. Jack himself hadn't blinked an eyelash at the mention of her mother's working in bars, and Mark had been appalled.

She supposed it was unfair to judge Mark. He was a product of his background as were she and Jack. Who was to say that Jack's opinion of her might not have been entirely different if Jack's father were someone successful and highly respected, like Mark's, if Jack's mother had been the pillar of the church and community instead of an irresponsible nonconformist type.

Rita rode beside Jack to the airport secure in the confidence that whether his sister liked her or detested her on sight, he would love her just the same. He would think she was beautiful and good, inside and out, and she'd feel both beautiful and worthy in his sight. Therein lay the key to the difference between her relationship with Jack and her relationship with Mark. Jack required no outside person's approval and Mark did. She'd sensed during the entire two years of her engagement to Mark that her position as his wife-to-be always rested on the foundation of his family's acceptance. In his own way Mark had loved her, but his love had been qualified.

Jack's love was unqualified. It wasn't predicated on anything. How unutterably sad that it wasn't sufficient. Love was never a cure-all for the problems in life. The fact that Jack loved her deeply and she loved him in return didn't change the realities of their situation. Jack had failed to educate himself in a profession. He had limited prospects for earning a living, not because he wasn't bright but because he was a dreamer with unrealistic ambitions. Eventually failure would break him, turn him into a bitter, disillusioned man. He'd move from one place to another, looking for the next sure winner, never satisfied, never finding what he sought. In the end all that mental brilliance and energy would be wasted.

Rita's intelligence reasserted the truth she'd known right from the start. Jack was the wrong man for her. He could make her pulse race with a glance or a brush of his fingertips. He could make her laugh, make her heart swell with joy, make her mindless with passion, but all that wasn't enough. She couldn't join her life to his, her future to his, and expect to be happy for long. She wanted a stable home with children, financial security, a standing in the community, none of which she would have with Jack, through no deliberate failing on his part. He was what he was, a handsome, wonderful man, a dreamer. She'd fallen in love unwisely. Now she was faced with two unhappy alternatives: unhappy with Jack. Unhappy without him.

Her mind told her that the second choice would be less painful over the long haul. Her heart sidestepped the whole issue. *Later. Decide later. For now, just love him. Let him love you.*

Chapter Thirteen

You're being very quiet." Jack smiled over at her questioningly. "I think you're going to like Beth, and I know she'll like you. Get ready for the third degree, though. She thinks it's high time I settled down and got married. So do I, for that matter," he added, picking up Rita's hand and bringing it to his lips.

"I'm sure your sister and I will get along fine. How on earth did she manage to get plane tickets at the last minute? Isn't this one of the busiest flying times the whole year?"

"Trying to change the subject before I work around to a marriage proposal?" Jack nipped her knuckles gently between his teeth. "To answer your question, she isn't flying a commercial airline. The plane she's coming in on is a company jet."

"That's a nice benefit. Does she work for the company herself or does her husband?"

"Her husband owns the company. Chuck's one of those computer software wizards you read about who started designing programs in their basements at age sixteen. In fact, he was mentioned in a feature *Time* magazine did a few months ago following up on computer software whiz kids of the seventies."

"I read that article." Rita's voice was faintly disbelieving. All the young men featured in the write-up were multimillionaires. Jack showed no signs of being impressed at his brother-in-law's fabulous success.

Rita wasn't quite so casual now about meeting Beth, but at first sight she liked her. Beth was a petite, vivacious version of Jack, with short blond hair, a golden California tan, and gray eyes like his, sparkling with life. After greeting Jack with exuberant affection, she turned to Rita and looked her over with open admiration.

"Gosh, you're gorgeous!" she exclaimed. "Where did this lucky brother of mine find you? You two might as well tell me everything, because I'll get it out of you!" she warned gaily.

"She probably will, too," said Jack wryly, standing with a golden-haired child hoisted on each hip. He was looking on with a thoroughly pleased expression. "Meet my favorite niece and nephew," he told Rita, exciting giggles and childish corrections that he had only one niece and one nephew. "That doesn't make you any less favorite," he teased. "Joanie here is five, and Billy is four. Kids, this is Rita. You can call her Aunt Rita," he added blandly, a wicked twinkle in his eyes. "Your Uncle Jack is planning to marry Rita soon."

"Jack!" Rita's shocked reproof blended with Beth's excited "Aha!"

"You should always tell children the truth," Rita rebuked.

"Well, in that case, I should change 'planning' to 'hoping,'" Jack added softly, his eyes making a personal contact with Rita's. He switched his attention to Beth, who was looking on with undisguised interest. "Okay, Miss Nosy. Don't wet your pants. Rita's here on vacation from Atlanta. We met on the plane coming out, and she's going back Sunday, which doesn't give me much chance to talk her into staying. Now you can see why I wasn't any more enthusiastic on the phone this morning when you called to say you and the kids were coming."

Brother and sister smiled at each other in quick, unspoken communication. Jack had been giving more than an explanation. He was apologizing for his lack of welcome, and Beth had accepted his apology. Standing by, Rita felt privileged to be witness to their sibling closeness, but it struck a disturbing chord of memory. She saw herself opening the door of her apartment and her sister Edna standing outside. There had been no warmth, no welcome, no understanding on Rita's part. Now she felt not only guilt and shame, but regret for what she had closed out of her life when she cut off all connections with her sisters.

"You've embarrassed Rita!" Beth exclaimed. "Come on, let's get these kids to mother's house. They're dying to get out on the beach. A swimming pool in their back yard and you'd think they never got to play in the water."

On the way to the parking lot, five-year-old Joanie pointed out the advantages of the ocean over a swimming pool and the pleasures of a sand beach compared to a backyard. After that, conversation took the natural and expected course, with Jack asking the children questions about themselves and then Beth about her husband and herself. Beth took care to include Rita, providing bits of background explanation as they were needed and casually sketching in an affluent, country club life-style. Rita listened carefully for a note of self-conscious pride or apology, but there was none. Nor was there any subtle congratulation or good-natured envy on Jack's part. Apparently brother and sister were both comfortable with her material good fortune and his lack of it.

"So tell me about you, big brother," Beth demanded of Jack. "What's this about moving to Maui? When I told Chuck, he said, 'You can bet your brother's on to something surefire. He came equipped with your old man's built-in business radar.' Daddy's ready to admit he was wrong, Jack," she added fervently. "The two of you need to get together one of these days and make up. But tell me about your latest money-making scheme. My brother's quite the self-made entrepreneur, as you already know," she added smilingly to Rita.

She sounded teasingly admiring, not derogatory. Rita listened with a new attentiveness to Jack's brief explanation of the housing construction venture that he'd already described to her. Somehow Beth's rapt interest gave it a credibility it hadn't had for Rita before, but then when Jack had finished, Beth was oddly hesitant, causing Rita to be doubtful all over again. Had Beth only been humoring Jack by seeming to take him seriously?

"Jack, you're going to need backers. Why not—"

"Forget it, Beth. I'm not about to ask Father for money."

"You wouldn't be asking him for *his* money!"

"No."

Beth made a frustrated sound. "You're so stubborn! The both of you! And so much alike! Rita, maybe you can be a peacemaker. If this bullheaded brother of mine does talk you into marrying him, do the family a big favor and insist on having a big wedding, with all the frills." She hesitated, seeing Jack's swift concerned look at Rita and his evident relief at what he saw in her face. "Have I said something wrong?" she asked uncertainly.

"I'd appreciate it if you'd let me air the family feuds, Beth," he said quietly. "I haven't gotten around to telling Rita about the Adams clan or the Kelseys."

The ominous warning in his tone deepened Rita's mystification. Apparently there was bad feeling between Jack and his father, which explained why Jack hadn't talked about him. But why had Beth urged Jack to ask his father for money that wasn't *his*? Had his father stolen or embezzled a large sum of money? Perhaps he'd even been in prison. Rita's curiosity was matched by her dread at learning the truth. Her empathy with Jack was strong, based on just the intuitive knowledge that his background had been a serious strike against him in some way, just as her own had been.

The conversation for the remainder of the drive was light but a little forced. Rita sensed Jack's thoughtfulness. With their arrival at the house, the constraint eased in the hubbub of carrying in luggage and contending with the children's excitement. Disclaiming any hunger, they begged to get changed into swimsuits immediately and go out on the beach. Rita's offer to keep an eye on them while Beth unpacked was firmly refused, by Jack.

"Beth can unpack later. I need you to help me in the kitchen. We'll make up a batch of sandwiches and have a picnic supper down on the beach."

Beth eyed them both speculatively and made quick work of ushering her two children out of the house.

Without a word Jack took Rita immediately in his arms and kissed her, deeply and passionately, with a new urgency that confused her. Opening her eyes when he had finally lifted his lips free of hers, she saw the intensity in his face and was vaguely alarmed.

"Jack, is something wrong?" she asked uneasily.

"Rita, I love you. Do you believe that?"

Rita stared up at him, her alarm turning into fear. Something was definitely wrong. She'd never seen Jack like this. He acted as though her answer were a matter of life and death.

"Yes, of course, I do," she whispered.

"I want to marry you, Rita, more than anything else in the world. Do you believe that, too?"

"Jack..."

"Do you?"

"Yes. Yes, I do."

He sucked in a deep breath as he hugged her close. "As long as you believe me on both those counts, everything will be all right. There're some things about me that are going to come as a surprise to you, Rita. It was stupid of me not to tell you from the first, but after what happened with Pendleton, I wasn't sure how you'd react. You didn't ask me questions, give me natural openings, and I thought there was time. Then all of a sudden Beth and the kids were coming. It crossed my mind just to let you find out gradually in the course of conversation, but I can't take any chances of losing you. I could ask Beth to keep quiet, but sooner or later you *have* to know."

"Jack, whatever it is, it won't matter." Rita smiled up at him protectively. "I love you no matter what your father is or what he's done. Who am I to judge someone else's family?" Her smile became gently apologetic as Jack looked down at her uncertainly. "I gathered from your conversation with Beth that there's bad feeling between your father and you and that it was probably caused by some wrongdoing on his part. Even if there was a big scandal or a crime involved, it wouldn't change the way I feel about you, Jack."

Jack's uncertainty had turned into blank bewilderment.

"Wrongdoing?" he echoed. "What are you thinking, Rita?"

Rita hesitated, wondering if she'd jumped to totally wrong conclusions. "Beth wanted you to ask your father for money that wasn't *his*. Naturally, I thought—"

Comprehension flashed in Jack's eyes, clearing away the puzzlement. "You thought he'd gotten money dishonestly," he said slowly. He cleared his throat, visibly gearing up his nerve. "Honey, Beth just meant that our father is a banker. He has a lot of influence in financial circles."

"A banker?" Rita repeated dumbly.

"We're not talking teller or loan officer," Jack said quietly. "He's the chairman of the board of one of the major banks in the country. Anybody who's anybody in banking or big business knows my father's name. He's a very successful, powerful man, and he wanted me to follow in his footsteps. I was a big disappointment to him. That was the reason for the conflict between us."

Jack watched her anxiously as she stared up at him, absorbing what he had told her.

"You really did drop out of Princeton, then," she murmured. "I didn't believe you."

He nodded. "That was the final straw, as far as my father was concerned. All the Adams men are expected to go to Princeton. My father did, and his brothers, their father, etc." Jack smiled coaxingly. "I'm the black sheep of the family."

Rita didn't smile back. She glanced over toward the open glass doors with their glorious view of the ocean and then back up at Jack, her expression sober and withdrawn.

"I can't believe I was so stupid, not putting two and two together. This house right on the ocean is probably worth a small fortune. Your mother has never worked because she hasn't needed to. Your father probably paid her a big divorce settlement and still gives her alimony." She frowned at him as he shook his head.

"There was no need for either. My mother inherited money. She was the only child of very wealthy parents. Please, I hope you won't let all this upset you," he pleaded as Rita pushed herself away from him. "None of it affects what's between us."

"I actually felt *embarrassed* for you because your mother didn't pay her bills! What a joke. No wonder you don't have to hold down a job! With both your parents rich, you don't *have* to!"

She tried to back away from him, but he caught her upper arms and held her.

"I haven't taken a red cent from either one of my parents since I dropped out of Princeton and joined the navy. I've made it on my own, Rita, and at the risk of blowing my own horn, I've done well for a man my age. Damned well." His hold on her arms eased and he slid his palms up and down in a gentle caressing motion. "You won't be marrying a poor man, honey, even if he is a college dropout."

"I can't marry you, Jack!" This time when Rita backed away, Jack didn't stop her. Her freedom to put space between them deepened her sense of tragedy. "It would never work," she added sadly, watching his hands longingly as he lowered them slowly to his side. "I learned my lesson with Mark. There's too much difference between your background and mine. Can you imagine how your father and all your other important relatives will react to your marrying somebody like me? The men in your family graduate from Princeton. In my family a high school diploma is a rarity. My mother worked in barrooms, Jack. We were poor white trash, everywhere we lived!"

Jack shrugged. "I've known for days what your mother did for a living, Rita," he chided her gently. "I know about all her divorces, the run-down places you lived in, your feelings of inferiority. None of that makes any difference to me other than making me wish I could make it up to you somehow. My feelings in the matter are the ones that count, not my father's or my relatives. I'm the one who wants to marry you and live with you, not them. So what's the real problem? Come on, out with it."

Rita met his eyes ashamedly. "How can I say I'll marry you now, when I wasn't sure before, when I assumed that your background was no better than my own? I loved you against all my better judgment, Jack. If I had agreed to marry you, it would have been a decision of the heart and not of the mind, and I don't honestly know that I would ever have said yes. You find that *amusing*?" she added unbelievingly as a slow smile spread across his face.

"Take it from me, sweetheart. You would have said yes. You are saying yes now, aren't you?" He held his arms open for her and urged her into them with his warm, eager gaze.

Rita moved toward him slowly at first and then with a rush. "Oh, Jack, I love you!" The words were squeezed out of her by the strength of his arms closing around her.

"I love you, too, sweetheart," he said in a low, happy voice. "Don't you worry about a thing from now on. I can promise you that I'm going to make you one hell of a good husband. You won't believe I can be such a boring, routine kind of guy."

Rita smiled into his shoulder and then rubbed her cheek against its solid warmth. "You, boring? Not a chance." She drew back and smiled at him. "That's why I fell in love with you in the first place, because you're so much fun. You love life, and when I'm with you, the world seems like a wonderful place. You're right," she said softly. "I would have said yes. But how were you so sure of me?"

Jack's smile lingered on his lips, but his eyes were very serious as he answered her.

"You had to say yes. Something like this doesn't happen more than once in a lifetime. I knew deep down when I got off that plane in Honolulu and left you standing there looking so sad and scared and alone that we'd be seeing each other again, here on Maui. Otherwise I wouldn't have been able to walk away. It happened fast with me, like lightning, and it isn't going to go away, ever."

He kissed her tenderly, reverently, and held her close, his cheek pressed against her head.

"I may not come across to you as the kind of guy you wanted in a husband, but you can depend on me, honey. It won't always be laughs and good times, but I'll do my damnedest not to let you down."

The quiet fervor in his voice brought tears to Rita's eyes. "My instincts told me from the beginning that I could trust you, Jack," she mused unsteadily. "Remember that take-off when I threw myself in your arms? That seems so long ago now. I feel like a different person. For the first time in my life, I'm *glad* to be me, even though there're some things about me I don't like."

"I'm glad you're you, too," he said tenderly. "And there's nothing about you I don't like. Now I guess we'd better see about making those sandwiches."

They talked about the immediate future as they worked together in harmony. Jack agreed with the greatest reluctance that Rita would have to return to Atlanta. She felt a responsibility toward her employer, and there were practical details to take care of. She had to dispose of her car and furniture and close out bank accounts, in addition to packing what she would bring to Hawaii with her.

"How long do you think it will take?" Jack wanted to know. "A week? Two, at the most, I would think."

Rita pretended to be indignant that he thought she could train someone to step into her job in such a short space of time.

"I was only teasing," she said reassuringly when Jack was silent and deeply thoughtful.

"I am being a terrible chauvinist, aren't I?" he said slowly. "Expecting you to uproot your whole life and come here where I want to live." He grimaced. "Atlanta, huh? This deal with Phillip hasn't gone so far that I couldn't pull out, you know."

Rita looked at him wonderingly. "Jack, are you offering to move to Atlanta with me?"

"It seems the only fair thing to do, since you're the one who's employed," he said ruefully. "Seriously, if your job means a lot to you—and I know you've worked hard to get where you are—I could adjust to living in Atlanta. It's a city where a lot's going on. There should be ample opportunities for someone like myself. Think about it. You don't have to make up your mind in the next ten minutes."

"I don't have to think about it," she replied promptly. "If you think you're sticking me in Atlanta when I could live here on Maui, you're crazy."

Jack looked at her searchingly. "Are you sure?"

"Positive."

Rita watched the relief spread across his face. "Thank you, sweetheart," he said fervently. "You don't have to work unless you want to, but I'm sure you wouldn't have any trouble getting a job here managing a clothing shop." His eyebrows shot up. "Or you might even start your own." He grinned. "If you decide you want to do that, I know a guy who can get you backers."

"I will want to work, I'm sure—until we have children. I do want to have children, Jack."

"So do I." He put down the spatula he'd been using and took her in his arms. "I wish we didn't have company," he said softly, kissing her. "I wouldn't mind getting started on it right now. Seriously, how long do you think it'll take you in Atlanta? If it's longer than a week or two, I won't be able to stand it. I'll have to come there and be with you."

Rita hugged him tight around the waist and leaned against him. Just the thought of days and weeks when she wouldn't see him and wouldn't be held close in his arms made her unbearably lonely.

"I hate the thought of leaving you, but I have to go back. There has to be a transition. I want to leave Atlanta and come here with a clear conscience, with the feeling that the loose ends are tied up right, not left dangling."

"And that the ties that have to be cut are severed gently," Jack added quietly, "not left to bleed and fester."

Rita slowly raised her head and looked into his face.

"You'll want to see your mother again someday, Rita. Probably sooner than you think. You're strong enough now to tell her that you were right in what you wanted but wrong in the way you went about it."

"How did you know?" she whispered. "But you don't know how afraid I am, Jack."

"I think I can empathize. When the time comes, I want to go with you. There's just one condition." He watched her give startled consideration to his offer and was deeply touched by her acceptance of it.

"What condition?"

"You have to be right there holding my hand when I look my father in the face and tell him basically the same thing." He smiled at her. "Honey, there isn't a relative on either side that we can't face up to together. And there's one of yours that I'm particularly looking forward to meeting."

The twinkle in his eyes served as a delightful warning that his sense of humor had been on hold long enough.

"One of my relatives? Who?"

"Your sister Edna. I owe her a tremendous debt. I want to have a nice present to give her when we meet." His grin was cautious. "I want to get her version of that night she showed up at your apartment—"

"Jack! There was nothing funny about that night!" Rita cut him off sharply.

"You don't see even a *little* high comedy in the situation? You and that stuff-shirt Pendleton and his snooty mother all standing around gawking at poor Edna like she'd just dropped in from outer space. She must have felt like she'd blundered into an exhibit at a wax museum."

Rita held her stern expression with difficulty.

"Mark's mother wasn't standing. She was...sitting." With the last word, Rita felt the corners of her mouth quirking. "I still don't think it's funny," she insisted with a grudging smile that was the beginning of the end of her resistance.

"I can see you don't," Jack agreed, chuckling, and the rich sound touched a spring of merriment inside her. She could no more keep from laughing with him than she could keep from loving him. It was happy, healing laughter, aimed at themselves and life's absurdity. It admitted their humanity, conceded their vulnerability, and celebrated their incredible good fortune in having found each other.

"Poor Edna," Rita gasped. "It must have been a nightmare for her." She smiled at him, her dark eyes brilliant with tears of happiness and mirth. "Jack, I love you so much! You make me laugh!"

Silhouette Special Edition

COMING NEXT MONTH

FOR NOW, FOREVER—Nora Roberts
Anna Whitfield couldn't have been less suited to become
Daniel MacGregor's heir-producing, child-rearing wife if she'd tried.
So why was the empire-builder moving heaven and earth to prove she was
his perfect mate?

SHADOW ON THE SUN—Maggi Charles
Although researcher Pamela Merrill and plantation owner Miguel Rivero
had barely met, their blazing passion rivaled the tropical sun. Yet Miguel's
tangled past shrouded their future in shadows.

ROSE IN BLOOM—Andrea Edwards
A place for everything and everything in its place: that was Rose Landen's
motto. Until devil-may-care Rick Weiller nonchalantly scrambled her
orderly existence with his soul-stirring kisses!

THE EXECUTIVES—Monica Barrie
When Ryan's seductive tactics distracted her from a crucial buy out, Talia
learned the hard way that mixing ruthless business and heady pleasure
often spelled romantic disaster.

GOLDEN FIRESTORM—Anne Lacey
Wynne knew that Indian activist Hawk Saddler was fiercely proud—
probably too proud to accept her and her "half-breed" children. Still, she
dared to dream their fiery attraction would burn away his doubts.

OBJECT OF DESIRE—Jennifer West
To American aristocrat David Winthrop, Angelina Zarsuela was wild,
exotic and utterly desirable. Though her dubious ancestry endangered his
blueblood ambitions, he had to have her...no matter what the cost.

AVAILABLE NOW:

FORGIVE AND FORGET
Tracy Sinclair

HONEYMOON FOR ONE
Carole Halston

A MATCH FOR ALWAYS
Maralys Wills

ONE MAN'S LOVE
Lisa Jackson

SOMETHING WORTH KEEPING
Kathleen Eagle

BETWEEN THE RAINDROPS
Mary Lynn Baxter

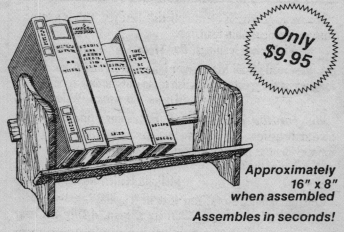